A Dilemma for Jamie
By: Angela Rigley
ISBN: 978-1-927220-10-8

All rights reserved
Copyright © Feb 2013, Angela Rigley
Cover Art Copyright © Feb, 2013, Brightling Spur

Bluewood Publishing Ltd
Christchurch, 8441, New Zealand
www.bluewoodpublishing.com

Names, characters and incidents depicted in this book are products of the author's imagination or are used fictitiously. Any resemblance to actual events, locales, organizations, or persons, living or dead, is entirely coincidental and beyond the intent of the author or the publisher.

No part of this book may be reproduced or shared by any electronic or mechanical means, including but not limited to printing, file sharing, and email, without prior written permission from Bluewood Publishing Ltd.

To Jack and Pauline
Best wishes
Angela Rigley

Other books in this series:

Looking for Jamie

Coming Soon:

A School for Jamie

For news of, or to purchase, these and other books from
Bluewood Publishing Ltd please visit:

www.bluewoodpublishing.com

A Dilemma For Jamie

by

Angela Rigley

Dedication

I would like to thank all my family and friends for their support, and dedicate this book to my granddaughter, Charlotte, as a thank you for her interest in my first book, 'Looking for Jamie'.

Chapter 1

"Mama, it's snowing." Eleven-year old Jamie Dalton pressed his face up against the nursery window. "And they're the biggest snowflakes I've ever seen." He turned to his little sisters. "We'll go out and build a snowman later, shall we?"

Picking up Annabella, who had started to grizzle, Tillie replied. "I'm afraid not, Jamie. The twins are much too little, and Auntie Ruby tells me this little one was coughing again during the night."

Fifteen-month old Alice toddled over to the window. Tillie noticed her red frock was becoming rather short. She would have to see about having new ones made for each of the twins. Something else to arrange.

Alice climbed onto the seat next to her brother and put her podgy hand into his.

He pointed outside. "Look, Alice, snow. Isn't it great?"

She nodded, cuddling up to him, her thumb in her mouth as usual, her golden ringlets contrasting with his darker hair. Beneath her little bonnet, her bright eyes—the image of her father's, and as blue as sapphires in her round face—beamed with love each time she looked at her big brother. Tillie couldn't wish for a closer relationship between her children and, although Annabella was so often confined to bed with illness, so hadn't developed such a tight bond, she knew Jamie loved her just as well. Although she'd wanted to call her 'Amelia', David had decided, on the morning of their christening that, as Alice had been named after Tillie's grandmother, he wanted their other twin to have his mother's name. So Annabella it was. They could always name the next baby 'Amelia'.

She patted her belly and, shaking her head when she heard her son whispering to Alice, "We'll ask Papa when he comes in, eh?" she placed the now sleeping Annabella in her crib and crossed the room to stand behind the pair at the window.

"I heard that, young man, and no, you mustn't bother your father. He has much more important matters to deal with. Anyway, he won't be back until late. He…"

She had been about to give him some bad news, but decided against it. There was no need to tell him just yet.

"Can I play with me train, then?" He climbed down from the window-seat.

"It's 'may', not 'can'. Please try to remember, but yes, and don't forget to put it all away afterwards. Nellie nearly fell over the carriage you left out last week. It was a good job she wasn't carrying anything or she would have fallen."

"Sorry, Mama, but it weren't my fault. Auntie Ruby called me for tea before I finished putting it away, and I forgot to do it later."

"You've always got an excuse, haven't you?" She ruffled her son's hair as Alice removed her thumb from her mouth and uttered, "Tain."

"Mama, she said 'train'," exclaimed Jamie, picking up the little girl in excitement. "She said 'train'."

Tillie tickled her daughter under her chin. "Aren't you a clever girl?"

"Say it again." Jamie tried to coax her into repeating it, but the thumb had been replaced and she was silent again.

"Perhaps she will later. Come on, let's get the box out, but don't make too much noise. Annabella needs her sleep."

After taking another look at the sleeping child, she helped him set up the track on the nursery floor.

Ruby poked her head around the door. "Need any help?" She came in, gesturing towards Jamie, who was playing happily, and mouthed, "Have you told him yet?"

Standing up and walking across to the window, Tillie whispered, "No, I was going to earlier, but lost my nerve."

Jamie reached over to pick up the engine that had come off the rail. "What's nerve, Mama?"

Tillie's eyes opened wide. Why did children hear the quietest-spoken word when they weren't supposed to, yet, when asked in a normal voice to do something they considered unpleasant, they apparently heard nothing?

Raising her eyebrows, Ruby smiled. "It's like bravery."

"But how can you lose it?"

Tillie shook her head, walking towards the door. "I'll let your Auntie Ruby explain while you carry on playing. I'll be back soon." Descending the stairs, she tried to work out how she was going to tell him about George.

"There's a visitor to see you in the parlour, milady."

She jumped at the sound of Purvis's voice. She hadn't heard the doorbell. "Oh, who is it?"

"It's Mrs Lumbley, milady. She seems a trifle flustered."

Tillie took a deep breath. "Thank you, Purvis. I'd better see what she wants."

What could Mrs Lumbley want now? Tillie's patience was wearing rather thin with her new neighbour. She'd only lived in The Old Farmhouse for six months and had already come calling three times with problems.

Tillie's change from housemaid to mistress of the house had come quite naturally to her, and she enjoyed the challenge most of the time, but occasions such as these taxed her abilities to the full.

Straightening her hair in the mirror as she crossed the hall, she entered the parlour, fixing a smile onto her face. "Mrs Lumbley, I hope I find you well."

Standing up quickly, the neighbour bobbed a curtsey, babbling, "My dear Mrs Dalton, I am very well, thank you. You know I hate to put you to any trouble, but…"

Tillie's eyes closed momentarily. This wasn't going to be a social visit.

"I was wondering if… Would you be able to lend me your gamekeeper for a few hours?"

Tillie hadn't expected that.

"Our gamekeeper?"

"Yes, that one with the black dog."

"Um…"

"You see, I need my sheep herding into their pen because of the snow, and my old sheepdog's poorly. He's probably on his last legs, if you know what I mean. I've tried all morning to do it myself, but the wretched creatures won't obey me. Just as

I think they're all in, one of them runs out, then the others follow and I have to start all over again."

The feather in the lady's hat waved in time to her head bobbing up and down as she spoke. Tillie couldn't take her eyes off it.

She realised Mrs Lumbley had stopped speaking. "I'm not sure, Mrs Lumbley. My husband won't be back until this evening, but I shall see what I can do. May I offer you a drink?"

"No, thank you, I've taken up enough of your time already, and I had better return home before the snow sets in and prevents the carriage from getting through. Good day to you. I shall await your gamekeeper as soon as is convenient?" She looked up hopefully.

"Um, well, I shall have to find out if he's amenable first." Tillie gestured for the lady to precede her out of the door. "Good day, Mrs Lumbley."

After she'd seen the lady safely ensconced in her carriage, Tillie went to the kitchen to see if Tom Briggs, the gamekeeper, was around, as she knew he called in for a cup of tea and some of Freda's renowned seed cake about that time of day. She was still a little bewildered about the strange request, and wasn't sure whether he would agree to it. They didn't have sheep of their own, but many of the tenant farmers did, so perhaps he'd helped out before. He was a kindly fellow, so she felt sure he would be obliging.

The smell of baking bread filled her nostrils as she entered the kitchen, finding the portly cook wiping down the large oak table.

"Good day, Ti—I mean, ma'am." Dear Freda, she still couldn't get used to addressing her by her title.

"Good day, Freda, has Tom been in yet?"

The cook straightened, looking rather surprised at the question. "No, ma'am, not yet. Did you especially need him?"

"Well, our new neighbour, Mrs Lumbley, would appreciate some help with her sheep. As you know, the master's helping with the funeral, and I didn't know what to tell her."

"Mm, she's becoming rather a nuisance, isn't she?"

Tillie shrugged her shoulders. "Well, I suppose it's understandable, being left a widow so soon after moving in. I try to help whenever I can."

"But do you think the master will get back tonight? The snow's coming down faster than ever." Freda opened the back door and a squall of icy wind blew in, forcing her to close it again quickly.

"Perhaps not, in fact I think I would prefer him to remain in Harrogate, rather than risk being lost in a snowdrift."

"I agree. Have you given Master Jamie the bad news yet?"

Shaking her head, Tillie turned to go out. "No, but I'd better get back up to the children. If Tom does make it in, please would you tell him about the request?" She was almost at the door when she remembered the reason she had come downstairs. "Ah, Freda, tonight's dinner…"

"Yes, ma'am, pork and apple sauce for the main course, as we agreed, but should I cook for the master?"

"Well…" Tillie decided to remain positive. "Yes, I think so. I know he'll try his utmost to get home, if only to say goodnight to the children. He can't bear to be away from them for long."

Nellie staggered in with a basketful of dirty washing. "And you, Mistress Tillie, he hates leaving your sight for the shortest of times."

Tillie reached out to help her. She knew the housekeeper was right, and felt exactly the same about her darling husband. Nellie shrugged her off, so, seeing a pile of clean linen on the side, she picked it up on her way out before anyone could stop her. They wouldn't let her do any of the household chores now she was mistress of the house, but she enjoyed helping out in small ways whenever she could get away with it.

Climbing the stairs, she thought about the change to her life. David had readily taken on the role of fatherhood to Jamie, and the birth of the twins had sealed their relationship. She enjoyed being wife and mistress more than she could have envisaged in her wildest dreams. If it wasn't for this…

Upstairs, Auntie Ruby had popped out to get him a drink, so Jamie carried on playing with his train, humming quietly. Alice picked up one of the engines and tried to put it on the track. It wouldn't sit properly, so he wound the key and showed her how to line up the wheels. "Like this, Alice."

"Tain." She took her thumb out of her mouth to say it again.

"That's right, t-r-a-i-n. Aren't you getting smart?"

She nodded, sitting back on her haunches to watch as the train tootled around the room.

What did his mama need nerve to tell him about? And why were they being so secretive? He hoped it wasn't anything to do with the reason his pa had gone away. Why would he go up to Harrogate and not take any of them with him? He would've loved to have seen his cousin, Sarah. He knew she was poorly, but he could have cheered her up.

The train stopped. Picking it up, Alice tried to wind it, but couldn't work out how, so passed it to Jamie. He rewound it and then set it back on its way.

Auntie Ruby returned, looking rather red and excited. She gave him his drink and then bustled about, smoothing down covers, picking things up and putting them back down again.

She suddenly came over and flung her arms around him, almost knocking the beaker out of his hand. He looked at her in surprise. She'd only gone out to fetch some lemonade. What had made her change into such a different person so quickly? He'd never seen her behaving so oddly. She was usually so quiet. But not like when he'd first come to The Grange. She'd definitely changed as she'd got older. That must be what the matter was—her age. He'd heard grown-ups saying it could be a cause of odd behaviour.

"Oh, Jamie, I can't keep it a secret any longer. I'm so happy," she declared, after she'd let him go. Picking up Alice, she planted big wet kisses all over her face, knocking off her bonnet.

"So I see, Auntie Ruby," he replied with a big grin. "Why?"

"You'll never guess."

He tried to think what could make an auntie so cheerful, especially one who was usually so gloomy.

Replacing Alice's bonnet, she tied the ribbons, squealing, "Sam's asked me to marry him."

"Oh." Jamie couldn't think why that should make her so happy. He thought they were already sort of betrothed.

"And I want you to be my pageboy, and Alice and Annabella to be my bridesmaids, and Sarah, of course. Isn't that wonderful?" She danced round the room with Alice, who was squealing with delight, even though she probably didn't know what her auntie was talking about.

Tillie heard the squeal as she approached the nursery. She rushed in. "Whatever's the matter?"

"Just Alice getting excited." Ruby had a huge grin on her face. She looked flushed and dishevelled. Tillie hoped she wasn't coming down with a fever.

Alice tried to jump, but her little legs weren't quite agile enough.

Putting the linen on the dresser, Tillie picked her up, scrutinising her face. "Why, what's happened?"

Ruby's face was still beaming. "It's nothing, Tillie, honestly."

"Well, it's a lot of noise for nothing."

Annabella began to cry in her cot.

"Oh, now look what you've done." Sighing, Tillie put Alice down, picked up her sister and went across to sit with her on the window-seat. The child was soon soothed, and Tillie, looking across at the subdued trio on the floor, felt guilty for raising her voice. Just because she was worried about David and having to tell Jamie the reason he'd gone to Harrogate wasn't an excuse to take it out on them. "Go on then, tell me what the hullabaloo was all about."

"I was just telling them..." Ruby began hesitantly, her face back to its usual frown.

"Auntie Ruby and Sam's going to get wed," Jamie finished for her.

"Why, Ruby, that's marvellous." Jumping up, Tillie

rushed over to embrace her sister. "It's about time. I'd begun to think he'd never make an honest woman of you. Why didn't you say something earlier?"

Ruby shrugged, as was her wont. "I daren't…in case he changed his mind."

"Oh, Ruby, will we never instil any confidence into you? No matter how hard we try, you're still the unsure, self-doubting girl you ever were." She gave her another hug. "But…Sam's away with the master, so when did he propose?"

"On Sunday, on the way back from church, just before we got the message from Harrogate about…you know what." She gestured with her head towards Jamie, who was watching the snow again out of the window.

"And you've waited all this time to tell us?"

She shrugged.

"And have you told anyone else?"

Ruby looked bashful. "No, not yet."

"Well, come on then, let's go down and spread the good news to Nellie and Freda, and anyone else who's around to hear it."

* * * *

By the afternoon, the snow had eased off. "Please, Mama, ca…may I go out now? Please." Jamie had already put on his old brown coat. It was too small to wear if he was going anywhere important, but just right for playing in. The sleeves were halfway up his arms.

"All right, while the twins are having their nap." Tillie looked in the drawer to find his hat and gloves while he laced up his boots. "But as soon as you feel cold, you come back in, you hear me? Your chest is still weak in bad weather, and I don't want a repeat of last year's pneumonia."

"Yes, Mama, I promise."

Tillie went downstairs with him, after checking the girls were asleep, and stood looking out of the back door at the white scene outside. Would David be able to get home through the snow? She wished there was some way he could get in touch to let her know he was safe.

She closed the door after warning Jamie once more not to get too cold, and bumped into Ruby, who was bending down picking up some carrots she must have knocked off the table.

"Oh, Ruby, I was coming to find you. Here, let me help."

"It's all right, I've got them." Ruby straightened up and placed the vegetables on the table. "What were you doing at the door?"

"Watching Jamie. He's gone out to build a snowman. He'll probably need one of these carrots for its nose."

"Oh, yes, and some coal for its eyes. Is there an old scarf and hat we could use?" Ruby picked out some coal from the scuttle and, putting on a coat from the back of the door, hurried out, calling, "I'd better go and help him."

Tillie smiled. Her sister was still not much more than a child in her eyes. She was so glad she was to be married. They hadn't discussed when the wedding would be——it would have to be in the New Year, with Christmas coming up—or where she and Sam were to live, or any other practicalities, but there were more important issues to be resolved. How had Sam and David fared in Harrogate? She couldn't wait for their return.

As she approached the nursery, she could hear Alice cooing in her cot. She knew it was the older twin as she could distinguish the slightly higher pitch of her voice. She would lie quietly playing with her rag doll, whilst her sister would want attention as soon as she awoke.

She went in, picked up the little girl and cuddled her.

"Mam, mam, mam," Alice repeated, stroking her doll's hair.

"Say 'pa...pa'."

"Mam, mam, mam."

Tillie smiled indulgently. She would keep trying to get her daughter to say 'papa' until the day she could surprise David with it.

Annabella awoke, grizzling immediately her eyes opened, so she put Alice on the rug and picked up her twin. "Hello, grumpy girly. Are you feeling any better?" She gave the child a cuddle, feeling her forehead. It seemed fine so, placing her beside Alice on the floor, she went to the cupboard and took out a box of coloured, wooden bricks.

"Let's see how tall we can build the tower today."

Try as she might, she could only manage to build two or three bricks at a time, for first one twin, then the other, would knock it over, giggling with delight as she pretended to be cross with them. Alice managed to lay four in a horizontal row, but Annabella scrambled them, scattering them across the nursery floor.

Just as Alice's bottom lip began to drop and Tillie could sense a fight brewing, the door was thrust open and Jamie came rushing in, his nose and cheeks red and glowing. "Mama, me and Auntie Ruby's made a huge snowman. Come and see it." He grabbed her hand, his wet, cold glove sending a shiver down her as he pulled her over to the window. "Down there, look."

Sure enough, on the lawn stood a magnificent snowman, a large carrot for a nose, and sporting a striped scarf and an old felt cap. "My, it's the best snowman I've ever seen," she exclaimed, extricating her hand. "Come and see, girls."

The twins toddled over to the window and climbed onto the seat.

"Noman," cried Annabella, "noman."

Tillie was delighted. Her younger daughter had made odd sounds up until then, but nothing definable.

"Yes, Bella, a snowman. Me and Auntie Ruby made it." Jamie looked so proud of himself, Tillie hadn't the heart to admonish him for using the nickname he'd given her. She rather liked it actually, but David insisted on using her full name at all times and, in this instance, she felt she should comply with his wishes. Sometimes, she found it rather difficult to go against her better judgement to obey him, but on important issues she did so. Whenever she could get away with anything, though, she used her gumption without letting on.

"Oh, Mama, can't I take them down to play? They'd love it."

"I'm sorry, Jamie, but it's time for their tea."

Nellie appeared with a tray and put on the small table.

"Are you having yours up here, Master Jamie, or coming downstairs to the kitchen?"

He pursed his lips as if he couldn't decide what to do, then looked out of the window again. "I think I'll go back outside in the snow. May I, Mama?"

Tillie paused with a spoonful of red jelly in her hand. "Just for a short while, then. It'll soon be dark." Annabella grabbed the spoon and put it in her mouth.

After Jamie had gone out, Nellie picked up a lump of snow that had dropped off his coat, and threw it into the washbowl, then turned to Tillie. "Have you told the boy yet, ma'am?"

She shook her head. "No, I've decided to wait until the master gets back, then we can tell him together."

"I suppose that would be best." Nellie picked up the bricks and put them back into the box, asking, "Where's Ruby? She should be doing this."

"She was helping Jamie with his snowman. Ah, here she is."

Her sister appeared with a jug of Freda's home-made lemonade, her ruddy face the complete opposite to its usual pale pallor. "Brr, it's cold out there," she muttered, placing the tray on the table, then rubbing her hands together.

* * * *

Jamie ran back outside. The snow on the lawn where he and Auntie Ruby had built the snowman was churned up, but over on the other side of the drive it was smooth and untouched, apart from a few birds' footprints. He wondered if they were called footprints when birds had made them, or were they clawprints? Some were bigger than others, probably made by crows or jackdaws. Others were tiny, more likely to be blue tits or…

A robin flew down and perched on the lower branch of the bush next to him. He stood still, not wanting to frighten it off. "Hello, robin redbreast," he whispered, reaching out his hand slowly. It was one of his ambitions to have a bird—not necessarily a robin, any bird would do—eat out of his hand one day. Not having anything to eat, it flew off. Perhaps next time.

Looking at the pure white snow, he longed to jump into it and make his own footprints, but wanted to enjoy the scene a little while longer before he did so. After a few seconds, though, he couldn't wait any longer. Closing his eyes, he counted to ten. Then, with a mighty yell, he sprang, jumping in with both feet together. "I'm a kangaroo, I'm a kangaroo!" he cried, waving his arms up and down to gain momentum. "I can jump really high."

The next leap was too high. He lost his balance and fell head-first into a large snowdrift, landing with such force his head was completely covered. As he opened his mouth to yell, it filled with snow. He could hardly breathe. The more he struggled, the deeper into the snow he became embedded. He began to feel really scared. Then he felt his coat being pulled. Spluttering, he regained his foothold and looked to see who'd rescued him. It was a young boy, dressed in what looked like rags.

"You all right?" the boy asked, brushing himself down.

"Um, I think so." Jamie rubbed the remains of the snow from his hair and his clothes. He looked the boy up and down again. He'd never seen him before.

"Who are you?" He felt slightly embarrassed at being saved by a stranger, one who wasn't even as tall as him.

"Bobby." The boy surprised him by holding out his hand.

Jamie shook it—mustn't forget his manners. "Where're you from?"

Bobby pointed into the woods.

"I didn't know there were houses down there."

"'Tain't a house, it's a hut."

"You live in a hut?"

Bobby nodded. "I gotta go now. Me ma'll wonder where I am."

Jamie's clothes were rather wet and he began to shiver. He didn't fancy staying out any longer, either. "Thanks for rescuing me," he called after the boy, who was running towards the woods. He received a wave in reply.

I wonder why I've never seen him before, Jamie mused as he hurried round to the back door, making sure all the snow was off him before entering the house. They wouldn't let him go out again if they knew he'd fallen in it.

* * * *

By eight o'clock, there was still no sign of David. The children were in bed and Tillie sat at the writing desk trying to compose a letter to her friend Emily Thompson, the vicar's wife, who'd helped her find Jamie three and a half years previously. She had already discarded the first two letters because her distracted brain wouldn't tell her pen the correct words, and she now gave up on the third.

Sighing as the candle spluttered, she put the pen down and walked across to the window, parting the curtains to peer outside. Through the gloom she could see it was snowing hard. It had started to come down heavy again at dusk.

"Please, God, let David get home safely," she prayed aloud as she pulled her wrap tightly around her. If he was coming home. He might have stayed in Harrogate if the weather was bad when he was due to set off.

After taking one more look through the window, she began pacing up and down the drawing room. Perhaps she should have told Jamie the bad news earlier in the day, but she'd wanted David to be with her for support. She knew he was going to be devastated, and was putting off the moment, imagining the sight of his little face crumpling when he heard that his cousin, Sarah, was very poorly with tuberculosis, and the doctors weren't sure whether she would pull through, and that her brother, George, had died.

She knew Jamie wouldn't be unduly concerned about George, as they had never got on very well, but he adored Sarah.

Eventually, lighting a new candle from the spluttering one, she sat down on the chesterfield and picked up a sampler she'd been stitching. Her ma had taught her how to sew when she was young, but she hadn't done any for so long she'd had to enlist Nellie's help to remind her. Usually, it relaxed her after the toils and troubles of the day, but that evening it only seemed to make them worse, so, after rectifying several mistakes, she conceded defeat and put the sampler down.

Hearing the door open, she jumped up, hoping against hope it would be David. It was Ruby.

"I'm off to bed. Do you want me to tell Martha to bank up the fire?"

They had hired Martha when Ruby had been promoted to nursery maid after the twins had been born.

Tillie looked across at the large, old grandfather clock on the wall. Ten o'clock. It couldn't be! She must have drifted off to sleep.

"Um, has there been any word from David?" Standing up, she rubbed her eyes.

Ruby shook her head. "No, he probably won't risk coming home in this weather. It's still snowing."

Tillie hurried over to the window and looked out again. All she could see were large white snowflakes drifting through the darkness. She sighed. "I suppose you're right," she murmured, walking across to the door.

"What about the fire?" Ruby asked again.

"Yes, ask her to bank it up, please. I can't see me sleeping well tonight, and I can soon poke it back to life if I have to come back down." As her sister turned away, she asked, "Are the children asleep?"

"Yes, all sleeping peacefully."

"Goodnight then."

Awaking with a start several hours later, Tillie sat up. She thought she'd heard something. Was it David? She felt the other side of the bed in case he'd crept in earlier without waking her, but it was cold and lifeless. Perhaps he'd been moving about in the adjoining room where he sometimes slept if he came home late, or if they had an argument, which was very rare. It had only happened once, actually…but she couldn't bear to think about that occasion, she just wanted him home safe and sound, tonight.

Pushing aside the sheet, she reached for her dressing gown, padded over to the door and opened it, stubbing her toe on the door jamb. Trying to stifle an exclamation, she stood rubbing her toe to ease the pain, moaning quietly.

Her eyes were becoming accustomed to the pitch blackness, but she still couldn't see if there was anybody there.

"Is that you, David?" she whispered. No reply. She repeated it, slighter louder, but there was still no reply.

She inched towards the bed, not wanting to bang into anything. It was empty. She burst into tears. Pulling her nightcap on more tightly, she made her way back to her own bed. Hopefully, it would still be slightly warm. Even though the tears had ceased, she lay awake, telling herself that David was probably tucked up snug and warm in Harrogate, so why was she so wound up? She wondered if it was still snowing but decided it was too cold to get out of bed again to check. Snuggling back down into the bed-covers, she eventually drifted off to sleep again.

Chapter 2

David tried to move his leg. It hurt like hell. Putting his hand up to his throbbing head, he felt a sticky patch on his temple.

A horse whinnied close by. No other sound could be heard as he tried to remember what had happened.

Then it all came back to him. There had only been a few flurries of snow in Harrogate, so he had thought he would be able to get home before the bad weather set in. He remembered getting worried as the snow began to fall heavier, then the last thing was the brougham overturning.

Shivering and brushing the snow off his coat, he tried to stand, but his leg wouldn't take the weight. The horse snorted again, so he shuffled towards her on his hands and knees until he felt her frightened breath on his face.

"Shush, old girl," he tried to reassure the agitated animal. She was lying down, still attached to the carriage by one of the shafts. Patting her smooth neck and stroking her mane seemed to comfort her, for she nickered quietly. Gritting his teeth at the pain in his leg, he snuggled up close, trying to dredge some heat from her warm body.

It dawned on him that it was no longer snowing. "That is something to be thankful for," he muttered, pulling his coat around him, wondering how long they had been there. They should have been home long before dark. Wondering what the time was, he took out his pocket-watch, but the light was beginning to fade, so he could not make it out. Sighing, he replaced it and lay back against the horse. She was breathing evenly and seemed to have gone to sleep.

Where was Sam, his groom who had been driving the carriage? He called him at the top of his voice. There was no reply, but the horse pricked up her ears. He thought she was going to try to stand, but he managed to sooth her and settle her down again.

The overturned carriage looked eerie in the fading light. His groom could be lying injured beneath it. He called again, but still no response.

Was Tillie worrying about him? Hopefully, she would have assumed he was staying in Harrogate.

He wondered whereabouts he was. Racking his brain, he tried to remember the last landmark he'd seen before they had overturned, but his mind seemed to be as impenetrable as the thick snow around him.

There had to be some way out of his predicament. He could not just lie there all night.

"Help!" he shouted. That disturbed the horse again. Flailing and bucking, she broke the shaft as she managed to stand, but then tottered into a snowdrift. Yelping in agony and gritting his teeth at the excruciating pain, he lunged forward to catch the harness before she could bolt. The broken shaft was dangling at her side, so he grabbed it, managing to seize the rein.

Gripping as hard as he could to the other side of the harness, he tried to pull himself up on to her back but, after three futile attempts, he was forced to abandon his plan. Sweat ran down his back, although his hands were frozen and his jaw ached almost as much as his groin.

The horse nickered again as he heard a movement behind him.

"Master?" Sam's shaky voice had never been so welcome.

The horse must have recognised him. She lifted her head and whinnied, almost pulling the rein from his grasp.

"Oh, Sam, thank god," David gasped, relief coursing through him. "Where were you?"

The groom limped over, rubbing his head. "Over there, behind the carriage. I think I must have been knocked out for a moment. How are you, sir?"

"Well…" David leaned against the horse for support.

"Hold on, sir, I'll fetch the lantern off the carriage."

"Good man." Barely able to stand, David clung onto the horse's mane, wishing she would stand still for a moment.

The groom was soon back with the lit lantern. "Do you

think you could get on her back, sir?"

"I have already tried."

"But if I help you up…"

Puffing and panting and in a great deal of pain, he managed to get onto the horse's back, but not being used to carrying riders, she tried to buck, almost dislodging him. Lying flat on her neck, he stroked her mane, whispering reassurances in her ear.

"Sam, how far do you think we are from home?"

"About a mile or so, sir, if I remember rightly."

"Do you think you would be able to walk with us? I am not sure I would find my way, even if I managed to stay on her back."

"Of course, sir."

Gritting his teeth at the pain, they set off, Sam carrying the lantern in one hand and the broken rein in the other. Before long, David felt himself slipping. He called out, "I am sorry, I cannot go any further. Every step feels like a knife being thrust deeper into my back."

The groom's agonised face looked up at him. He must have been in pain as well, but was bravely trying to hide it.

"If I could get up behind you, sir, I could support you." Sam looked around for something to climb onto. "Yes, over there, that could be a fallen tree. If I stand on that… Could you hold the light, sir?"

Sam steered the horse towards the tree and managed to cock his leg over her back and sit behind David. "Is that any better, sir?"

It was not really, but he would try and bear it.

Taking the lantern back from his master, Sam put an arm round David's waist, breathing heavily. With no saddle to cling onto, David did not feel at all secure as they set off. It was impossible to tell if they were still on the road. Everywhere was just a white sheet.

They hadn't gone much further when the horse lost her footing and slid down a bank. They were thrown over her head. David groaned as muffled hoof beats meant she had galloped away. With his leg bent at a peculiar angle, he was in so much pain he couldn't even open his eyes. He had no idea where Sam was. There was complete silence, and it was now dark as the lantern had been dropped in the fall.

He groaned. The fates were against him. He was doomed to die out there in the snow. Shivering from the cold as well as from shock, he began to pray as he pulled his coat around him.

Drifting in and out of consciousness, he was alerted by an intense, cold, wet feeling in his right arm. *Oh, my goodness*, he thought, yanking it away. *I must be in the river.* Telling himself not to panic, he tried to edge his body away from the water, cursing why it was not frozen over like everything else appeared to be. Then he realised he was actually lying on ice. His arm must have fallen through a hole. Barely daring to breathe, he managed to slither to what he hoped was safety.

Panting, and light-headed from the exertion, he thought be must be hallucinating when he felt hot breath on his face and a wet tongue licking his cheek. Then a faint light appeared, getting brighter.

"Jasper!" a voice called. The dog beside him barked, licked him again, and then ran back towards its master. "Hello, is somebody there?"

David recognised that voice. He could have wept as his friend, the Major, shone a light in his face. "Oh, my goodness, David, is that you?"

"Ri…ver," he tried to warn him. He did not want his saviour disappearing now that he had found him.

"Try not to talk, old chap." The Major clearly had not understood.

He tried once more. "Mind the river."

A lantern was hooked over his finger as he felt himself being lifted up. Visions of the pair of them falling into the icy water and their bloated bodies being washed out to sea slowly ebbed away as he was carried up the bank. He had never been so relieved in his life.

"Sam," David gasped, hoping against hope that his groom had not fallen in.

"Who?"

"My groom."

"Is he down there as well? I didn't see him." The Major stopped and looked down the bank. "Let me get you into the house, and then I'll come back and look for him."

He carried on, but after a few minutes they came to a stop.

"Sorry, old chap…but I'm going to have to put you down." Puffing and wheezing, the Major sat him down on what seemed to be a tree stump. "Not as fit as I used to be." He breathed in deeply, then blew his breath back out. "Days are gone…when I would carry a man a mile or so…to get him to safety."

Straightening his back, he put his hands on his hips, turning his head from side to side, then up and down.

"Right, off we go again."

Picking him up once more, the Major strode ahead, his breath warm on David's cheek as he inhaled and exhaled rhythmically in time with each step.

David recalled hearing about some of the heroic feats the Major had performed in the Crimean war, saving many of his comrades who would otherwise have perished. Now he believed them.

Before they had gone very far, he could feel himself slipping.

"Sorry." Putting him down on the snow, the old soldier sprawled next to him.

David tried to stand but his leg gave way immediately.

The Major wheezed, "It's not far now." Straightening, he put his arm around David's back and under his armpit, and they hobbled onwards.

The dog began to bark some way behind them. "Jasper!" the Major called. The dog barked again.

"Maybe he has found Sam."

David turned towards the sound, expecting the dog to come bounding up or, at the very best, to see his groom coming towards them.

"Leave me here, Major, and go back and find him."

"No, David, I suspect your leg may be broken," he puffed. "I've seen cases of broken bones that have been left too long without treatment…and they've never mended properly."

"But…"

"No arguments." They set off once more. David could see a faint light in the distance and concentrated his efforts on reaching it, although his head was becoming fuzzier with each step. Just as he felt they were going to make it, the old veteran stumbled and they both fell headlong.

He tried to sit up, but his friend had fallen across him and was not moving. Feebly, he tried to push him off, but didn't have enough strength. *This is it, I am definitely going to die this time,* he thought—quite calmly, much to his surprise. Closing his eyes, he resigned himself to his fate.

He nodded off, but a few minutes later was jerked awake as the old soldier gasped loudly, taking in a deep breath. Elation filled David as he felt him roll over.

"Sorry about that, old chum," mumbled the Major. "Since the campaign I sometimes have these odd episodes where I black out without any warning. Damned unfortunate, but I'll be as right as rain in a minute."

The lantern had miraculously stayed upright so there was still some light, but all David could focus on was the Major's ginger sideboards, looking strangely incongruous under the circumstances.

He felt himself being pulled along once more.

* * * *

David awoke with pins and needles in his foot. His leg would not move. It was splinted to a piece of board. Trying to make himself more comfortable, he gasped for breath as pain shot through him.

What was that strange rhythmic cacophony of sound emanating from the other side of the room? It sounded like…snoring? Where was he? He remembered the Major rescuing him from the snow. It must be him. But something niggled at the back of his mind. Something had not been right. Closing his eyes, he tried to cast his mind back.

"Sam!" he exclaimed. "We left him out there." Had anybody gone back to find him? He lifted himself up slightly so he could see the whole room. There was no groom there. Perhaps he had been put to bed.

He had to know. "Major!"

The snoring changed to a high-pitched whistle.

"Major!"

"Harrumph, harrumph."

"Major, please wake up."

The sideboards twitched and the Major sat bolt upright. "Oh, it's you, David. Thought for a minute it was my dragon of a wife."

David knew his friend had been widowed from his spiteful, ill-natured wife many years before. The poor man must have been having a nightmare.

"Did you find Sam?"

The Major rubbed his eyes and yawned. "Who?"

"Sam, my groom. You were going to see if you could find him."

"Oh, heavens, I must have fallen asleep after I put your leg in the splint and gave you the laudanum. Has that helped, by the way?"

So that was why he felt so fuzzy.

"Yes, I think it must have, but what about Sam? Were you or a servant not going to find him?"

"No servants left, old chap."

"What do you mean?"

"I only had old Jenkins, my butler—couldn't afford anyone else—and he passed away last week."

David's mouth fell open. How was he managing? How could a man of his advanced years survive in such a large house without any servants? And why had he not told anybody?

He must have nodded off again, probably the effects of the laudanum. When he awoke, he was alone. Then he heard someone stamping their feet in the hall.

"Hello…Major!" he called.

"Oh, you're awake." His host came in, taking off his coat.

"I've been out to look for your groom, but there's no sign of him. Our own tracks have been completely covered, so there's no way of checking any he might have made."

David tried to get up. The agonising pain stopped him. He fell back onto the sofa with a deep sigh. One of the springs was sticking into his backside, but there was nothing he could do about it.

The Major put another cushion behind his head. "How about a brandy?"

"That would be very welcome, even at this early hour, thank you."

Drinking his brandy, David looked around the room, dimly lit by the faint sunlight coming in the window. Barely any furniture remained, and a thin film of dust covered the few shabby items that were there, making him wonder how long it had been since the maids had left. He hadn't realised in what dire straits the old veteran had been living. Perhaps they could invite him to stay with them for a while, but would the once proud soldier be offended if it was suggested?

"Has it stopped snowing?" He tried to peer through the window opposite him. "I need to get a message to Tillie."

"It's stopped for the time being, but clouds are threatening over the hills towards the north, so I don't think it'll stay fine for long."

"How on earth am I going to get home?"

"Um, I've been thinking about that. I would lend you my carriage, but the wheel's loose and I haven't been able to get it fixed."

Jasper, who had been lying asleep on the hearthrug, lifted his head and howled.

"What's the matter, boy?" The Major stood up and patted him.

The bull mastiff shook itself then went across to the door, barking.

"Can you hear something?" The Major opened the door, looking out into the passage.

"Excuse me, old chum." He turned to David as the dog ran out. "I'd better see what the commotion is all about."

He disappeared, leaving David alone, frustrated at not being able to get up. The fire crackled and the wood the Major had put on it earlier burst into flames, giving him some welcome warmth. The Major must have removed his wet coat at some time, for he was wearing a maroon lounging jacket that was several sizes too large but much appreciated. Noticing there weren't any logs in the hod, he hoped there was a fresh supply in the cellar. Then he realised it wasn't a log that was burning, it was the leg of a table. It was no wonder there was not much furniture.

Longing to know what could be happening, his stomach rumbled, reminding him he had not eaten since stopping for lunch at the coaching inn the previous day.

The Major eventually came back in, out of breath. "You'll be happy to know…it's your groom."

"You have found him, where?"

"He'd been…" The old soldier flopped down in the armchair "…sheltering in the barn all night."

"In the barn? Why did he not knock at the door?"

The Major shrugged. "He said he did."

"How is he?"

"Well, he has some nasty cuts and bruises."

"Thank god that is all. I was so worried about him." David looked towards the open doorway as the dog came in and settled down on the hearthrug once more. "So, where is he?"

"Oh, I sent him to get help."

"Good, good, the Grange is closest, so I imagine he will go there, but I hope he does not upset Tillie. Did you tell him about my broken leg?"

"Yes, yes, of course, old chap."

He tried to work out how long it would take Sam to get to his house and back. It would be most of the morning, probably, so he might as well resign himself to waiting patiently.

His stomach growled again, and he hoped the Major could not hear it. If his misfortune was as great as it seemed, he might not have any food, and what he did have, he would need for himself.

He tried to make himself more comfortable, but there was no position that did not exacerbate the pain. He thought about asking for some more laudanum, then decided against it. He needed to stay alert.

"By the way, Major, what were you doing out in the dark last night, when you found me?"

"Um?" his old friend seemed to be nodding off. "Dark?"

"Yes, last night. Do you usually take a walk at that time of the evening?"

The Major sat up straight, brushing his bushy ginger hair back from his face. How long it was. How unruly. It must have been weeks since he'd had it cut, and there were several stains down the front of his waistcoat, so it could not have been cleaned for quite some time.

"Well, actually, I was just letting Jasper out for his last rendezvous with nature when I saw a horse cantering past. It was too dark to recognise who it belonged to, so I thought I'd better investigate. Jolly good job I did, what?"

"It certainly was. I am most grateful to you for finding me."

David kept expecting a maid to pop in, and found it most disconcerting that there were none. Once he was better, he would have to organise something for his friend. He could not let him stay in these dire circumstances.

"Would you like something to eat, old chap?" The Major's gruff voice broke into his reverie. "I think I may have some bread in the kitchen."

"Well…" David's stomach gave another rumble, and no matter how much he longed to decline the offer, it would be churlish not to. "Thank you, if it is not too much trouble."

"Not at all, old chap. I'm afraid to say that I don't have any kidneys or sausages, but I might be able to find an egg, although I haven't quite got the hang of how long to boil them to my satisfaction."

"An egg would be…thank you." David nodded.

Slowly lifting himself out of his chair, the Major disappeared through the door. The dog's ears pricked up and its tongue came out. It looked at David as if it was hoping for something to eat as well. He wondered when it had last been fed. It did seem to be much thinner than he remembered.

How on earth had the old soldier got himself into this situation? David knew he gambled a lot, but surely he would not have gone as far as to lose everything? He had heard of it happening, of men mortgaging their homes to the hilt, but the Major seemed such a sensible person, not at all the type to do that.

A loud clatter came from the kitchen, followed by an expletive. It was frustrating not being able to help but, even if he was mobile, he would not have the faintest idea how to boil an egg or even which end of a loaf of bread to cut. The dog looked up again momentarily, and then settled back down. Perhaps it was used to its master dropping things. His heart went out to the old veteran. It was so undignified having to fend for himself.

He did not have to wait much longer. The Major came shuffling in with a tray containing a boiled egg, a slice of bread and a glass of water. "Hope the egg's done to your liking, old chap." Placing the tray on a small table beside David's chair, he sat down opposite him.

Tapping the egg with his spoon, David cut off the top. Yellow yolk oozed out and ran down the sides. He tried to mop it up with the bread before the Major could sense his disgust, but the bread was so stale it just ran off it. He preferred his eggs hard-boiled but, not wanting to offend his friend, he ate it as fast as he could, trying not to make too much of a mess.

He realised his friend was not eating. "Are you not having any, Major?"

"Um…I had a bit of something while I waited for the egg to boil."

David didn't know whether to believe him, and finished the rest of his meal in silence. The Major was snoring loudly again by the time he had finished. He needed to wipe the sticky egg off his hands. On the dresser, just out of reach, was a rather grubby napkin, but he did not fancy using that. He would use his handkerchief instead. Reaching carefully into his pocket, he pulled it out and, spitting on it, managed to wipe off most of the gooey mess whilst Jasper lay forlornly on the rug, looking up at him with sad eyes as if accusing him of eating all the food. He reached out and allowed the dog to lick off the remainder of the egg.

"You could have had it all," he whispered. Reaching down to stroke his bony head, he was startled by a strange noise.

The Major jumped out of his seat, shouting, "That bloody canon's misfired again!"

The old war hero must have thought he was back in the thick of a battle.

David tried to calm him. "Major, you are at home, not on the battlefield."

His friend didn't look convinced, but sat back down, murmuring incoherently as the dog got up and padded across to put its head on its master's knee.

David had never seen his friend like this before. The wretched man was a wreck. Oh, where was Sam? Surely he should be back by now?

If only he could get up out of the damned chair! He needed to investigate whatever it was they had heard. It was not likely to be the thud of snow falling off the roof for he could see through the window that it was not thawing at all. Heaven forbid it was the roof caving in.

Well, he could not just sit there. He had to do something. He tried to ease himself out of the chair, but the splint on his broken leg protruded several inches past his foot and almost reached his armpits. If he could remove it… Reaching forward, he tried to undo the knots in the string, but they were tied so tightly it proved impossible.

Almost at his wit's end, he thumped the arm of the chair, throwing up a cloud of dust that almost choked him. Jasper must have picked up some of his agitation as he came across. "If only you could help," David sighed as he stroked the black head.

"Help?" the Major sat bolt upright. "You need help?

Major Duncan Ambrose Wallace of the Dragoon Guards at your service, sir." He stood up and saluted.

David looked at him in amazement. Perhaps he had better play along. "Thank you, Major, but your services are not required. You may relax."

"Relax? Mustn't do that, that's what they want us to do, then they can swoop in and take over." He grabbed David's arm and tried to pull him up. "Come on, man, we need to get out of here before they find us."

When David didn't stand, he put his arm round his back, yanked him up and dragged him along, oblivious to his cries of pain.

"Major, please stop!" The room was spinning.

"Mustn't stop now, we have to get you to safety."

David tried to disentangle himself but the veteran seemed possessed, pulling him out of the room, through the hall, and into the kitchen, where he deposited him unceremoniously onto a chair.

"We should be safe in here." The Major opened cupboards and looked under the table. "No sign of the enemy."

The pain was excruciating as David bent forward to try once more to get the splint off his leg, but the knots seemed to be even tighter. He could barely focus and thought he could see bone protruding through the bloody bandage.

The Major opened the back door and cautiously peered out. "We mustn't go out there, old chum, the enemy have covered the fields with snow to cover their tracks."

David could feel his face draining of colour and felt sure he was going to pass out. A low droning noise seemed to come from somewhere around his head, and he realised it was emerging from his own mouth. The sound must have alerted the Major, as he came over and knelt down beside him, raising his leg and resting it on a chair.

"Looks bad, old chum, I might have to amputate it."

David almost jumped off the chair in alarm, the dizziness suddenly clearing as he tried to push away the man he had considered to be his saviour. "No, no, believe me, there is no need for anything as drastic as that. Please…"

The Major ignored his pleas and took out a penknife. David screamed, trying to pull his leg away, but the Major held him in an iron grip as he sawed through the string on the splint. The second it snapped, David yanked the board, leaned on it and, with the Major's bent back for support, stood up and hopped over to the door. Panting and light-headed, he tried to open it, but the Major was behind him, breathing down his neck, pushing the door closed.

"I told you, you can't go out there. They're waiting for us."

"Major, the battle is over. It is safe to go out now."

"That's what they want you to think, then they can attack while your defences are down."

"No, Major, you must believe me. There is nobody out there." David tried desperately to convince the old soldier. He did not know how much more he could take and was forced to cling onto the Major's jacket to prevent himself from falling.

A knock came on the other side of the door and someone called, "Hello!"

Relief washed over David as he recognised the voice, but the Major turned the key in the lock. "See, I told you they were out there. Quick, hide under the table."

"Major, it is Sam. He has come to rescue us."

"Nooooo, it's the enemy, I tell you." Pulling David towards the table with one hand, he shouted, "Under there, hide!" He pointed the penknife towards the door.

"Sam, help!" David shouted, trying to pull away.

"Master?" The latch clacked up and down.

Putting his finger up to his lips in a ploy to make the Major think he was co-operating with him, David began to edge towards it, just managing to turn the key before the Major grabbed him again, yelling, "Don't let them in, you fool!"

The groom came bursting in. "What's going on, master?"

"The Major has…" David looked at his old friend, who had slumped to the floor, his arms around his head, crying like a baby. He turned to Sam. "Are you alone?"

"Yes, master, I've brought the pony with the trap, I

thought she would be the most sure-footed."

"We shall have to take the Major with us. We cannot leave him here in this state."

Jasper came in, yawning, ambled over to his master and sat down next to him. The wretched soldier was hunched in the corner, still blubbering.

Sam reached down to examine David's leg. "Can you stand on it, sir?"

"No, it is broken. I did have a splint on it during the night, but the Major cut that off when…" Closing his eyes at the memory of the terror he had felt when he had thought he was going to have his leg amputated by penknife, a shudder ran through him.

Sam gestured with his head towards the Major. "Do you think you'll be safe while I take some blankets and cushions and make the trap comfortable?"

David sat down on a chair. "Yes, make haste. There are some in the living room."

Sam hurried out, leaving David to contemplate on the next course of action. Would his friend come willingly, or did he still think he was surrounded by the enemy?

"Major?" he asked quietly.

The veteran shook his head, murmuring, "You'll regret that. They'll get us in the end."

"It is quite safe now, the enemy have retreated. We have won."

David did not know much about war, never having experienced it, but he hoped that would pacify him.

"Retreated, eh?" The Major stood up, looking all around him as if there might be unseen foes lurking in the shadows, then, as footsteps were heard, he cried, "Ha!" ran to the doorway and pulled Sam inside. He grabbed him round the throat, holding the knife dangerously close to his jugular vein.

"Major!" David yelled frantically. "Let go. Sam is one of us. He is on our side."

"Don't move, master!" Sam cried, his eyes pleading and desperate. "Please don't do anything rash."

The dog suddenly began a high-pitched wailing that

seemed to disturb the Major. "It's all right, boy, I've got it all in hand." He leaned forward towards the dog, giving Sam the opportunity to bring his arms up and knock the knife out of his hand. It clattered harmlessly to the floor. Kicking it across the room, he ran across to David and pulled him roughly towards the door.

David was reluctant to go, though. "We cannot just leave him, Sam, he is ill."

"But he almost killed me. Come on, sir, before he tries again."

David knew it made sense to put as much distance between them and the old soldier, but compassion got the better of him, and he looked back into the room. The Major sat weeping in a chair.

"No, Sam." He pointed to the penknife. "Pick that up and put it out of harm's way."

"But, sir…"

"Look at him, Sam, does he look dangerous now?"

"No, I suppose not."

Remembering seeing a walking-cane in the drawing room, David asked the groom to fetch it. Sam soon returned, then, understandably nervous, he cautiously approached the Major, making small noises as if he were calming a jittery horse. The Major didn't even look up as the groom took his elbow. He could barely stand, so Sam put his arm round his back and urged him forward.

Holding onto the backs of chairs and supporting himself with the cane, David gritted his teeth and followed. While the altercation had been going on, he had almost forgotten about the pain in his leg, but now it was all quiet, it had returned threefold. Light-headed, he had to blink repeatedly to prevent himself from passing out. Sam returned and he eventually made it to the door, after being almost tripped up by Jasper, who had jumped up to follow them.

Snow had started falling again as Sam squeezed them into the cart. Jasper lay under David's leg. The warmth from his furry body was very welcome as they made their way slowly back to The Grange.

Chapter 3

Jamie pressed closer to the window and peered out. "When will Papa be home? It seems ages since Sam went to fetch him."

"Well, Jamie, it takes a lot longer in these snowy conditions." Tillie picked up some of the bread Annabella had thrown on the floor, wondering, herself, why it was taking so long for her beloved husband to get home. She'd dozed fitfully most of the night, eventually assuming David had stayed in Harrogate.

Then that morning, Sam had rushed in. Not staying long enough to get his cuts cleaned up, he had briefly explained about an accident, that David was at the Major's house with a broken leg, and he had come for the pony and trap to bring him home. She'd wondered why the Major didn't have one but, to while away the time until they returned, she'd helped his valet, John, prepare a makeshift bed for him in the drawing room.

"Please stop throwing your food on the floor, Annabella," she grumbled in exasperation. There wasn't any point giving her more. Wiping her hands and face, she took her out of the high chair and placed her on the carpet next to her sister. Alice was playing quietly, having already finished her meal. How like their father they were. She would never stop rejoicing in the fact. But where was he?

"It's snowing again." Jamie sighed. "I s'pose that'll make 'em even later."

Tillie went across to join him, putting her arm around his shoulder as she looked out at the white landscape. The nursery window faced the drive, so they would have a clear view of anyone coming, but there was no sign of movement and it was already beginning to get dark. Where on earth were they?

She turned back into the room, on edge and snapping at the children for the slightest reason, which was very unlike her.

She usually had the patience of Job. Jamie remained on sentry duty at the window, twiddling with the tassel on the curtain tie and humming quietly to himself.

Unable to bear the tension any longer—she still hadn't told him about Sarah and George—Tillie jumped up and made for the door.

"Look after the girls for a minute, Jamie. I'll go and fetch Auntie Ruby."

Annabella immediately began to wail. Taking a deep breath, Tillie picked her up, rather more roughly than she'd intended, saying to Alice, "You be a good girl and stay with your brother." The child toddled over to Jamie. He helped her up onto the window seat next to him, putting his arm protectively around her.

"Papa'll be home soon, won't he, Alice?" Tillie heard him crooning to her as she went out.

Thank goodness she was not as needy and clingy as her twin.

* * * *

Jamie loved playing with his little sisters. He tried to think of a song to sing to Alice. He had already taught her most of the ones he'd learnt from Auntie Ruby, and every now and again he would make one up on the spot.

Singing,
"Hey, my lovely little girl,
You've got such a pretty curl,
Don't you know how lucky you be
To have a brother just like me?"

His finger twisted one of the blonde curls that had escaped from her bonnet. He received a big smile in return.

"D'yer like that one?" he asked with a grin, receiving a nod. "Thought you would. Me too."

She put her arms round him. "Thaimy," she lisped, planting a kiss on his cheek.

"I love you, too, my darling little sister." He felt very grown up, knowing he was in charge of her. "What shall we play now?" He tried to think of a game they hadn't played for a long time. "I know, let's play tiddlywinks."

Alice clapped her hands in glee. "Tink," she shrieked, making him blink in surprise. She was usually so quiet.

"I bet you can't remember what it is," he laughed.

"Tink," she repeated, as if to say that she certainly could. She climbed down and toddled over to the cupboard where their games were stored. Opening the door, she bent forward and peered inside before looking up at him with an enquiring gaze.

He reached in and took out one or two toys and some of the boxes. "I'm sure it was in here last time I looked," he murmured, rummaging around again. Then, his face beaming, he produced a small brown box. "Here 'tis, Alice. I knew it was in there."

Jumping up and down, she repeated, "Tink, tink."

They emptied the contents onto the carpet, and he placed the pot a few feet away. "Do you want to be red or green?"

She picked up a red one and threw it at the cup. It landed inside. Clapping her hands, a huge grin appeared on her face.

"Not like that, silly. That's cheating. This is what you should do." He picked up the large wink and pressed it on the edge of a smaller green one. It flew into the air and landed halfway across the room. "Oo, a bit too hard," he chuckled. He handed her a large one. "You have a go."

She tried but couldn't get the small wink airborne at all. She began to get rather impatient, saying, "Tink" with such ferocity he began to laugh. He was about to help her when the red one flew into the air and landed smack inside the pot.

"Hooray," he shouted. "You did it."

Jumping up, she shrieked. They danced round the room gleefully before he sat down again. "Now, I've got to do it." No matter how many times he tried, though, he just couldn't get his green wink into the pot. Eventually, he gave up.

* * * *

Tillie and Annabella met Ruby coming up the stairs with

her hands full of clean laundry.

"Why aren't they back yet?" her sister asked anxiously. "Sam and the master? I thought they would've been home ages ago."

"I wish I knew. I'm getting really worried." The child in her arms began to whine and wriggle. "Oh, for heaven's sake, stop it!" She was almost at the end of her tether.

Putting down the clothes, Ruby took the child from her. "There, there," she cooed, "Mama isn't feeling herself. Come on, let's go back upstairs." She turned to Tillie, who was almost in tears by this point. "Are the other two still in the nursery?"

Nodding, Tillie took a deep breath to calm herself. "Thank you, Ruby," she whispered as her sister walked away. "I'm sure you're just as worried as me."

There was something else she had a feeling she needed to tell David when he eventually did arrive home. She knew he would be ecstatic. It was what he'd been wanting, but she hadn't had it confirmed.

She met Purvis in the hall. "Why aren't they home?" she asked anxiously.

"If only I knew, ma'am." He opened the front door and peered out.

Edging past him, she stood on the top step, screwing up her eyes to see down the driveway. Where were they? They should have been back hours ago. All her senses were screaming at her to go out and look for them, but cold reason stopped her as snow fell on her upturned face.

But if I hadn't gone out to look for Jamie after Grandmama's funeral, she thought, *I wouldn't be standing here now.*

"Would you fetch my coat, please, Purvis."

"But, ma'am…"

"I can't bear the uncertainty any longer. I have to do something."

"But, Tillie…" The wrinkled face of the aged butler pleaded with her. "You know it would be absolutely foolhardy."

"I wondered where the draught was coming from." Nellie appeared behind them. "What are you doing out here? Is the master coming?" She squeezed past them and peered out into the gloom.

Purvis stood with his hands on his hips, his lips pursed. "No, Nellie, this foolish girl wants to go out and look for them, but I won't allow it."

"Of course you can't possibly go anywhere in this weather. Don't be so…" Nellie put her hand on Tillie's arm, but she shrugged it off.

"I don't care what you two say, I'm going."

She ran back into the house, her mind set. They couldn't stop her. Running to the cloakroom, she grabbed the nearest coat and bonnet, but was prevented from getting out of the room by the equally determined servants.

"Please let me pass." She was the mistress of the house. They should obey her.

"No, young lady, you are not going anywhere."

"I have to. Don't you understand? I can't just let them…"

Putting her hands on Tillie's shoulders, Nellie looked deeply into her eyes. "Think of those three children upstairs. What would happen to them if you didn't come back?" She then patted her mistress's belly. "And this one here."

Tillie gasped. She wasn't even sure herself, so how had the housekeeper guessed?

"I'm right, aren't I?" Nellie took the coat and hung it back up.

Realising she was defeated, Tillie let herself be led into the kitchen. With tears streaming down her face, she sat down at the table. "I just wish I knew why they're not home," she wept. "I feel so helpless."

Jamie came running in, but stopped abruptly. "Why're you crying, Mama? Papa ain't dead, is he?"

"No, Jamie," Nellie reassured him. "Your mama's just worried."

He went across and rested his head on his mother's shoulder. "Don't cry, Mama. He'll be all right."

Straightening, Tillie wrapped him in her arms. How could she have considered leaving him? She shivered and hugged him even tighter. "Oh, Jamie, what would I do without you?"

"Oo, I nearly forgot...Auntie Ruby sent me down to ask if you want her to bath the twins and put them to bed."

Tillie looked up at the clock on the wall. Was it that time already? Drumming her fingers on the table, she tried hard not to give in to her fears again. "Tell Auntie Ruby it's too cold to give them a bath, they had one last week anyway, but I'd be very grateful if she could get them ready for bed. I'll be up in a moment to say goodnight. Thank you, Jamie."

As he went out, she stood up suddenly, almost knocking over the drink Freda had placed in front of her.

"Sit yourself down for a minute and drink your tea," Nellie insisted. "You'll only work yourself up into a frenzy, and that won't be good for either of you."

She knew it made sense, but couldn't rid her mind of impending doom. She'd been so happy for the past three years. It had been almost too good to be true after the trauma of searching for Jamie all that time. Was it going to end in tragedy?

A disturbance at the front door aroused her. Were they finally home safe and sound?

Jumping up, she ran out of the kitchen, followed by Nellie and Freda. Purvis opened the door. But it wasn't her beloved husband who fell in through the doorway, his face covered in blood.

"It's Major Wallace!" cried Nellie.

Tillie brushed past his prostate body to look outside. "Major, where's David?"

"Had to get away." The veteran looked up at them with terror in his eyes.

"Who from?"

"The enemy."

They all looked at each other, baffled.

"But, where's David?"

"Did we make it?" the Major murmured.

"Yes, Major. But where's my husband, and Sam?"

They were obviously not going to get a meaningful answer from him. Tillie looked back outside. She couldn't make anything out in the dusk, could barely even see to the end of the drive, but she could tell there was nobody else there. She was so tempted to ignore what Nellie had said earlier and run out, but she was already shivering. Reluctantly, she turned back indoors.

The Major was in the drawing room, slumped in an armchair. Freda brought a bowl of water and some cloths and cleaned his face before applying some ointment to the wounds.

Tillie paced up and down, trying to remain calm. She turned to Nellie. "Do you think we ought to call out Doctor Abrahams?"

Nellie pondered for a moment as Freda came back in with some clean towels. "What do you think, Freda? Should we call the doctor?"

"Would he be able to get through in this weather? The Major looks settled now, he's even dropped off to sleep, bless him."

"But what's he done with the master and Sam?"

"I'll find John, see if he'll go out and look for them," Nellie suggested as she went out.

Tillie was working herself up into a state again. Raking her hands through her hair, she ran back to the front door and yanked it open once more. The darkness enveloped her as she took a step out. It was eerily quiet, the cry of a barn owl the only sound to be heard. Her beloved husband was out there somewhere, possibly lying in a ditch, hurt, bleeding, or even…

She couldn't contemplate the other possibility. Surely, she would have had a sign of some sort. No, she had to remain positive, for the children's sake.

Jamie came running up to her. "Mama, where's Papa?"

She turned and enfolded him in her arms. "I don't know." She was dangerously close to tears, but couldn't let him know how worried she was. Taking a deep breath, she closed the door. "Come on, let's play a game before you go to bed." Anything to take her mind off the situation. "We haven't played Snakes and Ladders for a long time, have we?"

"I think some of the bits are missing." He looked down sheepishly. "I forgot to put them away, and Nellie said she would throw them out if…" He grimaced.

"Oh, well, we can soon make some more. What else would you like to do?"

"Can I have another go at me new jigsaw?"

"Are you sure that's all there?"

"Yes, Mama, I always make sure me jigsaws are put away, 'specially the new one. It's got owls and nightingales on it." He looked up at her. "When's Sarah coming again?"

Should she tell him now? She'd been trying to find the right time all day. When she didn't answer straight away, he continued. "She loves birds, don't she?"

"My darling, there's something I need to tell you."

"About birds?"

"No, about Sarah."

"She's not hurt again, is she? Like that time in the park?"

"Well, not hurt, exactly."

He gazed at her, his brow furrowed. "I'm a big boy, now, Mama. I'm eleven. You can tell me."

She took his hand. "I know, Jamie, but you need to be brave." She took a deep breath before continuing. "Sarah is very, very poorly."

"She will get better though, won't she?" He raised his eyebrows, nodding.

"The doctors hope so."

"Phew, that's all right, then."

"But George…"

"I don't care if George is dead, he's horrible. Do you remember that time he—"

She had to stop him. She grabbed his arm. "But that's just it, Jamie, he is."

"What? Dead? Really dead? Oh, Ma, I didn't mean it." His stricken face fell. She wrapped her arms around him. "Why did he die?" he murmured into her bosom.

"You remember Uncle Victor had that nasty disease? Well, George caught it as well and wasn't strong enough to fight it."

He lifted his head and pulled away from her. "Is that what Sarah's got?"

"Yes."

"Don't let her die."

"Like I said, the doctors are hopeful she'll pull through." She looked into his eyes. "So we must pray that she does, and stay positive."

"Mm, I'll say loads of extra prayers tonight."

"That's the spirit. Come on, let's get the jigsaw out."

Concentrating on putting the pieces together, Jamie hummed quietly, occasionally stopping and looking thoughtful.

Tillie walked over to the window. Try as she might, she couldn't just sit on the floor, playing. Parting the heavy brocade curtains, she peered out into the night, remembering another night, many years ago.

She could visualise her mother pacing the floor, chewing her fingernails.

"Why isn't Pa home yet?" Tillie had asked. At twelve years old she'd been the only one still up. Her brothers and sister had gone to bed.

"I don't know. I'm getting rather worried. Nip down street, would you, and check whether Mr Potter's home. I think he's on same shift as your pa."

Pulling on her old brown coat and wrapping a thick scarf around her head, Tillie had run outside. She hadn't realised it was snowing so hard. She could barely see where she was going.

Reaching the Potter's house, she'd tapped on the door. Nobody had answered, so she'd knocked harder.

"There's no-one in, lass," a deep voice had emerged from the darkness. "Ain't you heard? There's been an explosion down Moorside pit. They've all gone to help."

"Oh, no, that's where my pa works!"

She'd flown back up the street. Her mother had been at the door, pulling on her coat. Getting closer, she could tell she already knew.

"Stay with the little ones, Tillie. I have to go and find out what's happening."

Her ten-year old brother, Matthew, had appeared, looking bleary-eyed. "What's going on?"

A Dilemma for Jamie

"You explain, Tillie, I need to be going." Her mother had joined the throng of people running down the lane that led to the colliery.

Tillie had quickly filled her brother in on what had happened.

"I'd better go and help," he'd called. Running back into the house, he'd got dressed and within minutes had followed his mother. Frustrated at not being able to do the same, Tillie had checked on her younger brother, Harry, and sister Ruby, who had luckily remained sound asleep.

Going back to the front door, she'd seen her next-door neighbour standing at her own doorway. Seizing the opportunity, Tillie had asked her to keep an eye on the children, and had run off after the rest of the village. Even though it was dark and snowing hard, she'd known the way and could see lights in the distance.

She'd soon caught up with an elderly man carrying a lantern. "Is there any news?" she'd asked anxiously.

"Yes, lass," he'd said, grim-faced. "About twenty men have been killed."

"Twenty? Oh, please God, don't let me pa be one of 'em!"

The man had been walking slowly, so she'd bade him farewell and run on ahead. Slipping on an icy patch, she'd grazed her hand, but had jumped up straight away.

The wailing and crying could be heard long before she'd arrived. That sound would always haunt her.

Shuddering at the remembrance of it, she wrapped her arms around her midriff, rocking side to side. Did she really want to remember any more? Resting her head back in the large armchair, she felt as if she was in a bubble. Jamie, playing across the room, sounded far away. Closing her eyes, she was once more back in the past.

The area around the colliery had been well lit up. Bodies were being carried out of the pithead on stretchers and each one caused the wail to increase. She'd found Matthew helping to carry the stretcher of a collier who'd raised a hand and waved to show he was still alive.

"Any news of Pa yet?" she'd shouted above the moaning and crying. He'd shaken his head.

She'd soon spotted her mother with a group of women and had run to them as another stretcher had been brought out. The whole group had moved towards it as one entity, leaning forward to see if the lifeless body belonged to them. A woman had broken away from the group, screaming, and the remainder had stepped back with a collective sigh, closing the gap that the hapless woman had left. Then another woman had run forward, crying with relief as a man with a bandage round his head had stumbled out.

Then the nightmare had reached its peak as she'd seen Matthew draw back the blanket covering the body of the next casualty. He had dropped to his knees, his head in his hands.

"Noooo…" she'd heard her mother yell as, pushing Tillie behind her, she'd run towards him.

"Mama!" Jamie was tugging at her sleeve. She could feel tears running down her cheeks. "Mama, what's the matter?"

Before she could reply, Nellie came running in. "Sam's home."

Tillie jumped up, wiping her face with the back of her hand, and pushed past the housekeeper. "Where are they?"

"He's in the kitchen, but…"

She raced out, wondering why the housekeeper had said Sam, rather than the master. Entering the kitchen, she looked round for her husband. Her mind registered Freda tending to the groom's face that was covered in blood. His arm was hanging limply by his side. But there was no sign of David.

"Where's the master?" she yelled, running across and grabbing Sam's shoulder. "Where is he?"

Sam flinched as he looked up at her with tears in his eyes. Tillie stared at him, waiting for him to speak. He looked down again, shaking his head.

She shrieked, "No! You don't mean…?"

For a few seconds, the room went deathly silent, then

everyone was talking at once, bombarding him with questions.

"Mama?" Jamie tugged at Tillie's apron, but she couldn't answer. She slumped down on the floor, too numb to cry, back in her bubble. She should have known that thinking of her father's death had been a portent of bad news. It was her fault her beloved husband was now lying dead in the snow. If she hadn't been thinking like that…

Chapter 4

Tillie had to know for certain. Jumping up, she declared, "He's surely mistaken. I'm going out to find my husband."

Brushing aside the protests from everyone in the room, she marched to the hall. Grabbing the first coat she found, she strode out of the front door.

"If I'd gone out earlier, I might have been able to save him," she mumbled. "They're not stopping me now."

Ruby came running after her. "If you're determined, then I'm coming with you."

"You get back to your fiancé. He needs you now."

"I know, but at least he's safe. You need me more. I'm coming."

Pulling the coat around her, Tillie realised it was one of David's. His cologne still clung to it. She breathed it in and quickened her step. The lantern Ruby was carrying gave scant light for them to see their way and they repeatedly slipped.

"How do you know we're going in the right direction?" Ruby gasped breathlessly after a few minutes. "We can scarcely see where we're going. I'm not even sure we're still on the path."

"I just know."

"But…"

"Ruby, save your breath for keeping up with me."

He can't be dead, he can't. Tillie strode out even faster, her head down, listening for any sound that could indicate that Sam had been wrong, but all she could hear was their breathing.

Suddenly a weird, wailing sound came from their left. They stopped.

"David!" Tillie yelled at the top of her voice. "Is that you?"

The sound ceased. They stood still, listening hard.

"David," she repeated quietly.

A Dilemma for Jamie

"It was probably a fox." Ruby pulled at her. "Let's go back, Tillie, we'll never find him in the dark."

"You can go back, Ruby, but if it takes all night, I'm staying out. I have to find him." She began to walk on when something shot past her.

"That was a dog, wasn't it?" cried Ruby.

"Yes, maybe it was David's new bloodhound and it can smell his scent. Which way did it go?"

"I'm not sure, it ran off so fast."

"Come on, Ruby, we have to follow it."

Changing direction, they followed the dog's paw prints in the snow. Fortunately, the ground was fairly flat and level.

"What's the dog's name, Tillie? We could call it."

"I don't know. He hasn't had it that long."

"It must have gone this way. I can still vaguely see some prints."

They increased their pace, screwing up their eyes and listening for any sound of the dog.

A closed gate loomed up before them. Ruby leaned over it. "We must have come the wrong way. A bloodhound wouldn't be able to jump over that, would it?"

"I'm not sure. Maybe if it had its tracking head on. Shh, is that the dog?" Tillie grabbed her sister's arm, then lunged at the latch on the gate, trying to open it. It wouldn't budge. "Oh, for goodness sake, open, you stupid gate!"

"Here, let me try." Ruby pulled at the latch, but she couldn't open it either.

"Mind out of the way. I'm climbing over." Without further ado, pushing Ruby aside, Tillie pulled up her dress and clambered up. Her petticoat caught on a nail. She yanked it off and jumped down the other side, then ran on, beyond caring whether her sister came after her or not.

She could definitely hear barking. "David!" she yelled again at the top of her voice, then croaked, "Please be alive."

The barking grew louder. Tillie's eyes were so full of tears that, even though they had become accustomed to the darkness, she couldn't see where she was going. A voice was calling from behind. That meant Ruby was following, but there was no time to wait for her to catch up.

The barking was now so loud that the dog must have been directly in front of her, but she still couldn't see it. She yelped as she fell over something. It was the shape of a body. A wet nose pushed into her hand and she wrapped her arms around the dog. "I think you've found him, you wonderful creature, you've found him."

Ruby came running up, panting. "Is it the master?"

"Shine that lantern over here."

Her sister did as she was bid. "It's him, but is he still alive?" Ruby looked anxiously into his face.

"I'm not sure. He's really cold, but I think I can feel his chest moving." His cheeks were freezing, so Tillie kissed his icy cold lips, blowing air into his mouth. He gasped slightly, so she repeated the action.

"We need to warm him up." Tillie began to take off her coat but Ruby grabbed her arm.

"Don't be foolish, you'll die of the cold as well."

"But we can't just leave him. What are we to do?"

A voice came from behind them. "Hello…Tillie, Ruby!"

Both girls jumped up at once. "It's Tom!" gasped Ruby. "Over here, Tom, over here."

Ruby ran back towards him, leaving Tillie in the dark once more. She lay down next to her husband, wrapping her arms around him. "It's all right, my darling, I'm here. We'll soon have you home," she crooned. "I knew you wouldn't be dead, I just knew it."

* * * *

Jamie stood and stared at Sam. He'd never seen so much blood before. His mama had started shouting, and then she'd run out, followed by Auntie Ruby. He'd been about to follow them, but Nellie had pulled him back. "No, Master Jamie. You stay here. We don't want you getting lost as well." So he'd had to stay behind, much as he'd wanted to go and help.

He thought about what his mama had told him. Was George really dead? No, he must have heard her wrong. After all, she hadn't seemed herself, had she? Wasn't that what Auntie Ruby often said about her? He wondered if he should ask Freda if it was true, but what with Sam and everything...

He sat on a stool, watching as the cook washed Sam's cuts and put ointment on them. Touching the scar on his own chin, he remembered the time he'd fallen over at the stile when he'd been going to Auntie Ruby's and, as it turned out, his grandmama's house soon after he'd first come to The Grange. She'd put some special ointment on him. He wondered if Freda's was as good.

"I think you had better go upstairs, Master Jamie," Nellie said. "The twins are on their own."

"But they'll be asleep."

"I know, but I would feel happier if there was someone sensible with them."

Feeling really special, he jumped down from the stool. It wasn't very often he was given *important* jobs. He was sometimes asked to mind the girls, just as a favour. Puffing out his chest, he whistled as he went up to check on his sisters. They were sleeping quite peacefully, so he sat reading his favourite book. After a while, he thought about going down to see if his papa was home. Just one more chapter, though.

* * * *

On the morning of Christmas Eve, Jamie ran into the lounge, jumping up and down excitedly, "Can I go and help pick some ivy and stuff from the woods?"

"As long as you do what Tom says." Tillie was determined to make an effort for the children's sakes.

Everyone helped decorate the house with the greenery, and she had to admit the holly with its bright, red berries, the baubles and the silver star on the tree did perk up her spirits.

On Christmas morning, the children were allowed to go in and wish their father a happy Christmas, and take him the presents they'd made, but he wasn't in a fit state to reply, let alone open them. She did her best to exclaim with delight as they ripped off the paper from their own presents, most of them being a surprise to her because Nellie and Ruby had bought them or made them. Being so few, she felt rather penny-pinching but, without David to help, and after nursing him day and night, she just didn't have the time or the energy to do much about them, just being glad to get through the day, slumping into an early bed.

* * * *

Some weeks later, feeling a lot better, David was able to talk, without shaking, about what had happened that dreadful day. "I don't know which was more terrifying: thinking I had landed in the river when the horse slipped, or the Major attempting to amputate my leg with his penknife."

"My poor darling, I can't imagine what you went through." Tillie sat in the chair beside his bed, holding his hand. "But tell me what happened after you left his house. Sam can't seem to remember much."

"I recall being squashed in the cart, trying to keep my leg straight. It was resting on top of the Major's dog and must have been a dead weight, for it kept wriggling."

"It must have been his dog that found you. Ruby and I thought it was your new gun dog."

"Thank God he did, or I would not be here now."

"Then what happened?"

"I thought the Major was asleep but then, all of a sudden, he grabbed the reins from Sam and stood up, yelling, 'Forwards, men, into battle.' He then whipped the wretched pony. It bolted and…" David shuddered.

Tillie stroked his face. "Don't tell me any more if it's too painful."

"The doctor says it helps to talk about these things."

"But surely not if it's going to upset you?"

He laid his head back on the pillows, closing his eyes for a moment, then opening them again quickly. "Better not do that. Each time I do, I see the cart careering out of control and breaking up as it overturned down a bank, sending us all flying in different directions."

He reached up to give Tillie a kiss as she straightened his pillows. "Now I understand how frustrated you must have been, my darling wife, the time you were forced to stay in bed when you were injured by that stray bullet. I feel like I have been in here forever. Thank goodness I do not need bleeding any more. Doctor Abrahams said it is not having any benefit."

"Yes, but you still have to remain in bed a few more days."

He lifted up the side of the counterpane and patted the sheet seductively. "Join me?"

Smiling wryly, she shook her head. "You know that would be impossible, with all the comings and goings, much as I would love to." Bending down, she gave him a lingering kiss.

"Well, could you not creep in during the night? Nobody would interrupt us then."

"The doctor said, 'no physical exertion', remember?"

"He is just a spoilsport."

"It's for your own good. You're lucky to be alive."

"I know, I know, so everyone keeps telling me."

"So be patient. You know I'm just as eager as you to get back to our loving relationship. In fact, it's driving me mad, not being able to lie down with you."

"My poor darling, I sympathise with you. But multiply that by a thousand fold, and you will have an idea of how I feel."

She brushed his dark hair back from his forehead. She rather liked it longer, but knew he would consider it not to be in a fashionable style, and would get John to cut it as soon as he was well enough.

She still hadn't told him she was expecting another baby. She'd been putting it off until the right time, but there never seemed to be one. Maybe now. She took a deep breath. "My darling, there's something I need to…"

A loud knock on the door stopped her. Eyes raised to the ceiling, she sighed.

"Come in," David called.

Jamie entered, holding his sisters' hands. "May we come in and say goodnight, Papa?"

"Of course, children." David struggled to adjust his position so they could sit on the edge of the bed.

"Are you better now, Papa?"

"Well, I'm getting there."

Alice took her thumb out of her mouth, kissed her father's hand, and then replaced it immediately.

David stroked her golden head, and reached over to do the same to Annabella. His face beamed as he surveyed his family, unaware it was going to increase.

Tillie would have loved to prolong the happy scene but, after a minute or two, could see David's eyes beginning to close. "Come on, children, your father must rest now."

"Goodnight, Papa. May we come and see you again tomorrow?" Jamie kissed the top of David's head.

David nodded as Tillie ushered the children out. "Take the girls up to the nursery, please, Jamie, and I'll be up in a minute."

Replacing her husband's covers, she rued that, once again, she'd failed to give him the important news.

"What were you going to say?" he murmured, not opening his eyes.

"Nothing, darling, it can wait."

Bending down, she kissed his cheek and ran her fingers over his face where the bruises had been. Only one or two small scabs still remained. Shivering in remembrance, she offered up a prayer for his miraculous recovery, and thanked God she hadn't believed Sam when he'd inferred that his master had died. Divine intervention had definitely been at play that night.

Approaching the nursery, she could hear singing and stopped to listen. Jamie's clear voice rang out, reminding her of church bells on Sundays beckoning them to morning service. She hadn't been since the accident but, now that David was recovering, she would make a special effort the following Sunday so she could thank God in person.

Ruby had been teaching the children some new songs. The twins could only utter occasional snippets, but Jamie knew them all off by heart and would often sing them to sleep.

Hesitant about interrupting the delightful sound, she paused but, wanting to say goodnight to the twins before they went to sleep, she opened the door quietly and crept in.

Both girls were tucked up in their cot, their nightcaps covering their ringlets. They looked so snug and warm. Alice's eyes were closed, her lips gently sucking her habitual thumb, and Annabella was lying next to her, curled up in a ball. They liked to sleep together when Annabella was well enough and unlikely to disturb her twin. A large grin appeared on her face when she saw her mama.

"Ma…ma," she murmured as Tillie bent down to kiss her. Her chubby arms reached out for a cuddle. Tillie enfolded her in a hug. Alice mumbled something without opening her eyes, so Tillie gave her a quick kiss on her cheek before covering them both up.

"They've learnt another new song today, Mama." Jamie whispered as he put his arm around her waist on the way out. "They want to sing it to Papa tomorrow."

"That's great, Jamie. I really appreciate all the time you're spending with them. It's helped me so much while your father's been laid up."

"Well, I thought I'd better learn 'em as many songs as I could before I go away to…that boarding school."

Tillie knew Jamie wasn't looking forward to going to school, but it had been arranged before David's accident. She'd argued for days, saying she'd lost him once and it would seem as if she was losing him again, but David had been adamant. "It's tradition in my family," he had insisted.

"What was it like?" she'd asked him.

He'd shrugged. "Not too bad, I suppose. You get used to it. Eventually, the other boys, and even some of the teachers, become like your family."

"I can't imagine what it's like, not having your brothers and sisters with you when you grow up."

"Well, sometimes Annie…" David had shrugged again. She'd known what he'd meant.

Jamie interrupted her thoughts. "Do I really have to go? I'd much rather stay here with you and Papa and the twins and

Auntie Ruby and…"

"I know, my darling, but your father insists, and I daren't go against his wishes while he's so weak."

Jamie's sad, solemn face almost broke her resolve, but she had to try to encourage him to stay positive. "Just think of all the new friends you'll make. You already know Sebastian from Upper Hall. He's been there nearly a year now, so he'll be able to show you what to do and how to conduct yourself. And anyway, it's not until September, so there's plenty of time yet."

"It's not fair. George doesn't…Oh, I forgot." He hung his head in sorrow. "I still keep forgetting that he's…dead. I know I didn't like him, but I didn't want him dead."

She hugged him. "Your papa's hoping Sarah will be well enough to come and visit us quite soon."

His eyes lit up. "Really? I'll write her a letter in the morning, shall I?"

"Yes, my darling, you do that. I'm sure it will help her recover more quickly. Now, off to bed."

"Aw, Mama, I'm not tired. Can't I stay up a little while longer?"

Tillie rolled her eyes. "I suppose so, just another half an hour."

Giving her a squeeze, Jamie ran off down the corridor, and Tillie went in search of Freda to finalise the menu for the following day. She didn't really think Sarah would be well enough to come for quite some time, but it was only a little white lie to keep him happy.

* * * *

Jamie sat chewing the end of his pencil, wondering what to write in his letter to Sarah.

Should he tell her about having to go away to school? He knew she had been going for a long time, but only day school. She didn't have to board. In fact, he remembered she'd been telling him about it on the way to the park, when she'd almost been killed, and he'd…But he didn't want to think about that. Everything had turned out well in the end, as his mama told him whenever he broached the subject. He didn't want to start having nightmares about it again.

He might as well tell her about the school. Mama had said it was a—what did she call it?—a milestone. Yes, that was it, an important milestone in his life.

Chewing the end of his pencil, he wondered if he ought to say sorry about George. Would she think he was being—he knew there was a word for saying something you didn't mean, he had heard his mama saying it—hippo something or other? But it wouldn't seem right to ignore it. Maybe he could put, 'How awful it was', or 'How upset you must be'. That sounded rather grand, but you said things like that in letters.

He finally decided on, *'I am really sorry about George. I bet you miss him,'* continuing with, *'I have been singing lots more songs to the twins. Annabella can talk much more than Alice.*

Oh, by the way, I have some really important news: I heard Nellie and Freda whispering when they did not know I was there. You will never guess what. Mama might be having another baby.'

That should cheer her up.

He finished with, *'I can't wait 'til you can come and visit.'* then sealed the letter, wrote her address on the front, and took it downstairs to put on the plate in the hall to be posted.

* * * *

David sat up as Tillie walked in. "Any news on the Major?" he asked as she put a cup of tea on his bedside cabinet.

"They say he's gone completely mad and been put in the asylum for his own safety."

"Poor man."

"But David, he almost killed you."

"I know, darling, but it was not his fault. It must have been the after effects of the war."

"You're so forgiving. I don't know if I could be as understanding. I almost lost you. I still shudder at the thought."

"Come here." David pulled her down to kiss her,

enfolding her in his arms. Settling on the edge of the bed, returning his kiss with fervour, she revelled in the comfort of his embrace. *Was it the time to tell him now?*

Seemingly reading her mind, he asked, "Was there something you wanted to ask me?"

"Well, there is something I need to tell you. I hope you'll be happy about it."

"Out with it, then."

She remained within the cocoon of his arms, her eyes tightly closed in case he found the news unsatisfying. "I'm expecting another baby," she whispered.

"I thought so."

Exhaling the breath she didn't realise she'd been holding, she pulled away and looked into his laughing eyes. "You…but how?"

"I have had my suspicions for a week or two. You have put on weight already."

"So why didn't you say something earlier? I've been going through hell, not wanting you to be upset in your state, in case you were unhappy about it."

"Unhappy? How on earth could you think that? It is marvellous news."

"But the twins are so young."

"You will cope, my darling, as you do so splendidly with everything that life throws at you." He kissed her passionately before continuing. "And would it not be a bonus if it was a boy?"

She raised her eyebrows.

"Now, do not go reading anything into that about me being unsatisfied with Jamie. You know I love him as much as if he was my own flesh and blood. I have adopted him and made him my heir, but…"

"You would like a son of your own. I understand."

"Are you sure of that?"

"Yes, of course, my dearest husband." Giving him a peck on the cheek, she stood up. She really did understand, but deep inside her, she felt slightly peevish. She knew it was silly to do so. She would love another little boy, herself, so why did she feel like this?

"That reminds me," she said. "We were going to invite Matthew and Jessie to come with their two youngsters, weren't we, before all this happened? Matty Junior must be three now. He was born just before we got married, and Lily's almost one. How time flies."

"As soon as I am well enough, we shall send them an invitation."

She tidied David's bedclothes before giving him another kiss on the top of his head. "Now get some sleep. The doctor said you can get up tomorrow for a little—I stress *little*—while."

He raised his eyes to the ceiling. "Really, Tillie, sometimes you treat me like one of the children. I was here when he said it, remember?"

"Of course, I'm sorry."

He stretched, raising his arms high in the air. "Anyway, my darling wife, I cannot wait to get out of this bed. I might even have a little rehearsal and have a wander round if I wake up in the night."

She looked up immediately, her eyes wide and mouth open, about to utter a protestation, but he grinned. "Only teasing."

Sucking in her breath, she shook her head. "You delight in vexing me, don't you?"

"Ah, my darling, but there is one way you could make sure I stay in bed all night…"

Her eyebrows shot up until she realised what he meant. "You never give up, do you?"

Laughing, he reached up and drew her resisting body towards his. "Just a cuddle, then, to help me sleep."

His hands caressed her swollen breasts and she moaned in frustration, as gently disentangling herself, she dropped a last kiss on his aroused lips and hurried out of the door. She'd been longing to ask the doctor when it would be safe to resume marital relationships, but it would be too embarrassing to talk to a man about it.

Chapter 5

David was already out of bed and dressed the following morning when Tillie went in to him.

"I am so excited, Tillie. Is that ridiculous? Who would believe a grown man could get so animated about leaving his bed to go outside?"

"Well, you have been in here a long while."

"Come on, wife, show me the way. It is such a long time since I left this room, that I have almost forgotten what the rest of the house looks like."

Laughing, Tillie helped him up as John arrived. "Sir, I haven't shaved you yet. You can't go out half-dressed."

"Do not bother about that today, John. I do not have time."

"But, sir…"

Tillie intervened, sensing that her husband was already tiring. "It's all right, John, maybe later."

David's face was already suffused with pain as John and Purvis helped their master down to the hall, where they put him in a wheelchair that had been made ready.

Jamie came running down the stairs as David slumped into the chair. "Papa, Papa, you made it," he squealed with delight.

David looked up at him, grimacing with pain, but obviously trying hard to smile.

"Can I see your bad leg, now, Papa?" Jamie continued, seemingly unaware of his father's agony. "Did they really have to cut it off?"

"Not now, Jamie." Tillie reached out to stop her son pulling up his father's trouser leg. "Your papa…"

"But you said I could see it when Papa was better."

"Later, Jamie."

Looking at her sideways, he took hold of her hand. "Isn't he really better?"

"Not quite. It's going to take a long time."

He reached over and kissed his father on the cheek. "Sorry, Papa. I just thought…"

David merely smiled and ruffled his son's hair as Nellie appeared. "Oh, Master, how good to see you up." Her face dropped as she looked questioningly at Tillie, obviously noticing the thin, pursed lips of her master.

"Take me…outside," David stuttered.

Nellie fussed, tucking the blanket around his legs. "Even though the sun's shining, it's still very cold out there. I'll fetch some more." She hurried off as Tillie began to push the wheelchair across the hall towards the front door. It was a lot harder than she'd expected, and she was forced to stop.

"Let me push it, Mama." Jamie grabbed the handles as she took a deep breath.

What had she been thinking about, in her condition?

"How are we going to get Papa down the step?" Jamie asked as John opened the large oak door.

"I'll take him." John took over as Nellie rushed up with two thick, checked blankets and wrapped them around her master, tucking them in tightly.

The sun felt warm on their faces as they walked down the drive towards the lawns. A robin began singing in the tree to the left, and Tillie watched her husband close his eyes. His face relaxed, a look of contentment replacing his earlier pained expression. The freezing winter had developed into a warm spring and the trees were full of buds. A host of yellow daffodils fluttered in the flowerbeds, their faint scent wafting on the breeze, and bright red tulips had their petals open to the sun.

The sound of babyish voices filtered through to her as Ruby came round the corner with the twins, looking snug in their blue coats and bonnets.

"Pa…pa," uttered Annabella who looked as if she was about to launch herself at her father, but Ruby quickly picked her up before she was able to.

Alice stood demurely at his side, smiling up at him. "Pa," she lisped before her thumb went back in her mouth.

Smiling, David reached out and stroked her head, but remained silent.

"Are you enjoying it, Papa?" Jamie asked, looking worried.

David merely nodded slowly.

"We'll just have one short tour around the garden, and then we'll get back." Tillie began to walk ahead while John pushed the wheelchair, and Annabella wriggled in Ruby's arms, so she was allowed to get down and run about. It felt so good to have the warm sunshine on them and to breathe the sweet, fresh air.

David began to cough.

"We'd better return to the house." Tillie quickly tucked the blanket in again and pulled his hat further onto his head. "We don't want you catching cold."

He shook his head vehemently. "No," he muttered in between coughs. "Not yet."

"But, darling…"

He grabbed her hand. His breathing evened out as the attack abated. "One more…minute."

She looked at John, who shook his head.

"We'll begin to walk back slowly," she conceded.

"Papa, you mustn't overdo it." Jamie patted his father's shoulder. Tillie had to smile as he looked up at her. "Must he, Mama?"

"No, darling, you're quite right, he mustn't, but he's too obstinate to take any notice."

She heard a wail from behind her and looked round to see Alice face down on the gravel. Annabella bent to try to pull her up but she resisted her efforts and lay screaming and kicking.

Tillie ran across and picked her up. "Oh, sweetheart!"

An angry weal was spreading across her forehead and blood oozed from her nose. "Oh, my goodness!" Tillie glanced back at David, torn between seeing to her wounded daughter and leaving her poorly husband.

Ruby hurried over and took the still screaming child from her. "She'll be fine. I'll take her in and clean her up."

"You go." David gesticulated towards her.

"I'll get the master back, ma'am." John began to push the wheelchair towards the door. "Jamie and I will settle him on the settee in the drawing room."

"Yes, Mama, don't worry." Jamie puffed out his chest. "John and me'll look after Papa."

Certain that her beloved would be in good hands, Tillie rushed after Ruby, catching up with her as she entered the kitchen. Alice had quietened down, but looked very pale. Ruby sat on a chair, put the little girl on her knee, and took off her bonnet.

Freda stood at the table, chopping vegetables. "What's happened?" Dropping a carrot into the saucepan at the side of her, she peered across at the little girl. "She looks as if she's going to…"

Alice vomited all over Ruby.

"Oh, my poor baby!" Tillie stared at her daughter as Freda grabbed a bowl and placed it in front of the child. She immediately threw up again into it. "Call the doctor."

"It's probably only concussion." Shaking her head, Freda wiped Alice's brow with a cool cloth. "There's no need."

"Only what?" Ruby interrupted, a puzzled expression on her face.

Freda explained, "Concussion, you get it with a bang on the head."

Ruby wasn't convinced. "Well, I've never heard of it. I still think we should call Doctor Abrahams. What do you think, Nellie?" she asked as the housekeeper appeared at the door.

"Jamie told me Alice had fallen over. Let me look at the lass." Nellie went across and stroked the child's head. "She seems fine now. Let's wait a while and then decide." She looked around the kitchen. "Where's Annabella?"

"Isn't she with Jamie?" Tillie cried, looking round in a frenzy.

"No, I didn't see her."

"Oh, my, surely she's not still outside on her own?" Yanking open the door, Tillie ran outside, calling, "Annabella!

Annabella!"

She felt sick to her stomach as memories returned of the desperation she'd felt when she'd been looking for Jamie, some four years previously. Followed by Ruby, she ran to the front of the house, to where Alice had fallen. There was no sign of her daughter on the gravel path or the shrubs surrounding it. Yelling as loudly as she could, she repeated her name, over and over, checking behind all the bushes, anywhere a small girl could hide.

"You stay out here, Ruby, and keep searching while I check to see if she went inside." She ran in through the front and into the drawing room. Jamie stood at the door, a book in his hand, and David lay on the settee, his eyes closed.

"Have you seen Annabella?" she cried.

David's eyes shot open as Jamie replied, "Not since we came in. What was all that shouting just now?"

"That was me. Didn't she come in with you?"

"No, Mama. I thought she followed you round the back."

Tillie crumpled into a heap on the floor, sobbing. "I can't find her."

Jamie jumped up. "I'll go and look for her, Mama, don't worry."

* * * *

Grabbing his coat from the back of the chair, he ran outside, pulling it on as he went. Calling his sister's name, he looked under hedges, behind bushes, and even parted the daffodils and tulips to look in between them. Nothing.

"She must have gone back in," he murmured, giving up and returning to the house in time to hear his papa saying, "Don't upset yourself, darling, not in your condition. She can't have gone far. Come, now, sit yourself down a moment."

Walking in, he saw his mama yank her hand away. "No! Don't you understand? I'll die if anything happens to her." Turning quickly, she knocked over a blue vase which smashed onto the floor with a loud crash, the coloured shards bouncing up and scattering as if in slow motion, reminding Jamie of

Annabella's blue coat.

"I've got to look for her," she cried, stepping round the broken vase as if it was of no concern. "I can't just sit here while she's out there."

She pushed past Jamie. He ran after her, trying to tell her he'd looked everywhere outside. She didn't seem to be listening to him, though.

He caught up as Nellie walked into the hall.

"Oh, Nellie, where is she?" Tillie pulled at the housekeeper's sleeve. "What am I going to do?"

"Now, just try to stay calm." Jamie had never seen the usually unruffled housekeeper look so worried as she took hold of his mother's arm. "Listen to me. Ruby's taken Alice up to bed, and she'll check if Annabella's gone to the nursery, John's trying the dining room and the other rooms down here, while Freda…"

Jamie felt as if someone had punched him in the stomach as he tried to grab his mama to stop her falling to the floor.

Chapter 6

Jamie's voice seeped through the haze. "Mama, please wake up."

Tillie sat up immediately, her head spinning. "Annabella…?" she murmured. The faint hum of voices around her turned to silence. She squinted at the faces above her, but none of them belonged to her daughter. "Annabella? Have you found her?" she yelled, jumping up.

"Not yet." Nellie pushed her back onto the sofa. "But everyone is out looking."

"Well, obviously not hard enough." Tillie pushed the housekeeper aside and stood up. Her head was still fuzzy, but she was determined she wasn't going to lie there while her darling child was missing.

"Tillie…" David reached out to her. She ignored him. She had to find Annabella, and nobody was going to stop her, not even her ailing husband. She ran across the room, thinking, *I must be strong. No more collapsing or silliness. That won't help at all.*

Stopping at the door, she turned. Nobody else was moving. "Come on, everybody, you've got to get out there and search. You can't give up."

Running into the hall, she saw Ruby hurtling down the stairs. "I've looked everywhere upstairs, Tillie. She's definitely not up there."

"How's Alice?"

"She's fast asleep, bless her, completely unaware of what's happening."

"That's one thing to be thankful for."

Wrapping her coat tightly around her, Tillie ran outside, followed by her sister and Nellie.

Sam came sauntering around the side of the house, whistling, his hands in his trouser pockets, as if he didn't have a care in the world. He stopped. "What's happening?"

Ruby ran to him. "Baby Annabella's gone missing. You

haven't seen her, have you?"

"Missing? How come?"

"Never mind the whys and wherefores," Tillie cried. "Have you seen her, or not?"

"No, I would have brought her back immediately if I had."

Tillie put her hands on her head, realising she didn't have her bonnet on. "I'm sorry, Sam, of course you would. I'm just desperate to find her."

"Where have you looked?"

Jamie was peering up the drive. "We've looked everywhere round here, Sam." Taking off his cap, he scratched his head, then his face lit up as if an idea had suddenly occurred to him. "Shall I go and look down by the lake, Mama?"

Tillie screamed. "The lake? No…please don't let her be drowned!"

Ruby took her hand and began to drag her along. "I'm sure she's not. Come on, we'll all go and make sure Baby Annabella isn't anywhere near the damned lake."

Not a ripple broke the mirror-like surface reflecting the sun and the trees surrounding it. It looked so calm.

Tillie stood looking into the murky, green water. Could her baby be down there in its depths?

"It doesn't look disturbed," Ruby volunteered as they all peered into it.

"Shall I wade in and see if I can see anything?" Jamie began to step nearer to the edge.

"No, Jamie, I don't want you getting wet through." Tillie looked across to the other side. "I'll walk round and check…"

David appeared in his wheelchair, pushed by John. "Any sign?"

"No, not a thing." Nellie patted his shoulder.

Sam pointed towards a dark shape caught on an overhanging branch several yards away. "What's that?" He charged towards it.

Tillie followed him, her heart in her mouth, praying, "Please, God, don't let it be her, please."

She caught up as he pulled out a sodden piece of frayed, green material. A collective sigh escaped everyone.

"Thank God." Tillie sank to her knees, relief flooding through her veins.

Jamie helped her up. "Good job it ain't Bella, eh, Mama? But I didn't never think it was."

She patted him on the head, realising, suddenly, that he was almost as tall as her. Pushing the thoughts to one side, she focused once more on the task in hand. Just because the piece of cloth wasn't her baby didn't mean she wasn't in the lake. Peering once more into the water, she shouted her name again, causing Jamie to jump. He took up the call as well, as they began to walk towards the woods on the other side.

Jamie began to slow down. He seemed rather agitated.

"Jamie? What's the matter?"

He stopped, looking back anxiously at David, who wasn't far behind. "Papa…the woods…"

"What?"

"Don't you remember what you told me?"

Tillie was beginning to get exasperated. "They're only trees, come on, what are we waiting for?" She hurried on again.

"But, Mama…" Jamie called after her.

She turned round at the fear in his voice. One look at his worried face, and she ran back to him. "What's wrong, Jamie? What are you so scared of?"

Jamie took off his cap and held it in front of him. "Papa told me, when I first come here…before you come…that I mustn't go in that part of them woods."

"Why ever not?" Tillie looked at David for some reasoning. "What's in there?"

David shook his head. His grey, pinched face betrayed his exhaustion. He was barely able to hold his head up. As concerned as she was about her daughter, she could see her husband needed to get back inside. What should she do? Go back with him or stay out searching? Her shoulders drooped. She turned to John. "I think the master needs to go home. He looks all in."

"Yes, certainly, ma'am. I was thinking the same myself."

David put up his hand as if to protest, but it dropped again as John turned the wheelchair. Tillie tucked his blankets around his legs and kissed him. She had made her decision. "You go back and get some brandy inside you. I'll stay out a while longer to look for…" Her voice broke, and she couldn't continue.

Nellie's arm came around her shoulder, and she heard her comforting voice. "I think you ought to be getting back in as well."

But she couldn't give up yet. Gently removing the arm, she turned to the housekeeper. "No, I can't go in until I've found her, but would you go with John and make sure the master's settled?"

The housekeeper nodded.

Jamie slipped his hand into hers. "I'll help, Mama. We'll find her, don't worry."

"Thank you, Jamie."

She stood watching the trio making their way back towards the house as Ruby took her other hand. "So will we, won't we, Sam?" Her sister looked up expectantly at her fiancé, who nodded as he shielded his eyes from the bright, evening sun, looking in the direction of the woods.

"Why did the master tell you not to go into the woods?" he asked Jamie.

"'Cos he said his brother was killed there a long time ago, and some people say it's haunted." He looked pensively from Ruby to Tillie before adding, "But he did say it was only ladies who thought that, so me and you could go and search, couldn't we, Sam?"

The groom smiled, putting his hand on the boy's shoulder. "Yes, lad, that sounds like a good idea. Come on, before it gets too dark."

They hurried off, with Ruby calling after them, "We'll carry on around the lake. Shout if you find anything."

* * * *

Jamie and Sam entered the woods. It seemed really dark after the bright sun outside. They stood still for a moment, listening. It seemed eerily still; no birdsong or animal cry broke the silence.

"You don't think it's haunted, do you, Sam?" Jamie took hold of Sam's hand, just as a precaution.

The groom smiled down at him. "No, Jamie, I don't believe in all that clap trap. Once you're dead, you're dead. Just think of how many people have lived since time began. If they all came back as ghosts, there wouldn't be any room in the sky, they'd all be bumping into each other."

Jamie tried to imagine hundreds of ghosts, all flying about, weaving in and out. "It would be funny, wouldn't it?" he laughed, startling a rook that flew squawking up into the tops of the trees. The raucous sound had him holding onto Sam's hand even tighter.

Something brushed against his sleeve. Holding his breath, he looked over his shoulder. Phew, it was only a twig. For a moment, he had thought it was a…a bony finger. *Don't be silly*, he told himself. *Ghosts don't have fingers. Do they?*

Sam stopped, holding his arm in front of Jamie. "Shh, what was that?"

Jamie heard a rustling sound coming from a clump of bushes to their right. "Annabella," they both called at once, running towards it. A speckled fawn with two tiny antlers bounded out. It stopped, its round, brown eyes full of fear, and then turned and leapt off into the trees.

They both let out a long breath. Jamie moaned, "Aw, I thought that was her, didn't you, Sam?"

"Yes, I hoped it was."

They continued further into the woods, pushing their way through bracken and low-hanging branches until they came to a ride, a break in the trees.

"She can't be in here, Jamie," Sam admitted. "There's no way she could have walked this far."

"Perhaps Mama and Auntie Ruby have found her. Shall we go and see?" It was getting quite dusky, and no matter what

Sam had said, Jamie was beginning to see all sorts of peculiar shapes, some of them very ghostlike.

Tillie wrapped her coat more tightly round her, shivering with fear that they would never find her little girl. She thought she heard a cry floating in the still air. Stopping, she pulled at Ruby's sleeve. "What was that?"

Her sister's head shot round. "What?"

"It sounded like a...a baby's cry."

"Where was it coming from?"

"Behind us, I think." Swivelling round, she looked back towards a copse to the left of the house.

Ruby turned to look. "Can you still hear it?"

"No." Tillie listened intently, but all she could hear were sheep bleating in the distance. It definitely hadn't been sheep she'd heard, but could it have been a child?

Then it came again. Ruby grabbed her hand. "I heard it that time. Come on." They began running back the way they'd come. There was no sign of Sam or Jamie near the woods. Tillie felt a moment's anxiety for her son, but pushed it away, knowing he was in Sam's capable hands.

"Jamie's tree house is in that wood over there," Ruby gasped breathlessly. "You don't think...?"

"No, she's too small...to climb the ladder." The stitch in her side was excruciating, but she tried to ignore it as they raced towards the copse.

Hardly able to breathe, she stopped, bending over double. Her sister had run on ahead but she came back, reaching out her hand. "Tillie, are you unwell?"

She couldn't speak. A stabbing pain seared through her body, making her scream. Eyes squeezed shut, she clutched her belly as another pain ripped through her. This was worse than a stitch.

She dropped to the ground with Ruby shrieking, "Tillie, what's the matter?"

She knew what was happening. She could feel a warm wetness running down her legs.

Ruby began to cry. "Oh, Tillie, not the baby?"

Nodding, she tried to stand. "I think so…but…we have to find…Annabella."

"Oh, my goodness. What shall I do? I need to get you indoors." Ruby looked agitatedly about her, then, reaching under Tillie's arm, she helped her up, repeating over and over again, "Oh, my goodness, oh, my goodness."

Tillie began to stumble in the wrong direction. Ruby tried to steer her the other way.

The gamekeeper approached, a gun in the crook of his arm.

"Tom, over here!" Ruby shouted.

His coat tails flapping, he hurried towards them, just as Tillie collapsed again.

"What's happened?" He bent down to help Tillie up. "Why are you out here?"

"Annabella's lost, and Sam and Jamie are searching the woods, and I think Tillie's losing the baby, and…"

"Slow down, Ruby." Tom looked at the maid with consternation. "We need to get the mistress home straight away."

"But…Anna…bell…" Tillie gulped, unable to bear the thought of abandoning the hunt for her little girl.

"Sam and Jamie will find her, sis. You need to worry about yourself." Ruby clutched her sister's coat, trying to keep her upright.

Tillie began to sob. "But I can't just leave her. She might be hurt, or…"

She doubled over in agony again, only being prevented from falling by Tom and Ruby each taking an arm.

Nellie ran out to meet them. Taking one look at Tillie's white, contorted face, she obviously reached her own conclusion. "The baby?"

Ruby nodded. "I think so."

"Oh, no." Nellie's face crumpled. "The poor master, not again."

"Never mind the master. What about poor Tillie?" Ruby yanked her sister away from the housekeeper and hurried her indoors.

A Dilemma for Jamie

"I didn't mean…" Nellie called after her. Tillie could feel her trying to grab her from behind. "Please, Tillie, I was only…"

"What's happening out there?" David's anxious voice came from the drawing room. "Have you found her?"

"No, sir," Ruby called. "It's the mistress, she's…I mean…we need to call for the doctor."

The chandelier in the hall seemed as if it was spinning out of control. The last words Tillie heard was her husband repeating, "The doctor?"

* * * *

Opening her eyes, Tillie looked at the linen sheets. She shouldn't be in bed. Lifting the bedclothes, she lowered her legs to the floor. A spot of red blood on her white nightdress caught her attention and desolation overcame her as she rubbed her belly with circular movements, consoling the baby she remembered was no longer there.

There's nothing to be gained from self pity. Miscarriages happen all the time, she tried to tell herself. *But what about Annabella?* She pulled up her nightdress, but her arms and head became entwined inside it.

"What do you think you're doing?" a voice came from behind her.

"Trying to get dressed. What does it look like?"

Strong arms pulled the garment back over her, before gently pushing her back onto the bed.

"Oh, no, you're not, young lady. You need to rest, after your…your miscarriage." Nellie sat down next to her, patting her in sympathy.

Tillie sat with her hands on her lap, exhausted after her futile effort at getting dressed. "What about Annabella?" she croaked. "You should have woken me when she was found."

"Well…um…" The housekeeper cleared her throat.

Tillie pushed her aside and jumped up again. "Do you mean they haven't…they haven't found her? She's still out there, on her own, in the…" She hesitated "the…dark?" Her voice trailed off. The sun was shining brightly through a chink in the pink curtains. "Have I slept right through the night?"

Nellie nodded, trying to pull her back onto the bed. "Yes, the doctor gave you some laudanum."

"You mean it's morning and she's still not been found?" Running wildly to the window, she yanked open the faded curtains, tearing a hole in the worn fabric. She'd been meaning to ask David if they could have some new ones, and the fact that she hadn't got round to it increased her aggravation.

She stared out at the grounds below while Nellie wrapped a warm shawl around her saying, "Everyone's searching for her, even the neighbours. They'll soon find her, don't fret."

"Don't fret? My little girl has been missing for…" She had no idea what the time was "…for goodness knows how long, and you tell me not to fret! I don't care what you say, I'm going down there."

Shaking off the shawl, she picked up the dress she'd worn the previous day. It was covered in dirt. Flinging it down, she marched over to the wardrobe and grabbed a dark grey one she hadn't worn since before the twins were born.

"Tillie…" Nellie tried to grab her again.

"You can't stop me. My mind's made up. Now, please, either help me get dressed, or go away and leave me to it."

The housekeeper sighed, clearly realising she was beaten. "All right, then, but don't go doing anything stupid. That wouldn't benefit anybody, least of all Alice. She needs you, as well, don't forget. Now, stop squirming, I can't…"

Tillie could feel her tugging at the dress, but it resisted all Nellie's efforts to fasten the buttons. Her shoulders drooping, she sat down in front of the dressing table, pushing her hair off her face. "You're right, as usual, Nellie."

How pretty her little girls had looked in their coats and bonnets. "Where is Alice? Has she recovered from her fall?"

"Yes, she seems fine. She's in the nursery. Ruby insisted on going outside with Sam, so Charlie Hodges's young daughter is looking after her. Charlie's out there searching as well, along with half the neighbourhood, like I said."

"So why can't they find her?"

"Nay, lass, if only we knew."

She changed into a different dress. "Is the master out there as well?"

"Aye, he hasn't been to bed."

"That won't do him any good."

"You're right, but you know how stubborn he can be."

Tillie thought she heard the housekeeper adding under her breath, "Even worse than his wife," but she chose to ignore it.

With Nellie's help, she gingerly descended the stairs and made it to a chair in the hall. She couldn't believe how weak she felt. Nellie was looking askance at her, shaking her head, but she looked away, not wanting to see the censure in her eyes. No matter how bad she was, she had to do her part in finding her daughter.

The front door opened and Jamie came running in. "Mama, Mama…they think…they've found her," he puffed.

She jumped up. "Where?" Before he could reply, she grabbed him and hugged him to her. "Oh, Jamie, thank God." She ran to the door. "Where is she?" she repeated.

He pointed to their left. "There, on the other side of the vegetable garden."

"Well, I can't see her. Why don't they bring her in?" she yelled as Nellie helped her into a coat.

"'Cos she's stuck down a well."

"A well?"

"Yes, an old one that Tom thought had been filled in."

"How did she get down there?" She looked from Jamie to Nellie, her brow puckered.

"Don't know, Mama. Tom heard a cry and when he went to see what it was, he…"

"That must be what we heard yesterday," Tillie howled, remembering the cry she and Ruby had been about to investigate. "Oh, my poor baby girl! She must have been down there all night. Please, God, help them get her out."

They followed the sounds of shouting and saw a crowd of people with ropes and ladders, all staring at a hole in the ground. Seeing David in his wheelchair, she ran across to him.

"Why aren't they getting her out?" she wailed. "David, do something!"

Her husband's anguished face looked up at her. "The hole's too narrow for anyone to get down."

"Well, can't they just make it bigger?"

The huntsman at the annual neighbourhood hunt, Charlie Hodges, broke away from the group of men. "To do so, Mrs Dalton," he raised his voice above the noise, "we need to dig the earth out from around the sides, but that could cause the ground to cave in on top of your daughter."

"So what are you going to do, then?"

"We're still trying to work out the best course of action."

Pushing aside some of the men surrounding it, she peered down the tiny hole, hoping to catch a glimpse of her daughter, but only blackness stared back at her. "Bella, darling," she called. "Mama's here."

She listened for a reply, and heard a faint mewing sound. "Oh, sweetheart, hang on, we'll soon have you out."

She turned to Charlie. "Can't you just drop down a rope for her to grab, and pull her up?"

"We've tried that. The poor little mite couldn't have known what it was for."

"Oh, my God, what are we going to do?"

Sam and Ruby hurried across. "Oh, Ruby," she cried, burying her face in her sister's coat and clinging onto her, her legs so shaky she could hardly stand.

Nellie came up behind them. "Ruby, I think your sister needs to get back indoors." At Tillie's shake of the head, she continued, "There's nothing either of you can do out here, and you haven't eaten all day."

"I couldn't eat at a time like this, Nellie. Food's the last thing on my mind."

"I know, but you have to keep your strength up. If—I mean—when, they get this little lass out, she's going to need her mother healthy, not half dead." She gently ushered Tillie away from the scene. "You know it makes sense, so come on."

Tillie took one last look at the ugly, black hole. The thought of her baby lying down there, cold and hungry, sent a shiver down her spine, but she felt so wobbly and light-headed that she let herself be led away towards the house. Every now and again she turned around to see if any progress was being made, but it didn't seem to be, everyone was still standing scratching their heads.

Ruby helped her into the house, while Sam returned to the well.

* * * *

Jamie stayed close by, desperate to pick up a shovel and help with the digging, but they wouldn't let him. He grabbed Sam's arm. "Why can't I do something?"

The groom flinched. "Because it's too dangerous. You'd probably be more of a hindrance than a help."

Jamie let go, remembering that Sam had been badly injured in the accident when his father had lost part of his leg. "Oh, sorry, does it still hurt?"

Sam nodded, bringing his arm up across his chest and holding it with his other hand. "Sometimes."

Jamie turned his attention back to the well. "But I want to help."

"I know, but the best thing you can do is look after your pa. Make sure he's warm enough, and that sort of thing."

His father was slumped in the chair, his face as white as a sheet. Jamie ran over and covered up his legs. "Do you want me to get you another blanket, Papa, or a cup of tea or anything?"

His papa merely shook his head, slipping his hands under the cover.

"Do you think Bella will be out soon?" Jamie fidgeted from one foot to the other, unable to stand still. He received a slight nod in reply.

"That's good." Beginning to feel cold, he clapped his hands together. "I hope they don't take long."

He chatted away about anything he could think of, only receiving grunts as replies, but at least it took his mind off what the men were doing. Feeling helpless at not being allowed to do anything, talking was the only option left to him.

* * * *

Freda brought a steaming mug of tea to Tillie and Ruby in the lounge and asked whether any progress was being made.

"Not really." Ruby sat down and cupped her mug in both hands.

Tillie could feel her sister looking at her sympathetically, but kept her head down, hardly having the strength to raise it. A huge sigh escaped her. Why were the fates so against her? What had she done to deserve so many trials and tribulations? No sooner had she dealt with one, than another cropped up. It just wasn't fair.

Freda's sympathetic hand on her back opened the floodgates and, burying her face in the cook's apron, she sobbed.

"There, there, let it all out, then we'll get you tucked up in bed where you belong. I'm surprised at Nellie letting you out of it in the first place, in your condition."

Recovering, Tillie replied, "Don't blame her. I had to go. I couldn't just lie there." Sipping her tea, she could hardly hold the mug steady. She looked at Ruby. "Do…? Um…did they see whether it was a boy or a girl?"

Her sister looked vacant for a moment, then answered, "Oh…the baby?" Shifting awkwardly, she looked uncertainly at Freda, before mumbling, "A boy."

Tillie sighed. "Poor David, he so wanted another son."

Freda took her hand. "There'll be plenty more chances, I'm sure. Concentrate on getting yourself well. You look all in. Why don't you go to bed?"

She could feel her eyes closing. She was so weary, but she couldn't go to bed, not while Annabella was still down that awful well.

"No." She forced her eyes open. "No, I can't."

"Well, put your legs up and rest here, then."

She felt herself being covered over.

I must not go to sleep, I must not…

Chapter 7

The grandfather clock in the hall chimed twice as Tillie stirred. Two o'clock already? Glancing around the room, she found she was alone. Throwing off the blanket, she stood up but, overcome by dizziness, she flopped back down. They hadn't woken her, so her daughter must still be down that hellhole. She had to get out there.

Trying once more, by holding onto chairs, she managed to get across the room and into the hall. There was nobody about, not even Purvis. The large, oak front door almost proved too much, but she managed to ease it open and squeeze through. A fresh breeze hit her as she stepped outside to the sound of loud voices. She staggered over to the spot where her daughter had been found. The whole neighbourhood seemed to be there, some digging, others standing around, pointing or scratching their heads.

Spotting David looking pale and wretched, with Jamie hopping up and down beside him, she went across to them.

"Hello, darling." She kissed her husband's dry lips.

He looked up at her, his eyes bloodshot, eyelids red and drooping.

"How far have they got?" she asked.

He shook his head slowly as Jamie pointed to his left. "Those men there are digging another hole."

"What for?" asked Tillie.

"Well, Sam says that the plan is to, um—I think that's what he said—to dig this other hole close by and then tunnel across to where they think Bella is, and…and get her out." Raising his arms as if he was lifting something, Jamie looked at his father for confirmation. "That's right, isn't it, Papa?"

David gave a slight nod.

Closing her eyes, Tillie took a deep breath, then whispered, "Will it work?"

She sensed David shrug his shoulders as he leaned his

head against her arm. Stroking his hair, her head shot up as a shout was heard from the work site. Not waiting for Jamie and David to catch up, she ran across to see what was happening.

Two of the men were staring down the new hole, arguing. "I told you it was too risky."

"Well, I thought it would work."

They looked up as Tillie pushed them apart. All that could be seen was soft churned up earth in a small dip.

"What's happened?" she yelled. "Where's the hole?"

"We tried to—"

"You mean *you* thought you'd take shortcuts," the other man intervened. "And look where it's got us."

Tillie was at screaming pitch. "So start again!"

Charlie Hodges came across, and Tillie grabbed his arm. "Mr Hodges, tell them to get digging. Please, they can't stop."

"Yes, ma'am." He turned to the men. Some had already restarted, Sam and Tom amongst them, but others were standing about uncertainly, leaning on their shovels.

"Come on, men." He gestured towards those who were standing idle. "All of you, get to work, and make sure you shore it up properly this time." They obeyed, and the hole soon began to reappear.

The huntsman turned to Tillie, who was shivering uncontrollably. "Ma'am, I think you and David should go in. I'll send somebody to let you know how we get on."

She shook her head. "I've only just got here." She had to stay. She couldn't desert her little girl now. Closing her eyes, she drew in a lungful of air.

Be strong, be strong.

But however much she fought the weakness, she couldn't prevent strong arms from steering her away. She turned back to David in a daze. However bad she felt, he looked ten times worse.

John broke away from the men, his clothes muddy, his boots even more so, and took hold of the handles of the wheelchair. "I'll take the master in," he said.

Tillie held onto the side of it for support as they left Jamie with the men.

David started coughing when they entered the house. Freda ran off to the kitchen, returning with hot toddies. Tillie sank onto the sofa while John helped his master sip some of the hot drink before settling him on the larger sofa and scuttling back outside. David's coughing fit abated, his eyes closed and his head drooped onto his chest.

Putting her drink on the side table, Tillie could feel her heavy eyelids closing. "I must not go to sleep," she murmured, but it wouldn't hurt to shut them just for a moment.

* * * *

Her stomach gave an almighty rumble as Tillie thought she heard the clock chime five. David looked dead to the world, his mouth slightly open. He didn't look as if he was breathing. She jumped up, panic stricken, and stumbled across the room, falling on top of him.

His eyes shot open as he jerked and spluttered.

"Thank God," she cried, resting her head on his chest as they both fought to get their breath back. "My poor darling, forgive me for waking you like that, but I thought…" Blowing out her breath, she composed herself as he held her close. They lay together silently for a while until Freda came in carrying yet another tea tray.

"Oh, thank you. Just what we need." Tillie removed David's arm from her chest and sat up, watching the cook pour the milk into the cups. "Do you know what's happening?" she asked weakly, although she knew they would have been told if there had been any news.

"Last I heard they were making some progress."

Freda handed Tillie her tea and she took a sip. Nectar couldn't have tasted any sweeter. "But she's still not out?"

The cook shook her head. "No, but it shouldn't take much longer."

"Really?" Putting down her cup, Tillie jumped up. "I need to get out there, then."

Freda put a restraining hand on her arm. "Finish this first, Tillie."

Her mind registered that the cook had addressed her by her name, rather than her title, but in the circumstances, she couldn't care a jot. Nellie did it all the time.

Why did she feel so weak? She'd only lost a baby. Sighing deeply as Freda went out, she sat back down, saying to David, "I'm so sorry, my darling."

Her husband's face had lost some of its grey pallor. He looked across at her. "Uh?"

She reached out her hand, but was too far away to touch him. Letting it drop, she murmured, "About the baby. It was a boy, you know."

He nodded.

"I'm sorry," she repeated. "I know how much you wanted another son."

He merely shrugged.

She wanted to know what his reaction was to—what she thought he would consider—the devastating event, but was none the wiser. Maybe when they both felt stronger, they would be able to discuss it properly.

Freda reappeared at the door. "Shall I start cooking dinner, ma'am?"

"I suppose so." Even though her stomach was still rumbling, Tillie couldn't really face the prospect of sitting down to a meal.

"I've baked extra bread and taken sandwiches out to the workers."

"Thank you, Freda. That was thoughtful of you."

The cook hesitated, as if to say something else, but bobbed a curtsy and left.

"Oh, how much longer are they going to take? Surely, she should be freed by now." Tillie thumped the cushions in frustration as the door opened and Jamie came running in. "They've...they've nearly got her out." He grabbed Tillie's arm, pulling her off the sofa. "Come on."

Tillie looked at David. Clearly realising there was no way he could follow them, he waved his hand at her. Not needing any further encouragement, she grabbed Jamie and ran.

An air of expectation hovered in the still evening. "Please,

God, please, let her still be alive," she prayed over and over again.

Ruby ran up to her. "They've nearly done it," she cried, gripping Tillie's shoulder, causing her to flinch, but the pain seemed to calm her as she gulped air into her lungs. Still praying quietly, she edged closer to where the men were heaving on ropes and pulleys.

Sam came over, his hands, clothes and boots covered in mud, his brow shining with sweat.

Ruby looked up at him with concern. "You shouldn't be doing so much, with your bad arm."

"I'm all right," he replied. "I have to do my share."

The men at the edge of the hole moved forward, blocking Tillie's view. Then a shout went up, causing the air to vibrate with sound.

She could feel Ruby shaking beside her. Clinging onto her with one hand and Jamie with the other, Tillie moved closer. She still couldn't see what was happening.

The shouting stopped and a hush descended. Tillie held her breath as the people in front of her parted. A little shape, completely wrapped in a blanket, was brought to her.

"Noooooooooo." Tillie fell to her knees, sobbing.

Chapter 8

David pushed his valet away. "That will do, John. Nobody is going to be looking at me."

"But, sir, I haven't finished."

"It does not matter whether I still have a few whiskers on my chin. Leave me alone."

He could not have felt worse if he tried. He had thought the pain of losing his young son, Freddy, all those years ago, had been unbearable, but the agony he was experiencing now was insupportable.

As John tidied up, he inhaled deeply, trying to stop his hands from shaking. He knew he should apologise to his valet but didn't have the energy. He had enough to cope with without pandering to his servant's hard-done-to feelings.

"Would you like me to help you dress, sir?" asked John, standing very erect, his hands behind his back.

"Yes, I suppose so."

He really did not want today to happen. How was he going to bear up and not break down in front of the family? He was the master. He should be the strong one on whom they all depended.

As John helped him into his black trousers, he wondered how Tillie was coping. He had barely spoken to her since it had happened. She would be just as devastated as he was, if not more so. Women seemed to feel that sort of thing worse than men, but he could not find the words to comfort her. How could he console her, when he felt so wretched himself?

He heard movements in the adjoining room. She must be getting up. He would dearly love to go in and say something. But what? All the platitudes that people usually said at such times sounded so trite. They did not help at all. No, better to remain silent.

John put the final touches to his black tie. "Did you want to stay up here until it's time, sir?"

"Just get me out of this room, John, please. I have spent enough time in here recently to last me a lifetime."

* * * *

Jamie had been told not to open the curtains, for some reason. It was daylight outside, but he could just make out his little sister lying there in her white cashmere dress. How could she be dead? She looked so normal, just as if she was asleep. Her chest looked as if it was moving. Reaching out to trace one of the scratches on her white cheek, he pulled his hand away. He hadn't expected her to be so cold.

Putting his hands together, he said a short prayer. He didn't know if there was a proper one to say.

Auntie Ruby came across, putting her hand on his shoulder. "It just isn't fair, is it, Jamie?"

Shaking his head, he tried to keep the tears at bay. He had to be strong now. Papa had gone to bed as soon as he'd heard the awful news, and hadn't got up since. And his mama...well, she walked around like a ghost, pale and unsmiling. The black clothes she wore didn't help. She had to wear them, everybody did, but somehow, they looked so much darker and solemn on her.

Knowing what to expect this time, he stroked the little face once more before turning away.

Auntie Ruby patted his head. "Do you want to stay here on your own, Jamie? I need to go up and check on Alice."

He shook his head. "I'll come with you. If she's awake, I can play a game with her. Keep her occupied." *Me, too,* he thought.

Lady, his Labrador, jumped up as he moved away. She didn't actually belong to him, she was a family pet, but he looked after her most of the time. He fondled her soft head. "Where's Goldie?" he asked. Her ears pricked up at the mention of her pup. Goldie was Jamie's. She'd been given to him soon after he'd arrived at The Grange so she wasn't actually a pup any more. "Don't you know? Never mind, she can't be far. You stay here and look after Bella."

The dog seemed to understand, for she lay back down, licking her paws.

Jamie followed his auntie upstairs. Alice was still asleep, so he took out some paper and sat down to draw—black shapes, all intertwined, with large open mouths.

Auntie Ruby finished folding some of Alice's liberty bodices and vests and went over to look at his sketch. "Oh, Jamie, that's horrible. What's it supposed to be?"

He shrugged. "Don't know. It just seemed to flow out me pencil."

"Well, I don't like it. Put it away and do something nice. You'll scare poor little Alice with pictures like that."

Folding the paper so his little sister wouldn't see it, he put it to one side and sat chewing the end of his pencil. "I can't seem to draw nothing good at the moment, or write any happy stories."

"I know. It's such a miserable time. Poor little Alice keeps asking for Bella."

"I bet she can't understand where she's gone." Jamie stood up and walked over to the window. "Do you really think Bella's gone to heaven?" He pointed up to the sky. "Right up there?"

"Well, that's what the vicar says when anyone dies: 'If he or she was an upright citizen, he or she will go to heaven, and children go anyway'."

"Will I?"

"Yes, Jamie, of course you will, if you stay a good and honest person." Turning him round to face her, his auntie playfully slapped his cheeks. "But you aren't going to die for a very long time. You'll probably live 'til you're about…eighty."

"Phaw, eighty's very old. Even papa isn't nowhere near that."

She looked wistful. "No, nor was Grandmama. Do you remember her, Jamie?"

"Yes, when she cleaned up me face after I fell down."

"I still miss her." She put the clothes into a drawer. "But I sometimes feel as if she's still with me."

"What, like a ghost?" Jamie shivered, remembering what

he had been thinking earlier about his ma.

"Well, no. I...I can't really explain it." She reached down to pick up Alice, who had awoken. "Anyway, now we've got to look after this little girl and keep her safe. We don't want anything happening to her."

Jamie kissed his sister. "No, we don't," he repeated, tickling her under her chin. "Do we?"

The child giggled, her thumb in her mouth. Auntie Ruby began to dress her. "You'd better get ready for the funeral."

"Nellie said children don't usually go to funerals but I can go if I want, 'cos I'm a big boy."

"Do you want to, though? Don't you think it'll be too upsetting?"

Jamie thought for a moment. "I remember going to one when I lived with the gypsies. I can't remember who died, but it was fun. Everybody had a great time."

"Well, this one won't be fun. It'll be really, really sad."

"Oh. But I could hold Mama's hand and look after her, couldn't I?"

She hugged him as Alice ran off to play with her doll. "Yes, Jamie, or you could stay here with me and Alice."

"Why? Aren't you going?"

"No, I've got to look after your little sister. She's too young for that sort of thing."

"Oh." He went back to the window. The bright sun made him blink. It wasn't the sort of day you'd expect to be burying someone, especially a little girl.

A movement down on the drive caught his eye. He squinted to see what it was.

"It's Papa," he exclaimed. "He's outside, on his own."

Auntie Ruby joined him at the window. "So it is. I wonder where your ma is, or John."

"How did he get down the steps? I'd better go and see if he needs help." He ran to the door.

"But, Jamie, you're not changed," she called after him, but he didn't turn back. He charged downstairs. The front door was wide open.

A faint cry came from behind one of the bushes. He

found his father on the grass, his wheelchair upturned beside him, the upper wheel spinning, as if it had a life of its own.

"Papa?" He touched his father's face.

His blue eyes opened. "Jamie?" he muttered.

"We're here, Papa." He reached down to pull him up as John came round the corner.

"Oh, my God. What happened?"

"I don't know," Jamie replied. "I just found him like this."

John lifted his master while Jamie righted the wheelchair and, between them, they managed to get him into it. His face was more ashen than usual, but he didn't complain. In fact, he hardly made a sound.

Jamie's insides were churning. He was so scared his beloved papa was going to die. He followed John into the house, his fists clenched at his sides.

Nellie met them as they entered the hall. "I was wondering where you had all got to…" she began.

Jamie interrupted her. "Papa fell, Nellie. I found him. It was so horrible. He ain't going to die as well, is he?" Tears began to fall down his cheeks as he grabbed her arm and pulled her towards the wheelchair.

She patted his hand. "No, dear, of course he isn't." But the worried look on her face didn't calm his fears. "Go and find your ma, she needs to be here."

"Where is she?"

"She's probably in her chamber, dressing…"

Jamie didn't wait to hear any more. He ran up the stairs, two at a time, and banged on her door. "Mama, may I come in?" He couldn't just burst in, in case she wasn't decent.

His mother opened the door, looking very bleary-eyed, still in her nightgown. "Jamie, what's going on?"

"It's Papa, he fell down."

"What do you mean?"

He grabbed her arm and tried to pull her out.

"Come on, he fell out of his wheelchair when there was nobody there."

"Just a minute, Jamie, I can't go downstairs like this. I

need to dress."

"But, Mama, I think he's going to die."

"What?"

"Please, Mama, you've got to come now."

Grabbing a robe from the back of the door, she hurtled down the stairs after him.

"David, my darling." She dropped to her knees beside him. He half raised his hand but it flopped down again. She grabbed it and put it up to her face, looking around at everyone.

"What happened?"

"We don't know, ma'am," John replied, straightening his master's blanket. "I brought him downstairs, not half an hour since, and left him in the morning room. I thought he would be safe in there."

"Oh, David." Tillie put her arms round him. "Has anyone sent for Doctor Abrahams?"

"Yes, ma'am."

"The funeral...must not miss it," David stuttered.

"Well, wait 'til the doctor's been. Just rest for now. We have another hour or so before they...before we..."

Jamie felt so useless just watching. He picked up a glass of water from the table. "Do you want a drink, Papa?" Receiving a nod, he held up the glass to his father's lips. "Is that better?"

Another nod. He put the glass back down and looked at his mother. "He will be all right, won't he, Mama?"

"Yes, Jamie, I'm sure he will."

"It's just that..."

"I know, darling, after all that's happened, it's hard to take in. Pray that he will recover."

Jamie's brow puckered. "I prayed that Bella would be brought out safe, and that didn't work, did it?" He ran out, ignoring his mother's voice calling him back. What was the point in praying if God didn't listen?

He ran out of the house, down the drive and into the woods, where his tree house still nestled in the branch of the oak tree. He still played in it occasionally. Climbing up the ladder, he clambered over the top rung and curled up into a ball in the corner. Too numb to cry, he just lay on the hard boards with his head on the cushion he always left there.

Why did people have to die? First George, then Annabella and now, possibly, his papa. He'd been scared he was going to die earlier in the year. But he'd got better then, and that had been a lot worse. He sat up. Maybe, he would get better now.

A blue tit landed on the rail next to him. Was it the same one that often came? He wasn't sure.

"I'm sorry, Bluey. I don't have any crumbs today," he whispered. The bird hopped onto the floor, picked up one that he must have left on his last visit, and flew off.

He wondered if his squirrel friend would come to keep him company. It came most days he was there and would even eat from his hand. Not today, though.

"I s'pose I better get back. I don't want to miss Bella's funeral," he muttered. "Whatever a funeral is."

He wasn't sure what would happen. He'd missed his grandmother's, and Auntie Ruby had said it wouldn't be like the gypsy one.

He climbed back down the ladder and ran to the house. The doctor's carriage stood in front of the door. He ran even faster.

The doctor was coming out of the drawing room with Nellie as Jamie entered the front door. "He will be all right, won't he, Doctor? Please, please say he will." He pulled at the man's sleeve, uncaring of his bad manners.

Nellie tried to pull him off. "Master Jamie, please…"

The doctor patted him on the head. "Yes, young man, your father's just a bit shaken up. He'll need to rest."

"Oh, fanks, fanks." Jamie hurried in to see his papa laid back on the sofa, his eyes closed.

"Is he really going to be better, Mama, like the doctor said?" He put his arms round his mother's waist and hugged her tightly, burying his face in the soft material of her dressing gown. "He is, isn't he?"

His mother squeezed him. "Yes, Jamie. Thank God."

Perhaps He had been listening, after all. "I'm sorry, God," he whispered, looking up to the ceiling.

"Up you go and get changed then. It'll soon be time."

"Yes, Mama." He turned to go out, then asked, "Is Papa coming to the funeral?"

She pulled a face. "I'm not sure."

Feeling guilty at doubting God's help, he said every prayer he could think of to try to make up for it. He changed into his new black suit. The middle button on his jacket was particularly difficult to button up so, fastening all the others, he left that one undone. Hopefully, nobody would notice. He brushed his hair extra well, and then remembered he hadn't washed his hands and face.

"Oh, bother," he muttered, wondering whether it was worth getting undressed again. No, he could make do with a quick wipe. Surely, everyone would be too interested in Annabella to notice if he had a smut on his face.

After a wipe with the flannel, he tried the button again, but the buttonhole was just too small and stiff. With a deep sigh, he gave his trousers a quick tug, straightened his tie, smoothed down his jacket and opened the door. There wasn't a sound to be heard.

Standing on the landing, he hesitated, afraid to go down. Drumming his fingers on the banister, it occurred to him that maybe it was so quiet because they'd gone without him. He hurtled down the stairs and almost ran into Nellie coming out of the drawing room.

"Ah, Master Jamie, I was just coming to find you. Let me look at you." Smoothing down his hair, she tutted as she checked behind his ears before wiping his cheek with her apron. "I see you've made do with a cat's lick. Never mind. Come on."

At least she didn't notice the button, Jamie thought, keeping his hands in front of him as he followed her.

Alice ran up to him and he picked her up. "Jem," she said, poking him in the eye.

"Ouch, you little minx. That hurt." Putting her back down, he bent to tell her she shouldn't do that but, looking into her face, the spitting image of her dead sister, he just couldn't bring himself to scold her. He hugged her before Auntie Ruby took her hand and dragged her away.

This was it, then. The funeral. A large man, wearing a very tall hat and dressed in black as everybody else, put the lid on the little coffin, then picked it up and carried it outside.

Jamie hung back, unsure what to do. His mama was quietly crying into a black handkerchief. She looked so pale and sad, so he took her hand, looking for his father. There he was, in his wheelchair, his face grey, his eyes closed, tears dribbling down his cheeks.

As they went outside, it looked as if everyone was crying except him. Was there something wrong with him? Why wasn't he? *Because you have to be the brave one*, a little voice in his head told him. *You're not a young child anymore. You have to be grown up.* But all the grown-ups were crying. Perhaps it was because he wasn't grown up then. He couldn't decide what the reason was, as they followed the hearse towards the church.

Somebody began to sing. Jamie recognised the hymn, 'Amazing Grace'. He'd heard it in church the previous Sunday. Wondering who it was, he turned and saw his mama's friend, Mrs Thompson, the vicar's wife. He hadn't realised she was there near the back of the line of people following them. A few others joined in. His mama didn't, though. Each time he looked up at her, he could see she was still crying, although most other people had stopped. She still kept hold of his hand, so he felt safe.

After a short service in the church, they filed out to the graveyard. They were all crying once more, some people really loudly, as they stood around the grave. Jamie watched them lower the little coffin into the hole, and it suddenly hit him. He was never going to see his little sister again. Never teach her songs, or read her stories. Tears pricked at his eyelids, then gushed down his cheeks. His body was racked with sobs. His mama held him close. She was sobbing as well.

He vaguely heard Vicar Thompson saying something about dust and ashes and then somebody passed him a box of soil. He didn't know what to do with it. He just stared at the brown stuff. Eventually, his mama took it from him and, taking out a handful, threw it onto the top of the coffin. He thought, for a heart-stopping moment, that she was going to jump into the hole with it. Grabbing her coat, he pulled her back. She was still weeping uncontrollably. He felt so helpless. His papa was also crying bitterly, his hands covering his face. Who could he turn to?

Mrs Thompson appeared out of the crowd, took his mother's arm and led her away a short distance from the grave. Jamie didn't know whether to follow, or try to console his father. He looked so fragile and ill, slumped in the chair. He had to go and help him.

Putting his arm around his shoulder, he begged, "Oh, Papa, please don't cry."

His father grabbed his hand and sobbed even more. Jamie squeezed his eyes shut, trying so hard to be brave. Nellie came across and gently untangled him.

"Come on, now, sir," she said to his father—quite harshly, Jamie thought. "Take the master back, please, John. He's had quite enough for one day." Jamie could see the valet rigidly holding the handles of the wheelchair as he walked away, his back stiff and straight.

She then turned to Jamie. "You, too, Master Jamie. You go with your papa, and help John get him back."

"What about Mama?" he asked, anxiously looking for her. She was already walking away, supported by her friend.

"Mrs Thompson will look after her. You go with your pa. He needs you now."

Chapter 9

Jamie sat on a blanket on the lawn showing Alice how to make daisy chains. He pushed his thumbnail into the stalk of one daisy and gave her another one to push through it, but her podgy fingers split the stem every time.

"Never mind," he said, patting her hand. "You just watch."

She nodded, put her thumb in her mouth and sat back.

"I want to get it finished for Maisie. She'll be here soon."

"Maithie," she lisped.

"Yes, you like playing with her, don't you?"

Another nod.

Jamie knew that having his friend come to play was helping Alice recover from the death of her twin. Nellie had told him so. He enjoyed her company as well. She spoke normally now, not like when she'd been found by the Button family before his mama's wedding to Uncle David, as he used to call his papa. She hadn't been able to speak at all then.

"There she is." He jumped up. "Look, Alice, can you see her? The one in the yellow dress?"

He helped her up and they ran towards her. Detaching her hand from her foster mother, Mrs Button, Maisie approached shyly. Jamie led her and her younger sister, Charlotte, to the blanket. Jamie knew she wasn't actually related to the family. It was just easier to call them 'sisters'.

"We…I've made you a necklace."

"It's lovely."

He put it round her neck. It fell apart, but he soon put it back together.

"Me," said Charlotte. "Me have one."

"Yes, all right, I'll make you one as well."

Mrs Button interrupted. "Would it be all right if I leave the girls with you, Jamie? I need to speak to your housekeeper and cook."

"Yes, Mrs Button, of course. We can make loads of necklaces."

The children sat down as she went inside.

"I heard me ma talking to Pa yesterday," said Maisie, rather sadly. "They were arguing."

"What about?"

"Me."

"Why would they argue about you? You haven't been naughty, have you?"

"No...at least, I don't think so." She looked thoughtful for a moment. "I hadn't thought of that. Oh, I hope I haven't." Her sad, violet eyes looked up at him. "Perhaps that's why."

"Why what?"

Her sister grabbed her arm. "Me have one."

"Here, Charlotte, have mine." Maisie took off her daisy chain and put it around the youngster's neck. "You don't mind, do you, Jamie?"

Shaking his head, he tried to make sense of what she was saying. "So...?"

"Pa said...and now Ma's gone to ask if I can...if there's..." She burst into tears.

"Aw, don't cry." Jamie didn't like to see her crying, and he still hadn't the faintest idea why she was.

Charlotte gave her a hug. "Don't cwy, Mawy." Her new family still called her Mary, the name they had given her when they'd first taken her in, unable to speak due to the shock of her mother dying in the fire at Mrs Curtis's house.

Maisie calmed down and began to explain. "They say I'm old enough to go into service now."

"Oh." Jamie wasn't sure what that meant, but it sounded worrying. "You're ten, aren't you?"

"Um, yes, I think so. Not really sure."

"Well, I'll be twelve next month, and I'm sure you're two years younger than me, so you must be about ten. When's your birthday?"

Shaking her head, she shrugged.

"Don't you know?" he asked.

Charlotte looked up from the beetle she'd been trying to push off the blanket. "My birfday on Thunday. I'll be thix." He thought that having no front teeth must be why she couldn't speak properly.

"Ma said I can share Lottie's birthday," Maisie said flatly. "I always share somebody's."

"Who's Lottie?"

Charlotte pointed to her chest. "Me."

"Oh. Well, isn't that better than not having one?" Jumping up, Jamie grabbed her hand. "I know, let's go and ask Freda if she'll bake you a cake."

"Cake." Alice's face beamed as she put up her arms to be picked up.

Brushing some grass off her green dress, Jamie fastened her apron ties and took hold of her hand.

But Maisie remained seated. "No, I don't want to be no bother."

"She won't mind, she loves baking."

"I like cake," Charlotte piped up, her face glowing.

"Come on then, let's go and ask her." Jamie tugged at Maisie's arm.

"But, Ma…" She still seemed reluctant to go.

"Surely your ma won't mind?" Jamie asked.

She looked down, saying slowly, "She's gone in to ask if there's a pos…position for me."

What was she talking about?

She continued, "As a scully maid or something."

What? He must have misheard her.

"But you're not old enough to be a *maid*." Then memories of Katy, the young servant who'd been at his Auntie Annie's house in Harrogate when he'd visited four years previously, flitted through his mind. She'd only seemed as old as Sarah, who'd been eleven then.

"Oh. But there's no need to worry. If you came to work here, I could look after you." He'd thought that would cheer her up, but it didn't seem to.

Martha, the parlour maid, came out with a tray of lemonade. Maisie still looked miserable as the drinks were handed out. Jamie didn't know how to comfort her.

He sat back down and swallowed his juice. "That was nice, wasn't it?"

"More, please," said Charlotte, holding out her beaker. The maid filled it again. Maisie sipped her drink, her face downcast.

"Your ma's talking to Nellie," Martha said bluntly to the young girl. "And she don't seem very happy."

"Did you hear what they were saying?" asked Jamie.

"Not really. Not my business."

Jamie couldn't get used to the maid. He'd heard the other servants moaning about her, and her abrupt manner meant he couldn't get as close to her as he was with the others.

They finished their drinks and she took the tray away.

Mrs Button came out. Her face didn't give anything away, and it wasn't his place to ask.

"Come on, Mary, Lottie. Time to go," she beckoned to them. The girls jumped up and ran to her.

"Goodbye, Jamie." Maisie waved as they walked off.

He waved back, then turned to his little sister. "Well, Alice, we still don't know, do we? Shall we go in and see if anyone will tell us?" It would be good to have someone of his own age around.

The little girl nodded. Her thumb firmly in her mouth, she took Jamie's hand with her free one.

* * * *

Tillie sat up with a jerk, sweat soaking her body. Opening her eyes slowly, she pushed her hair off her face and let out her breath.

If only the nightmares would stop!

Leaning back onto the pillows, she tried to rid her mind of the terrifying images of her daughter running through the woods, being chased by large black birds, or floating face down in the lake, being pecked at by ducks and herons, but each time she closed her eyes, they were there again.

The hands on the clock at the side of her bed pointed to

five o'clock. Was that all? Why hadn't she closed the curtains before she'd gone to bed? At least, then, the sun wouldn't be streaming through the window. Maybe she could get back to sleep if she covered her head with the sheet. But then she might have another…

No, she might as well get up, but quietly, so as not to wake David in the adjoining room. It seemed as if he couldn't bear to touch her, or even hold a decent conversation since Annabella had died. He'd cocooned himself in a blanket of grief, and she couldn't get through to him. Some days he barely left his bed. She worried that the estate affairs were being forsaken, but he assured her everything was being dealt with.

She needed to speak to him about Jamie, as he was still insisting that boarding school was the right option for the boy, but she was getting more and more upset at the thought of her son leaving home for weeks on end. When she'd been in prison, the pain of not knowing where he was had sometimes overwhelmed her.

Her mind was made up. She was going to put her foot down and say he was not going. Although, when David's mind was set on something, it was hard to get him to change it. But she had to. She just had to.

Wrapping herself in her dressing gown, she went down to the kitchen to make a drink. Sitting at the table with a mug of hot tea, she stroked her belly, thinking about the baby she'd lost. What would they have named him? They hadn't got round to discussing that. At the rate they were going, hardly even speaking to each other most of the time, it would be a long time before she conceived another one.

Freda came in, yawning and adjusting her cap. The look of astonishment on her face made Tillie smile, despite her sorrow.

"Good day to you, Ti…I mean, Mistress," she blurted out, lifting up the kettle.

"I've already filled it, Freda. It should be boiling again by now."

"You didn't need to be doing that." The cook shook her head.

"You know me, Freda. I still can't get out of the habit of…you know." She shrugged, not in the mood for explanations.

Freda put the kettle back on its hook and felt the teapot. "Anyway, what are you doing up so early? You should be resting, not getting up at this unearthly hour. Only us servants need to do that."

"I couldn't sleep."

The cook poured herself a cup of tea and put it on the table, then put her hand on Tillie's shoulder. "It will get better, you know, easier, like."

"Well, Freda, things can't get any worse, can they? This year has been the year from hell. First, George dies, then the master and Sam have that horrific accident, then Annabella and the baby…" Putting her head in her hands, she began to sob. "I can't take any more. I just can't."

"There, there, my dear, let it all out. It's about time. You've been much too brave." Freda took her in her arms and rocked her. "It don't do to bottle things up inside you. It has to come out some time."

Her heart was breaking. She had no control over the tears. Each time she thought she'd recovered, she would start again. Freda cuddled her, stroking her head and running her hand up and down her arms. She thought she could hear the cook sniffing as well. That made her cry all the more. Having been so wrapped up in her own sorrow, it hadn't occurred to her that the servants would be as upset as the family. They kept themselves to themselves and weren't allowed to show their feelings. Feeling guilty that she hadn't considered them, she cried even more.

Eventually, Nellie's voice pervaded through the mist of tears. "Come now, lass, come on." She felt herself being prised from Freda's arms as she heard the housekeeper say, "Pour the lass another cup of tea."

Sitting back, she tried to pull herself together. The handkerchief Freda had given her was sodden. Reaching into her dressing gown pocket, she found a dry one and blew her nose. Taking a deep breath, she opened her mouth to speak, but all that came out was a shuddering sob.

Taking a sip, she nodded in apology to the two ladies who were looking at her so solicitously, then went back upstairs.

Sitting on her bed, she tried to calm herself, but the tears began to fall again and, curling up into a ball, she lay down and gave in to them once more.

* * * *

David turned over in bed. Something had woken him up, a moaning sound, no—more a keen wailing, coming from the adjoining room, Tillie's—or, to be truthful—their room. He listened harder. Maybe it was the wind blowing through the eaves? But he had never heard it do that before. It had to be his wretched, tormented wife. Ever since the funeral, she had been walking round like a spectre, no colour in her cheeks, her face a picture of misery, and he had felt powerless to help her.

How could he make her feel better? What could he say to ease her pain?

Absolutely nothing. He couldn't even come to terms with it himself, so how could he alleviate her suffering?

Pulling the covers over his head, he tried to blot out the sound. His own eyes filled with tears at the thought of her, lying in that big bed, all alone, with no one to shoulder her burden. That should be his task. He was her husband, the master of the house. He ought to be in there with her.

Go and comfort her, his conscience told him.

I know I should, but… His head was reeling from the opposing thoughts whirling round inside it. *What if she pushes me away? What if she does not want me?*

Then he heard Nellie's voice added to the medley. "Get in there and just put your arm around her. That's all she needs."

He looked up. He hadn't heard the housekeeper come in. But the room was empty. He shook his head, wryly realising that, being used to following the housekeeper's advice for so long, he did not even need her physical presence to know what she would say.

Pushing back the covers, he began to do as the voice had ordered. But the crying had stopped. Tillie must have gone back to sleep. No point disturbing her now. He lay back down.

* * * *

Pulling up his trousers, Jamie tried to work out how he could persuade his father to let him stay at home and not go away to boarding school. He had promised Maisie he would look after her now, so he couldn't go. That was, if she was definitely coming to work as the—what did she call it?—scully maid. Nellie hadn't said anything about it last night, so he decided to ask her first thing. It might be one of the things that would make his papa change his mind.

Buttoning his brown shirt—he didn't have to wear black if he didn't want to—he hesitated, thinking about his cousin, George, how he'd tried to get him into trouble when he'd first arrived at The Grange. His sister, Sarah, had stuck up for him. He loved her and hoped she was better from the illness that her brother had died from. But George dead! He still couldn't believe it. Would he be up in heaven? He'd been naughty. Did naughty boys go to heaven? He'd been told that they didn't, so where would he be? Something else to ask his mama about—when she was feeling better, of course.

He brushed his hair and, before putting on his cap, checked his face in the mirror. Oh, dear, he'd been too tired to wash it before he'd gone to bed and hadn't realised there was a black mark on his chin. Reaching over to the wash bowl, he wrung out the flannel and spread it out, giving his whole face a good wipe.

"S'pose I'd better clean behind me tabs as well," he muttered, knowing that Auntie Ruby would pull his ears forward and inspect them, saying, 'You could grow potatoes behind those ears' if he didn't. He decided, though, that his neck would do. It could wait 'til next time.

On the way downstairs, he wondered whether it was worth trying to get Auntie Ruby, and even Nellie, on his side against the boarding school thing. Surely they wouldn't want him to go? Then he remembered being told that his father had gone to Eton with Nellie's approval. Maybe not Nellie, then. But Auntie Ruby—yes, he felt sure he'd be able to rely on her. Look at all the help he gave her with the twins when he wasn't doing his lessons.

His father would have to find a proper governess for him. The old lady from the village, who'd been giving him lessons up until then, Miss Augusta Hetherington, was getting married, so Auntie Ruby had told him. She wouldn't be able to come any more, even if she was still needed. He wondered why an old lady like her would want to get married. His auntie had said she wasn't old, and that he wasn't to let her hear him say so, but her wrinkly chins and long nose told him otherwise.

Freda looked up from the dough she was kneading as he entered the kitchen. "Good morning, Master Jamie. You're up early."

"Do you think I should go to boarding school?" he blurted out.

"Well, it's not up to me."

"I know, but what d'yer think?"

Turning the dough over, the cook pressed her knuckles into it, shaking her head. "If your father says you're to go, then that's it."

"But…"

"If it were up to me, I'd say you should stay here with your family, especially after what's happened. But it isn't."

Jamie put his arms round her plump waist and hugged her. "Thanks, Freda."

Nellie walked in, looking rather surprised to see Jamie hugging the cook. He let go, knowing there was no point trying to get the housekeeper on his side.

She repeated what Freda had said earlier. "You're up early."

"Um, Maisie said, yesterday, she might be coming to work here." He looked from one to the other. "Is she?"

"What's that got to do with being up early?" asked Nellie, folding some towels she'd taken down from the overhead airers.

"Nothing, I was just wondering."

Freda put the dough into a bowl and covered it with a cloth before placing it near the fire. He tried to remember why she did that. Something to do with it rising up. He'd often watched it, imagining it taking off into the air, the cloth flapping at the sides, but had never seen it do so.

"Is she?" he persisted.

"Maybe. It hasn't been decided yet." Nellie picked up the piles of towels and took them out.

He turned to Freda.

"It's no good asking me," she said as he opened his mouth to speak. "I've told them I could do with some help, so now it's up to the master."

"I'm sure he'll say yes. I'll go and ask him."

He ran out, ignoring the cry from the cook. She was probably only going to tell him not to bother his papa, but he needed to know.

He ran into Martha on his way out. All the other servants greeted him warmly whenever he met them, but she didn't even smile. Never mind, he didn't have time to worry about her. He had to catch his papa before he came down. Halfway up the stairs, though, he changed his mind. Perhaps it would be better to speak to him while he was eating his breakfast. But then, his mama would be there, and they didn't seem very happy when they were together, hardly spoke to each other, so would that be a good time or not?

He stopped, full of indecision. Perhaps he should get his mama on his side first. He sensed that she didn't want him to go.

While he stood pondering, Auntie Ruby came out of the nursery, carrying Alice. "You're up early, Master Jamie."

Why did everybody keep saying that?

"Have you seen Mama?"

"Do you mean this morning?"

"Err, yes." Of course. She was bound to have seen her yesterday! Sometimes his auntie said the stupidest things.

"No, I haven't. I've only been to the nursery. What's the rush?"

"Well…do *you* think I should go to boarding school?"

She patted his head as Alice wriggled, trying to reach her brother. Jamie took her and planted a kiss on her cheek.

"Jaim," the little girl said, a huge grin on her face.

"You can nearly say my name now," he said proudly, handing her back to her auntie, who carried on towards the stairs, with Jamie following. Alice was still smiling at him over her shoulder, and he pulled faces to make her giggle.

"So, do you think I should, Auntie Ruby?" he asked, his lips forward in a pout.

"I beg your pardon?"

"Go to boarding school?"

Auntie Ruby turned to face him. "It's what your papa wants, Jamie."

"I know, but I really don't want to go, and Maisie might be coming, and Alice needs me and—"

"It's not up to me." She shook her head. "But, if it was, then I would say no."

He leaned his head on her arm. "Thank you, Auntie Ruby. That's what Freda said as well." He looked up, his head to one side. "I don't s'pose you'd say that to Mama?"

She sucked in her breath. "I don't think it would make much difference, Jamie, the way your mama is at the moment. She's grieving so much for little Annabella and the baby she lost, I can't seem to get through to her."

"Bella," said Alice, looking around excitedly as if she thought her twin was going to appear.

"Ah, no, Sweetiepie, she's not here," Jamie tried to console her.

"Bella," she repeated, more urgently.

He looked at his auntie. "She doesn't understand that she's never going to see her again, does she?"

Auntie Ruby shook her head, her eyes filling with tears. "Come on," she croaked. "Let's see what there is for breakfast."

Jamie was still no further forward in his search for deliverance from the dreaded school. His father had his breakfast tray taken up to his bedroom. His mother didn't appear either, and when he told Nellie he was going up to see her, he was told not to disturb her.

He wandered outside. Should he go down to his tree house? For a change, it didn't really appeal to him, but he began to walk in that direction, anyway. He remembered the boy who had rescued him from the snowdrift in the winter. What was his name? Bobby. That was it. He'd said he lived in a hut, and had pointed towards the woods on the other side.

Satisfied that the puffy clouds overhead weren't going to rain on him—he'd been scolded the previous week for getting wet—he decided to go and investigate. Maybe he could make friends with Bobby. He'd never had a proper friend, apart from Maisie. He knew Sebastian from The Upper Hall over the hill, but wouldn't really call him a friend. The only other boy he knew was George, and he was—he couldn't bring himself to say the awful 'D' word. Not that he'd been friendly anyway. He'd been really horrible, but he shouldn't think like that. Nellie had told him that you shouldn't think ill of the dead.

The clouds had all disappeared, so he skipped towards the woods. It would be colder in there, where the sun couldn't get through the trees, but he decided he would be warm enough with his thick brown jacket.

Pulling his cap further onto his head, he entered the woods, passed his tree house and carried on. He shouldn't get into trouble for going further, as the place where his papa's brother had been killed was down the other end.

Whistling through his teeth, although he still hadn't got the hang of doing it properly, he sauntered along, pushing low-hanging branches aside when they got in his way. There was only a very narrow track to follow. It couldn't really be called a path.

He stopped. He'd heard something over to his right. It hadn't sounded like any of the birds whose calls he knew. He'd been learning them and recognised all the common ones, blackbirds, jays, and pigeons, even owls. But it hadn't sounded like any of them. Half excited and half nervous, he carried on a little further. There it was again.

Eyes peeled, he peered through the bracken and ferns. He couldn't see anything unusual.

He almost jumped out of his skin as something shot by, not ten yards from him. Or could it have been *somebody*? It had moved so quickly he hadn't had a chance to tell.

"Hey." He jumped again as a voice spoke in his ear.

Turning quickly, he saw a boy in a tatty grey shirt and ripped trousers standing behind him, so close he could see his brown eyes. It was Bobby. "You scared the daylights out of me!" he cried. "How did you get behind me so quietly?"

Bobby merely grinned, his arms folded in front of him.

"Are you on your own?" Jamie asked, glancing around.

The boy nodded.

Slightly unnerved, Jamie looked down at him, not knowing what else to say. He shifted from one foot to the other. Now that he'd found him, he wasn't sure what to do next. Perhaps it wasn't such a good idea. Then he felt his sleeve being pulled.

"Do you want to see where I live?" Bobby had found his voice at last. "It's only over there." He pointed to where smoke could be seen curling up through the trees.

A whiff of it wafted across to Jamie. What a wonderful smell! All woody and…smoky. Closing his eyes, he breathed in deeply through his nose. "Yes, please," he replied.

They waded through the ferns and were soon in a clearing surrounded by very small buildings. Jamie remembered Bobby telling him he lived in a hut. He'd imagined it to be like a shed, but when Bobby took him inside, it reminded him of a gypsy caravan. Two beds stood at one end, a table at the other with three chairs, and a fire burned brightly in the middle—not that a gypsy caravan would have had a fire in it.

A very small lady wearing a dirty white shawl full of holes was standing at the table, pulling the fur off a rabbit. Jamie had seen Freda do that before. It came off in one piece, once you chopped off the feet. He hoped she wouldn't be gutting it while he was there. He knew the innards smelt absolutely foul.

She looked up and smiled, showing two black teeth amongst some whitish ones.

Jamie didn't know if he should take off his cap. He knew it was good manners to do so when you entered someone's house, but would you call this hut a house? He decided to do it, anyway. He twiddled it round in his hands.

The lady turned to her son. "Aren't you going to introduce us, Bobby?"

"This is me ma," he said, putting his arm around her shoulder.

His ma raised her eyebrows. "And who is this fine young gentleman?"

That made Jamie feel very grand. Even though he was only eleven, he felt like a giant beside his new friend and his mother who only came up to his ear.

Realising that Bobby didn't know his name, he put his shoulders back and said, "I'm Jamie."

"Well, good day to you, Jamie," she replied. "And where have you sprung from?"

Before he could reply, Bobby said, "'E lives up at big 'ouse I told you about."

Her eyebrows raised again as she looked him up and down. "Oh, you do, do you?"

"Yes, ma'am."

"Well, we don't stand on ceremony here, lad, so you can put yer cap back on."

Jamie did as he was bid, feeling even taller with it on.

Bobby pulled at his sleeve again. "I saw a bird's nest yesterday. Want to come and see it?"

"What sort of bird?"

"A blue tit."

"Oh, yes. Is it far?"

"Nay, only across the wood."

They went back outside as Bobby's mother began to cut into the rabbit.

Just in time, thought Jamie as he followed his new friend out of the camp and through the woods, *before that horrible stink escapes.*

He could see the smoke drifting upwards again and sniffed. "What's that fire burning?" he asked.

"That's the charcoal. It has ter burn for a few days afore it's ready."

Ready for what? he wondered, but didn't like to ask. "It's got a lovely smell, hasn't it?" he remarked instead.

"Has it? I never noticed."

Further into the woods, he heard voices.

"Oh, no, that'll be me sisters and cousins," moaned Bobby. "Keep low and they might not see us."

"Why don't you want them to?"

"'Cos they'll only want to join us, and they're girls."

"What's wrong with…?" Jamie began to ask, but Bobby put his finger to his lips. "Shh."

Through the trees Jamie could just make out four figures sitting in a circle, giggling. They skirted by them until they came to a clearing.

Bobby pointed to a group of bushes covered in ivy. "It's in there," he whispered. "The nest."

As they approached, a bird flew out. "'Tis a blue tit," Jamie whispered. "You're right."

"'Course I am. I know all me birds," Bobby whispered back.

They edged closer. "Are there any babies inside?"

Bobby nodded, and Jamie carefully pulled back the ivy and peeped inside. Sure enough, five gaping mouths opened. He quickly replaced the ivy and moved back. Bobby had a quick look as well before they turned away.

Jamie suddenly felt very sad. He remembered when George had looked into a nest and been about to touch the babies inside, but Sarah had stopped him. Why did he keep on thinking about George? He hadn't even liked him. So many things reminded him of his dead cousin.

"What's up?" asked Bobby, looking puzzled. "You don't look very happy to see 'em."

"Have you ever known anyone what's died?" Jamie stopped and looked at his friend.

"Them birds ain't dead."

"No. I don't mean them. I mean, like…family?"

It was Bobby's turn to look sad. "Aye, me brother. He

died last year."

"It's horrible, isn't it?"

"At least he's in heaven."

Annabella would be, but was George?

Bobby began to run ahead. "But we ain't dead," he called, flinging his arms in the air. "We can run and sing and…anything we like."

"Yes," replied Jamie, "we can, can't we?"

They danced around the clearing, singing at the tops of their voices, just to show how alive they were, until the four girls appeared. They stopped as the tallest one came up close to Jamie.

"'Oo's this?" she asked with a sneer, jabbing at his chest.

The other three stood back, holding hands. The two little ones didn't look much older than Alice, but the other one… The prettiest green eyes he'd ever seen stared at him from behind the other girl's shoulder. His knees went weak. He wasn't sure if it was from the sight of her or the taunts of the taller girl.

Bobby stood up straight and declared proudly, "This is me mate, Jamie."

"Ha, you ain't got no mates."

Dragging his gaze away from the girl with the green eyes, Jamie turned to the one who'd spoken. He stood closer to Bobby and said, "Yes, he has. I'm his friend."

"And where've you come from? I ain't seen you before."

"'E lives up at big 'ouse, so there," Bobby retorted, poking her in the ribs.

"Oo-er, lives up at big 'ouse, does 'e?" she mocked, pushing him and making him stumble.

Jamie reached out and caught him before he fell. "Don't do that," he cried. "You're bigger than him."

"Oo, fancy boy, think you're 'is hero, do yer?"

"No, I just don't like people being pushed around."

Sticking her head in the air, she pranced around, her finger pushing her nose up, singing, "Fancy boy, fancy boy."

Jamie had never thought of himself as being above anybody else. In fact, when he'd first come to The Grange he'd spoken like a ruffian, but in the four years he'd been there he'd been taught to speak properly, so he probably seemed like it to her.

He pulled Bobby away. "Come on, Bobby. Let's go."

Sticking out his tongue at the horrible girl, his friend followed him.

"I'm sorry if that's your sister, Bobby, but I don't like her," Jamie said as they made their way back towards the smoky compound.

"Nay, she's me cousin. The other one's me sister, and the little one in the pink dress."

All their clothes had been ragged, but Jamie couldn't recall any of them being pink, not even Bobby's sister's. He hadn't looked beyond her long fair hair and those eyes… His heart began to thump, just thinking about her.

"Oh, that's good," he said casually.

They reached the clearing where the huts stood in a circle, and Jamie decided he'd better return home. They would probably be wondering where he was.

"Are you coming in?" asked Bobby.

Jamie could hear the girls giggling in the distance behind them. They must have followed. "No, thanks, I have to get back." Waving his arm in the air, he crossed the clearing.

"Will you be coming again?" called Bobby.

"P'raps," he called back. He would have to think about that. Much as he'd love to see the green eyes again, he would be too embarrassed if the horrible one started making fun of him. He wasn't used to that sort of thing. It had made him really uncomfortable.

Making his way through the trees, he realised he didn't even know Bobby's sister's name. Maybe he would go again. Then he could ask quite casually what it was.

Hacking through the ferns, they seemed thicker than he remembered, and he could still smell smoke. That meant he was near Bobby's camp. But he'd been walking for ages. He should be further away than that. Was he going round in circles? He began to feel scared. He couldn't go back and say he was lost. That girl would definitely laugh at him. No, he would have to try and find his way on his own, making sure the smoke was behind him.

Chapter 10

Tillie turned over in bed and stretched. The clock downstairs in the hall began to chime. Counting the chimes, she reached twelve. Twelve? That couldn't be right. She couldn't have slept the whole morning. Picking up her bedside clock, she checked what that said. "Oh, dear, it is."

Pushing back the bed covers, she stepped out onto the cold floor, wriggling her toes as she tried to reach the rug. Pulling it towards her, she stood up, but was forced to sit back down. She sighed. When would she feel normal again? It seemed like she'd been poorly for ever and couldn't remember what it was like to feel well.

Taking a deep breath, she stood up again. It was at times like these that she wished she'd agreed to Nellie's suggestion that she have her own maid, but she'd been so determined that she would manage without one. Perhaps it was time to concede. Maybe she would have a word with David, if he was in a good mood, of course.

Wrapping her dressing gown round her, she padded over to the door, yawning.

The door opened. "Ah, you're awake," Nellie said.

"Only just," Tillie admitted. "I was wondering if a bath could be arranged. I feel filthy. A bath would perk me up."

"Just what I was going to suggest. A long soak would do you the world of good."

"I'd better go down and sort out tonight's dinner menu with Freda first. I forgot last night." Tillie tried to get out of the door, but Nellie urged her back in.

"No need," said the housekeeper, taking her arm and sitting her back on the bed. "It's all arranged."

"But how does she know what I want?"

"Years of practice."

"Oh." Tillie slumped down onto the bed, watching as her bath was brought in and filled with water. Taking off her nightclothes, she stepped into it and, closing her eyes, lay back and luxuriated in the soft, warm water, rubbing her hands over her belly as if to heal it.

Tears pricked at her eyes once more, but she was determined not to give in to them. She had to be strong. She couldn't wallow in self-pity any longer.

The water soon began to cool, so she sat up and soaped herself, wondering if David was up. Before the accident, he'd loved washing her back and would sometimes climb in with her, not that they got much washing done. They could just fit in, if she sat with her back to him, with his arms around her, while he…

Would they ever get back to normality, what with his bad leg and everything else that had happened?

Rinsing off the soap, she stood up and reached for the large fluffy towel Nellie had left hanging over the chair. Wrapping it around her, she sat back on the bed, enveloped in its softness.

It was unusual for Jamie not to come and say good morning. He must have been told not to disturb her.

Someone knocked on her door.

Speak of the devil, she thought. *Here he is.*

"Just a minute, Jamie, I'm not dressed," she called.

"It isn't Jamie, it's me," she heard Ruby call back.

"Oh, come in, then, if you don't mind me in a state of *dishabille.*"

Ruby came in carrying Alice. "A state of what?" she asked.

"It's a new word I read in one of my books. I've been dying to try it out for ages."

"Well, sis, you sound a lot happier today, I'm glad to say."

"That's what having a long, warm soak does for you." She didn't add that the crying fit she'd had earlier had also washed away a lot of her desperation and hopelessness. But she realised it had. "Anyway, how's my darling daughter?" She leaned over and gave Alice a kiss, gripping the towel tightly.

"She's wonderful, aren't you, gorgeous?" Ruby grinned as Alice giggled.

"And where's my Jamie?" Tillie looked behind them, expecting him to appear.

Ruby looked surprised as if it hadn't occurred to her that he wasn't around. "Oh, I expect he's out playing somewhere."

"Has he had his lunch?"

"No, we're all running slightly late today, I don't know why. I'm just taking Alice to get hers. I expect Jamie'll be waiting downstairs. It's not like him to miss it."

"But he hasn't been in to say hello this morning."

"Well, I'll go and find him while you dress. He won't be far." Ruby took Alice out as Tillie rummaged in her wardrobe for something bright and cheerful to wear. Then she remembered she was still in mourning, and would have to wear the customary black for some time yet. The clean dress was one that she didn't really like, it didn't fit properly and the crepe was scratchy, but it would have to do.

Suitably dressed, with a necklace of jet, and a locket containing some of Annabella's hair round her throat, she sat down at the dressing table to brush her tangled hair. That took quite a while as it was full of lugs. Ruby still hadn't come back up, or Jamie. Tying her hair in a bun for quickness, she hurried downstairs.

David called out as she passed the drawing room. "Is that you, Tillie?"

"Yes, dear." She rushed in to him. He lay on the sofa, a grimace on his face. "What is it, darling? Are you in pain?" Reaching out, she took in his still-handsome face, the gorgeous blue eyes that she loved so much.

"Could you just…?" He hesitated, looking deeply into her eyes. "It is nothing." Shifting his position to make room for her, he patted the space beside him. "Come and sit with me for a while. How are you feeling, my darling?"

She was taken aback at the unexpected endearment. It'd been some while since he'd even spoken to her civilly, let alone with any warmth. "Actually, I'm feeling a lot better today, thank you." Reaching over, she kissed his lips. He kept his eyes closed as she pulled away. Was it because he hadn't enjoyed the kiss? Had he only been polite, asking how she was?

Confused, she began to stand but, with his eyes still shut, he took hold of her hand. "Do not go yet." He pulled her into the crook of his arm, and she lay with it wrapped around her, her head resting on his chest, but much as she was enjoying the unexpected intimacy, she was still wondering why she hadn't seen her son. Perhaps David knew where he was.

"Have you seen Jamie this morning?"

"No, come to think of it, I cannot say that I have."

"I haven't either."

"But you have only just got up, have you not?"

"Yes, I know, but…" Her right arm was turning numb with lying on it, so she sat up. "It doesn't matter. It's just that it's unusual for him not to come and say good morning, that's all."

David smiled, looking up at the clock. "I think it would have to be 'good afternoon' now."

Shrugging her shoulders, she smiled ruefully. "Yes, I suppose."

She stood up, eager to see if Jamie was in the kitchen. "Are you sure you're not in pain? Is there anything I can get you?"

Pushing his lips forward in a pout, he replied, "Another kiss would be nice. That is, if you are not too busy."

Sighing, she reached forward. "I'm not busy, I'm just concerned about Jamie, that's all." She kissed him and straightened up.

"He is eleven years old, Tillie, not seven any more. You wrap him up in cotton wool sometimes. I expect he is down in his tree house or somewhere."

"Yes, probably."

"And, do not forget when he goes away to school, you will not see him for weeks. You need to get used to it."

"Yes, well, that's something I need to speak to you about."

"Not now. Go on, if your son is more important than sitting with me." He waved her away. "Please, would you pass me that newspaper before you go?"

Your son? It was always 'your son', unless the boy did

something to be proud of, then it was 'our son'.

Giving him the paper, she had to admit that she did feel sorry for him, bored to tears, unable to get about on his own. She made a mental note to come back and spend some time with him once she was sure Jamie was safe. They could play a game of cards. Jamie liked playing cards, so he could join in as well.

She hurried out, bumping into Nellie in the hall. "Do you know where Jamie is?" she asked quickly. "I haven't seen him today."

"Um…Ruby was just asking the same thing. I haven't actually seen him since breakfast. But he won't be far."

Tillie didn't miss the look of concern on the housekeeper's face. Grabbing her arm, she looked her in the eye. "You are worried, though, aren't you? I can tell."

"Well…not worried, exactly."

Raising her arms behind her head, Tillie ran into the kitchen, yelling, "Where is he? Where's my boy?"

Nellie followed her, calling, "Please, Mistress, don't get upset. There's bound to be an explanation."

Freda and Ruby were outside the back door. Tillie joined them. "Is he out there? Can you see him?"

They both shook their heads. Ruby handed Alice to her and began to run towards the woods, calling, "I'll check his tree house."

Nellie put a reassuring hand on Tillie's arm. "I'm sure that's where he'll be. Don't fret."

"But what if he's so upset about going away to school that he's run away?"

"Now, what good would that do, running away? Where would he go?" Freda shook her head as she went back inside to finish preparing the vegetables for the evening meal.

"Freda's right," said Nellie. "Running away wouldn't do any good, would it? He'd be even worse off than ever."

"I know, I know. It's just that after the awful time I had before, and everything that's happened…"

"I understand, Tillie, sorry—Mistress—I really do."

"No, you don't, Nellie. You can't possibly know what

I've been through. I sometimes wonder how I have the strength to cope with all the trials that God showers on me."

"You do cope, though. You're a very strong person. I really admire how well you deal with everything that besets you." The housekeeper took her by the arm. "Come on in."

Tillie shook her head.

"Well, at least have a cup of tea."

Tillie had to smile. That was the universal panacea—a cup of tea. One would be very welcome, though.

She let herself be drawn back inside. There was a plate of sandwiches on the table, so she sat down in front of it with Alice on her knee. "Eat up," she prompted.

"They aren't hers, she's already eaten." Freda quickly removed the plate, and placed a hot cup of tea in its place. She then seemed to have second thoughts and put the plate back, saying, "But you might as well eat them."

"They're Jamie's, aren't they?"

"Well, they were, but you have them. I can make him some more as soon as Ruby brings him in."

Eating the bread automatically without tasting it, she let her wriggling daughter climb down from her lap. "Don't go away, though, Alice, sweetheart. I don't want to have to go searching for you as well," she muttered between bites.

Freda took the little girl to the sideboard and handed her a large crumbly biscuit out of a coloured tin. "I know you're not usually allowed to eat between meals," she told her. "But I don't think your mama will mind today."

Alice's face lit up as she toddled back to show off her prize. Tillie hadn't the heart to take it from her, so she picked her up again and put her back on her knee, watching her eat it. She seemed to be enjoying it so much. Oh, the joys of being a child, and relishing such small treats without a care in the world!

Finishing the biscuit, Alice climbed down and pointed to the tin, saying, "Scit."

"No, darling, you can't have any more."

The child's bottom lip stuck out. "Scit!" she cried.

Tillie jumped up and pulled her daughter away from the

tin. "Mama said 'no more'. Please be told."

Alice began to cry.

"Now, see what you've done, Freda," Tillie yelled at the cook. "If you hadn't given her a biscuit in the first place, she wouldn't be crying for more now."

Seeing the look of indignation on the cook's round face, Tillie knew she was being unreasonable, but the phrase 'a child should be seen and not heard' sprang to mind. Not that she ever lived by that rule. She thought, unfashionably, that children should be allowed to express themselves, but sometimes it seemed very appropriate.

Sighing, and not looking Freda in the eye, she picked up the child. "Come on, let's go out and look for your brother." The crying ceased as the thumb was put back in. Fortunately, her daughter wasn't prone to having long tantrums.

Tillie decided that Alice's full-length navy blue dress would be quite warm enough without a coat, so setting the little girl's bonnet straight and tucking in her curls, she went outside, wrapping her own shawl around her.

Ruby could be seen in the distance running back from the woods. She was alone. Picking up Alice, Tillie hurried in her direction and, as she got nearer, could hear her sister gasping for breath. She was shocked to see her dress was torn, her white apron covered in black and green blotches, and the petticoat underneath ripped. She was carrying her mop cap, and her brown, tangled hair looked like she had been pulled through a hedge.

"What on earth happened to you?" asked Tillie as her sister drew level. She also had a nasty red cut on her cheek.

Alice put out her arms for Ruby to take her, but she was bent over double, trying desperately to get some air into her lungs.

"Not now, sweetheart," Tillie told her daughter as she waited for Ruby to speak. "Auntie Ruby can't take you yet."

The little girl began to squirm, wanting to be put down, so Tillie decided that it would be easier to let her have her way. "Keep hold of Mama's hand, though," she cautioned her.

Ruby caught her breath enough to speak.

"He's...not...there."

"Well, I rather gathered that." Tillie waited for her to continue. When she didn't, she asked, "But why are you so dishevelled?"

"I fell down the ladder...and got...caught up...in a...thorn bush."

"Are you hurt anywhere else besides your face?"

Her sister shook her head, putting her hand up to her cheek, and bringing it back down with a spot of blood on her finger. "And then...fell down a ditch."

"Oh, you poor girl." Tillie pulled some twigs out of Ruby's hair and brushed down her dress.

"Any word?" Ruby asked, ripping off a bit of her torn petticoat to dab her face with.

This time it was Tillie's turn to shake her head. "No." She inhaled deeply, casting her eyes over the landscape. Suddenly, she saw a movement out of the corner of her eye. Turning to see what had caught her attention, she saw a large brown hare running across the field, then another. They both bounded off, leaving Tillie even more deflated than ever. But something else was coming into view, down at the bottom near the woods. *Probably just another hare.*

"Is that him?" she asked Ruby, who had been looking the other way.

Her sister turned and, shielding her eyes from the sun, exclaimed, "It is, it's him."

Tillie grabbed Alice, who had been sitting quietly playing in the grass, and they began to run towards him, calling his name.

He looked up, took off his cap and waved it as he ran towards them.

"Oh, thank you, God," Tillie gasped as they hurtled down the field. "Thank you, thank you."

"Where've you been?" yelled Ruby as they came within reach of him. "We've all been worried sick."

Jamie pulled up, a look of surprise on his face as he noticed Ruby's ripped clothes. "Auntie Ruby, where've *you* been, more like?"

"Don't be cheeky, Jamie," Tillie half-heartedly admonished him as she handed Alice to her sister and enfolded him in her arms, closing her eyes and breathing in the earthiness and smoky scent clinging to his thick brown jacket. The smell rather surprised her, but she didn't care where he'd been, she was just so thankful he was back.

"You're a bad boy, scaring us all like that," Ruby continued, but Tillie straightened and put her hand on her sister's arm.

"Never mind chastising him, Ruby. Just be glad he's safe."

"But…" With an offended look, her sister opened and closed her mouth as if she was vying with herself to say more to the boy.

"Please?" Tillie looked at her beseechingly before taking Jamie's hand and walking back up the field. Ruby soon followed.

"I made a new friend," Jamie said excitedly.

Tillie wasn't sure if she'd heard him properly. She stopped. "What do you mean?" *A friend in the woods?*

"His name's Bobby." He then rubbed his tummy. "I'm hungry."

"I'm not surprised," said Ruby, catching up with them. "You've missed your lunch." She looked as if she wanted to say more, but kept quiet after noticing Tillie's raised eyebrows. "You'll have to tell us what you've been up to when you've had something to eat," she said quietly.

Tillie smiled at her in silent recognition of her reticence, and they made their way back. Ruby was forced to put Alice down when she got too heavy, and the little girl could only make slow progress through the rough grass, so Jamie offered to carry her, but could only do so for a few yards as his arms ached as well.

Carrying her daughter the rest of the way, Tillie told Jamie to run on ahead and let his papa know he was safe.

"But he can see I am," he replied, obviously unaware of the panic he'd caused.

"Well, just go and prove it to him, please, there's a good

boy."

He disappeared up the drive and round the back of the house.

As he ran, he breathed a sigh of relief. *I won't tell no one I got lost in the woods. I think I got away with it. Mama don't seem too worried, but Auntie Ruby will prob'ly give me a telling off when she gets me on me own. I could tell she were a bit cross with me.* He could revert to his old way of talking when he was on his own. It was so much easier. He tried really hard to talk proper when he was with his mama and papa, and Auntie Ruby tried to tell him what words he should use, but she wasn't as good as them, and wasn't as strict.

He hurried into the morning room after managing to avoid Freda, whom he could hear rummaging about in the pantry. His papa wasn't there. Running out into the hall, he bumped into Nellie.

"There you are, young man. Where on earth have you been?" she asked, grabbing him by the shoulders and checking him over.

Aw, if he'd realised she was there, he would've hid 'til she'd gone. "Just down the woods," he replied, forcing a smile, then added quickly, "Where's Papa? Mama told me to tell him I'm safe."

"You've already seen your mother?"

"Yes, ages ago." *Try to make it look like I've been back a long time.*

"Oh," Nellie's eyes opened wide. They looked browner than usual. He suddenly realised he was the same height as her. He must have grown while he was out. He reached up and laid his hand flat on the top of his head, and moved it over the top of the housekeeper's.

"I'm as tall as you now, Nellie," he declared, hoping that it would take her mind off the reason he was late.

She pushed him away. "Never mind that. Where *is* your mama?"

It hadn't worked.

"Oh, she's...she's outside with Auntie Ruby and Alice,"

he said quickly. "I need to see Papa."

"Isn't he in there?" She pointed into the room he'd just come out of.

Weren't grown-ups stupid? Would he have asked if his father had been there? About to raise his eyebrows and tut as he'd seen Auntie Ruby do many times, he thought better of it. Best to make his getaway. "P'raps John took him to the garden."

Opening the front door, he noticed a twig sticking out of his pocket. Thank goodness Nellie hadn't seen that. He hurried out and hid behind a bush, emptying both pockets and shaking out his cap to make sure there wasn't anything left inside it. He'd given it a good shake before he'd left the wood, but another wouldn't do any harm. Satisfied that he was twig-free, he began to search the gardens.

If his father wasn't there, maybe he'd be in his bedroom. But he never went up there in the daytime, it was too much of a palaver to get up and down the stairs. He didn't really know what a 'palaver' was, but he'd heard his papa say it and thought it was a magnificent word. He rolled it round his tongue, repeating it over and over, "Palaver, palaver."

He wandered round the gardens for a while, thinking that it would be best to keep out of everyone's way. A blackbird hopped onto the lawn near him, making him think of Sarah. She'd shown him a blackbird's nest the first day he'd met her. He hoped she'd received his letter and wondered when she would be coming to visit.

Thinking of his cousin also reminded him of the girl he'd met that morning. Oh, she was beautiful! He wished he knew her name, he couldn't keep thinking of her as 'Bobby's sister' or 'the girl with the dazzling green eyes', but he would probably never see her again, so it didn't matter.

He picked up a twig, possibly the same one he'd just thrown down, put it in his mouth, chewing the end of it like he'd seen Sam doing, and began strutting round the lawn, his head in the air, pretending he was at a ball. His parents had held a few at The Grange, and he'd often crept down and peeped through the banisters at the people below him in their fancy clothes, dancing or standing talking, unaware that they were being watched. One time, swaggering along the landing, throwing his arms out as he'd seen one of the men in a fancy shirt doing, he hadn't heard Nellie come along. She'd sent him back to bed, but he'd still heard the music and pictured everybody enjoying themselves. Maybe one day he'd go to one of these grand balls and meet the girl. But no, she wasn't likely to move in the same circles. She looked really poor.

Then he remembered that gentlemen didn't chew twigs, they smoked cigars. Taking the twig out of his mouth, and holding it between his fingers, he blew out pretend smoke.

Papa always says he'll make a gentleman of me, he thought, *so I need to get in some practice.*

Holding out his left hand as if it was around a lady's waist, he danced around the lawn, the pretend cigar in his other hand. They weren't the proper steps, but that didn't matter. Maybe his papa would show him when he was better.

His hands dropped to his sides. His papa's leg was never going to get better, and he would never be able to dance again.

He sat down miserably on the grass. Poor Papa, not only would he never dance again, he wouldn't be able to walk on his own either. It was only the bottom half of his leg they'd cut off, but he would always need someone to support him, or else be pushed around in the wheelchair.

Jamie tried getting up as if he only had one leg. Kneeling down and leaning on his hands, he bent his right leg behind him and tried to raise himself up on his left one. It was impossible. He just couldn't do it.

Slumping back, his stomach began to rumble, reminding him he'd missed lunch. Dare he go and ask for some? He'd probably die of starvation if he didn't, so he got up and casually walked inside, hoping that everyone would have forgotten about the morning's shenanigans. That was another lovely word he'd recently learned, another one to roll around the mouth. Shenanigans.

Martha was the only person in the kitchen. She looked up from the table where she was cleaning the silverware on some newspaper, and pointed to a pile of sandwiches on a plate.

"Your meal's there," she told him curtly before carrying on rubbing.

"Thanks," he replied, grabbing the plate and rushing back outside. He wasn't usually allowed to eat his meals anywhere but at the table, either in the kitchen or upstairs in the nursery, but the smell of the polish would spoil his meal—so would the company.

Sitting in the garden on one of the many benches, hidden from view of the house, the same old thought kept creeping into his mind—boarding school. If only he could forget about it. His papa kept saying he was lucky he hadn't been sent before, because most boys went as soon as they were eleven, and he was nearly twelve. He didn't want to go at all. The horror he'd felt when his mama hadn't returned to the barn still haunted him occasionally, and he was worried that he might start feeling like that again while he was away.

As soon as his papa was in a good mood, he'd talk to him about it again and try to explain. Not that he hadn't tried a few times already, but he would be extra—what was the word?—pers…perstistent. He would stand up like a man and…well, he would try his hardest.

"There you are, Jamie." His mama's voice broke into his thoughts. She looked down with raised eyebrows at the empty plate. Had he eaten the food? He didn't remember doing so. He hoped she wasn't going to tell him off for eating it outside, but she didn't say anything, much to his relief. She put Alice down, and the little girl immediately ran over to him and put her arms up.

"My darling little sister," he crooned, thinking, *you're the lucky one, you won't ever have to go away. You're a girl.* Not that he would have wanted to be a girl. They had to dress up in fancy dresses. He wouldn't like that. And they had to do sewing and broidery and stuff like that. They couldn't go shooting. His papa had once said he'd take him on a shoot. But that had been before the accident.

"So, why are you hiding away out here?" his mother asked. "Did you tell your father you were safe?"

"Oh, no, I couldn't find him." Jamie had completely

forgotten he was supposed to do that.

"So, he doesn't know?"

"Um, no, s'pose not." He looked down guiltily. "I got hungry and forgot to carry on looking."

"But he wasn't in the drawing room when I passed it just now." His mama looked very harassed. "Why do people keep disappearing? What's the matter with everyone?"

* * * *

David read the newspaper without much enthusiasm. It only contained bad news. A man had been murdered in a nearby village. He tried to remember the person, but could not bring his face to mind. Some cattle had been stolen, and a sheep had got wedged in between two trees and had had to be rescued.

One headline said that a young boy had absconded from school the previous week and had not been seen since. That made him sit up and take notice. He knew the family well. The boy's name was Sebastian. It was the same school that Jamie was to attend in the autumn. With a sigh, he turned over the page. He did not want Jamie seeing the story. His son was already reluctant to go and would not need any further excuse to get out of it.

He rested his head back against the sofa. Was he being unreasonable in insisting on him going? It had been a spur of the moment decision that had escalated. He, himself, had gone to Eton and he had thought it would be the best thing for Jamie, as he had virtually no interaction with other boys of his own age at home.

There was no way he could back down now, even though he knew that Tillie did not want her son to leave home and live with strangers. He smiled ruefully. *Her* son? Jamie was also *his* son. He had legally adopted him, so he was as much his as hers.

Tillie had seemed rather concerned that Jamie had not been seen all morning. It was not unusual for him to go down to his tree house and spend a few hours there, but he always told someone he was going. He would go and find out.

"Damn this gammy leg," he muttered as he put down the newspaper and tried to get up. Why was John never around when he needed him?

His wheelchair was beside the sofa. Could he get into it on his own? Reaching over, he managed to pull it towards him and, standing on his good leg, swivelled round and plonked into the chair. Pushing himself up with his arms, he twisted his body so he was comfortable, and began to push himself across the room by reaching down and turning the wheels manually. It was much harder than he had expected, and he hadn't made it to the door when he had to stop, his arms aching, and his lungs devoid of breath.

As frustrated as he felt at not getting very far, he was elated that at least he had done it on his own. Things were looking up. Maybe he would not be quite so dependent on others from now on.

John came in, looking appalled. "Master, how did you get there?" He began fussing round him.

"I did it, John. I did something myself, without any help." David leaned back, smiling but exhausted.

"But, master, you're not well enough to be doing things like that."

"It is time I pulled myself together."

"But…"

"Now I am in here, take me outside."

After wrapping him in a blanket, John manoeuvred the wheelchair down the front step by going backwards. "Where do you want to go, master?"

"Round the back, through the garden."

They came to the summer house. David was weary, but the warm weather was such a delight he did not feel inclined to go back indoors. "Leave me in here, John. I shall have a nap. Maybe you could go in and check that Jamie is back."

"If you're sure, master." The cover was tucked in again and the valet left.

Leaning his head against the summer house wall, David closed his eyes.

A Dilemma for Jamie

Voices woke him some time later. They belonged to Tillie and Jamie. "Thank goodness, the boy had been found," he muttered.

Could he get himself out without John? The small step should not be too much of a problem if he was careful. He wheeled himself over to the door. Would it be easier to go backwards? At least he would not get catapulted out if it went wrong. He tried to turn the chair round. That was easier said than done. Many backward and forward manoeuvres later, he was lined up.

Chapter 11

Tillie brushed some grass off Alice's new maroon dress. She was growing out of all her old clothes. Children weren't obliged to wear mourning, but Tillie felt that a dark-coloured dress would be more appropriate than the pink one she'd wanted her to have. She herself would have to wear black for a few more months. It was only right to do so in respect of her other little girl. Tears began to well up in her eyes at the remembrance of the dressmaker coming prepared to make two dresses and being told that only one was required. Little events like those caught her off-guard. She was beginning to manage her grief to a degree, but then something would happen to start her off again.

A sudden shout from behind them brought her back to the present.

"That sounded like Papa," cried Jamie, running towards the sound. "Papa," he called. "Where are you?"

Wiping away her tears, Tillie picked up her daughter and followed him. "David?" she yelled. Her ill-fitting dress was too long, and she almost tripped in her haste.

"Over here, by the summer house," she heard David's strangled reply.

Rounding the corner, her worst fears were confirmed. Her husband lay on the ground, his wheelchair upturned beside him. "Not again," she croaked, hurrying towards him. Jamie had already reached him and was trying to help him up.

"Where's John?" she asked crossly. "He's supposed to be looking after you."

"I am not a child, Tillie. I do not need 'looking after'."

"Well, you know what I mean." Putting Alice down, she helped Jamie lift him up to a sitting position. "Are you hurt?"

Shaking his head, he tried to right the wheelchair.

"I'll do that, Papa," cried Jamie.

David sighed, his shoulders visibly drooping.

Tillie reached out to help him. "Are you sure you're not hurt? You might have—"

"Stop fussing, woman." He pushed her arm away. "I told you, I am fine."

Helpless, and offended by his attitude, Tillie stood up. Alice began to whimper, so she picked her up, burying her face in the little girl's soft bonnet.

Jamie tried once more to help his father up.

"Leave him, Jamie, I'll go and find John. You can't do it on your own, you'll hurt yourself." She turned away so he wouldn't see the frustration and hurt on her face.

From the sounds they were making behind her, she could tell he wasn't taking any notice of what she'd said, but she certainly wasn't going to help now. David had made his wishes very clear. He didn't want her there.

Nellie met her on the way in. "Mistress Tillie, have you thought any more about young Mary coming to work here as the scullery maid? Freda says she manages but finds certain tasks difficult now she's not getting any younger. It would definitely help that wretched Mrs Button. She's pregnant again and can't afford to keep Mary on."

Tillie hadn't given the idea much thought, and wasn't in the mood for discussing it.

Ruby appeared from behind her. She must have been listening, for she replied, "I think it would be an act of kindness, don't you, Tillie? After all, where would we have been if we hadn't been taken in by the master?"

"But she's so young, it doesn't seem right."

"She's older than I was when I first came," said Ruby.

"Yes, but you had me to look out for you."

Nellie took her arm. "And Mary will have all of us to look out for her. We're not going to treat her badly and make her work her fingers to the bone like some households do. She'll have to knuckle down and work hard, of course, to earn her keep, but Freda will make sure she doesn't overtax her."

Tillie knew it made sense, but wondered if David ought to be involved in the decision. "Shouldn't we consult the master first? He's—"

"Consult me about what?" her husband's voice came from behind them. She turned to see him being wheeled in.

"It's nothing, master," replied Nellie. "It's a decision for me to take. You don't need to be bothered about it."

He seemed riled that he was being excluded. "I am master of this establishment. I would like to know if any changes are to be made."

Tillie was still feeling upset about, what seemed to her, his callous attitude to her earlier. "Well, if you want my opinion, I think it's a good idea, but I'll let you fight it out between you." She turned and left them to it. Let him have the final say, if that was what he wanted.

Ruby followed her and tugged at her sleeve. "Is there anything the matter, sis?"

Tillie passed Alice to her. The little girl was practically asleep. "No. Thank you, Ruby. Would you please put Alice down for her nap? She's well overdue."

Ruby took the child after giving her sister a knowing look, and took her off to the nursery.

On her bureau, Tillie had a half-written letter to Emily that really ought to be finished, but would she be able to write it without venting her perturbed feelings? As good a friend as the vicar's wife was, she didn't want to saddle her with her problems, especially as she was due to have her baby at any time.

As she stood in the hallway, trying to decide where to go, Jamie came running up. "Is it true that Maisie's coming?"

"If that's what's been decided, then yes."

"That's good. I'll have someone my own age to play with."

"Maisie won't have time to play, Jamie. She'll be too busy working."

"Oh." He seemed to consider that for a moment. He then looked puzzled. "Why does everyone call her Mary?"

"Because that's the name the Button family gave her when they found her wandering in the fields, unable to speak, when…you know…" Tillie didn't like to talk about that horrific time when she'd left Jamie in the barn to go and find some food after she'd taken him and Maisie there to escape the fire. Maisie had run out, and Tillie had been too guilt-ridden to go after her.

Jamie screwed up his face. "I don't really remember much of that. But why don't they call her Maisie now they know that's her real name?"

"Maybe we will when she gets here. We'll have to ask her which name she prefers." She ruffled his hair, thinking it needed cutting.

He seemed to consider that for a moment, then, nodding, he turned and walked away.

"Get on with some of your school work, Jamie," she called after him. "You've been slacking lately. Just because Miss Hetherington is laid up with the flu, doesn't mean you…" Her words tailed off. He was well out of earshot. He'd waved an acknowledgement before rounding the corner, so she hoped he would heed her, but it was probably a slim chance.

Giving a deep sigh, she wondered how to ease her fraught feelings. Nobody seemed to need her. David had made it quite plain that he didn't want her 'fussing' over him, as he put it. Alice was asleep. Jamie had hopefully gone off to do some spelling or drawings. Perhaps she should have sat down with him and made sure he did. If Miss Hetherington was still poorly the following day, she would definitely take some time and help him, but not at that moment, not in the mood she was in.

Maybe some fresh air would be beneficial. Poking her head out of the door to see if it was warm enough to go without a shawl, she decided it was, so, tying her bonnet in place, she wandered down towards the lake. The antics of a mother duck fascinated her as it waddled along the edge, followed by ten ducklings. The one at the back couldn't keep up, and kept getting left behind. The mother, seemingly unconcerned at her offspring's slowness, looked around briefly before jumping into the water, followed by the other babies. The smallest one at the back finally caught up. Tiny wings flapping, and squawking loudly, it hurled itself in and, legs paddling madly, tried to catch the rest of its family.

Shaking her head and wondering how many of them would eventually survive without being eaten by foxes or birds of prey, Tillie turned away. When would the pain of losing her own baby ease? Wrapping her arms around her body, she carried on. With no particular destination in mind, and her brain not really engaged in where she was going, she found herself a while later in the village.

"Good day to you, Mistress Dalton," a voice she hadn't heard for a while greeted her.

Oh, no, thought Tillie. *That's all I need, Mrs Lumbley and her problems.*

She turned towards the lady, trying to turn her grimace into a smile. "Ah, good day, Mrs Lumbley. I hope you are in good health."

"Well, actually…"

Tillie stood patiently listening while the lady regaled her with her life history.

"I'm sorry to hear that," she eventually managed to say once she was able get a word in. "But I'm afraid I must leave you now. I'm…" She tried desperately to think of an excuse to leave without appearing rude. She mumbled something incoherent and, nodding her head, backed away.

Hurrying down the main street, anxious to avoid bumping into any other neighbours, she stepped off the pavement to skirt around a couple walking really slowly in front of her, and was almost knocked over by a boy on a bicycle. She hadn't thought to look behind her. The boy yelled as he swerved across the road into the path of an oncoming horse. The bicycle overturned, landing the boy in the middle of the road. Luckily, the rider pulled up in time before the horse could trample him.

Running across to the boy, she asked anxiously, "Are you hurt?"

The horseman climbed down and together they helped him up.

"No, ma'am. Thank you, ma'am," he mumbled, pulling on his cap, keeping his face hidden.

"I'm so sorry," she added. "Is your bicycle damaged?"

She knew that was what the contraptions were called, as David had shown her a picture of one in a newspaper, saying that he was thinking of getting Jamie one for his birthday.

"I hope not, 'cos it ain't mine," he replied.

"Whose is it then?"

The boy seemed reluctant to reply. He shifted from one foot to the other as the horseman picked it up. Then he grabbed it, put one foot onto the peg behind the back wheel, scooted for a few yards before lifting himself onto the saddle, and rode off without another word.

"Well, that was most odd. He rushed off without so much as a 'by your leave'," said the horseman. He turned back to Tillie. "He didn't catch you, did he, madam?"

"No. I'm fine, thank you, sir, just a bit shocked at seeing a boy like that riding such a contraption down the main street."

"Oh, one sees them all the time nowadays. It's becoming quite a fad."

Whether it was a fad or not, Tillie decided there was no way she was going to let Jamie have one of the infernal machines, no matter what David said. They looked much too precarious.

Bowing her head, she took her leave of the gentleman. "Thank you for your help, sir. Good day."

Climbing back onto his horse, the man doffed his hat and said farewell before continuing his ride.

Tillie was still shaking. Even though she'd stepped back onto the pavement when the boy had ridden off, she still felt vulnerable. There seemed to be so much more traffic than usual, carriages and riders and even a few more of those dangerous bicycles.

What was she doing there in the village anyway? She'd better return home. Straightening her bonnet, she turned back. Passing a millinery shop, a pretty red ribbon in the window caught her eye. How lovely that would look on Alice, something to brighten her day. Etiquette said that everybody else still wore the customary black, but her little girl didn't have to.

With her hand on the door latch, about to go in to buy a

length of the bright ribbon, she realised she hadn't brought her reticule, so didn't have any money with her. She had only intended going for a short walk round the estate, and it hadn't occurred to her to bring it. How fortunate she had remembered in time. She would have looked so foolish if the shopkeeper had already cut the ribbon and she hadn't been able to pay. It wasn't one of the shops that they usually frequented, so they didn't have an account there.

Sighing, she turned away. She really did need to pull herself together.

Another bicycle wheeled past her, this time ridden by a young lady. Appalled, Tillie stopped. The lady's skirt revealed her ankles and part of her legs as she pedalled. Tillie looked at the other people walking along the street to gauge their reactions. Nobody seemed in the least bit shocked. They didn't even appear to have noticed. What was the world coming to?

Hurrying along, she tried to make sense of what she'd seen. How long had she been hidden away in her own little world, not noticing that life was changing outside? She wasn't sure whether she liked the change, but knew in her heart of hearts that she would have to get used to it.

Leaving the village, she hurried down the lane, thinking back to the strange behaviour of the boy who had almost run her over. Why had he scooted off so quickly? He'd said the bicycle wasn't his. Perhaps he'd stolen it.

Approaching the house, she hoped nobody had noticed her absence. They all had enough to contend with, without worrying about her. The hem of her black dress was covered in mud. It hadn't rained for a day or two, and there hadn't been any particularly muddy puddles, so she couldn't understand why she'd got in such a state. She would have to apologise to Nellie.

Jamie came running out as she was about to open the door. "Mama, you've been gone ages."

She kissed the top of his head. "Have I? I hadn't noticed."

Nellie came bustling over. "We were worried sick."

Tillie raised her hands in the air, sighing. "Am I not

allowed to go for a walk? Do I have to have permission to do anything?"

Seeing their anxious faces, she relented. "Look, I'm sorry if I caused a stir, but I just…I only wanted…" Her voice trailed off as Ruby came out with Alice. Her sister didn't berate her as she had expected her to. With a sympathetic look, she handed her daughter over to her, saying, "Say goodnight to your mama, Alice."

Tillie cuddled the little girl. Had she really been gone so long that it was her bedtime?

"Night, night, my little darling," she cooed. "Sweet dreams."

Chapter 12

Jamie lay on the lawn playing with Goldie. That morning, Mrs Button had brought Maisie to work in the kitchen with Freda. He'd tried to make her welcome by offering to help her but had been told to go out and play. She'd looked so lost in the black dress and white apron that seemed much too big for her. Her black curls had been swept up and hidden beneath a white mop cap, and her violet eyes had looked really scared. He'd felt so sorry for her.

It just didn't seem fair that she should have to work at her age, while he lazed about, doing whatever he wanted, at least for the time being. The dreaded boarding school hadn't been mentioned lately.

He jumped up and threw the ball to Goldie. She immediately retrieved it. That was another good word he'd learned recently. He loved learning new words, especially ones that made you move your lips, like 'retrieved'.

He wondered if it would be the right moment to speak to his papa. Throwing the ball again, this time as hard as he could, he decided he would—what was the expression he had heard his mama use? Something like 'take the cow by her horn'. Yes, he would definitely do that.

Taking a deep breath, he called Goldie, who was rooting around in a clump of weeds in front of a hedge. The dog looked at him but didn't return straight away.

"Where's the ball, Goldie?" Making his way over to her, he hoped it would spur her on to pick it up. But the weeds were stinging nettles, and he didn't fancy going in and being stung. He knew how much that hurt, even if you spat on a dock leaf and rubbed it on the tingly bit.

A loud raucous cry made him turn round. A magpie landed in the field not far from him. It looked at him for a moment, its beady eye unblinking, before flying off again.

Oh dear, that's bad luck, thought Jamie, looking round to

see if its mate was anywhere near. Auntie Ruby had told him that one single magpie on its own was something like a portent of doom—whatever that meant—unless you saluted it. He quickly did so before it flew out of sight, hoping he wasn't too late.

Hearing voices on the other side of the hedge, he crouched down and held onto Goldie, trying to make himself as small as possible. He'd heard Tom saying there'd been poachers on their land in the last few weeks and that they could be violent.

One of the voices sounded familiar. Carefully reaching forward so he wouldn't get stung by the nettles, he parted the hedge enough to see through it. He gasped; he was right. It was Bobby with two older men. Well, perhaps not men, they were probably about sixteen or seventeen years old. He was about to call out to his friend when he noticed one of the older boys was carrying a stick, and hanging from it were several large fish.

Letting go of the branch, he let it fall back. He definitely didn't want to be seen. But what should he do? He couldn't snitch on his friend, but it was his duty to inform Papa or, at least, Tom, if he found anything wrong.

The voices faded away. He sat back on the grass, breathing a sigh of relief that they hadn't seen him, but then Goldie began to growl. Before he could work out what had alarmed her, he was grabbed from behind and lifted up so his legs were dangling in mid-air.

"Gotcha," a deep voice cried. "What do you think yer doing, spying on us?"

"I…" Jamie could barely speak. His throat was being squeezed by the hands holding him tightly round his neck, and he felt as if his eyes were bulging out of their sockets. He was terrified he was going to be killed.

"Put him down, Jake," he heard Bobby say. His voice sounded rather shaky. He was probably scared of the big lad as well.

Just when Jamie thought he'd breathed his last breath, he was released roughly and fell in a heap on the ground. Rubbing his sore neck, he looked up at his attacker. He looked like a larger version of Bobby, but he hadn't said he'd got an older brother.

Goldie licked at his face, but the youth pushed her roughly aside. He wanted to tell him not to treat his dog like that, but daren't. She sat on her haunches, panting, obviously afraid.

He felt a hand on his shoulder and turned to see Bobby's anxious face. "Sorry 'bout my cousin Jake, he's a bit rough."

"You know this lad?" the boy called Jake asked Bobby, pushing him aside.

His friend nodded. "Yes, his name's Jamie."

"So, how d'yer know him, then?"

Bobby looked hesitant. Before he could say anything, the third lad spoke. "Never mind all that. We need to get back."

Jamie could see he was trying to hide the fish behind his back.

"What you looking at?" The boy asked with a sneer. "Think you can see something?"

Jamie shook his head. "No," he tried to say, but all that came out was a croak. He shook his head again.

"Well, there ain't nothing to see, so you'd better bloody well tell nobody, if you know what's good for you."

Jamie's eyes opened wide at the swear word, but he quickly looked away. Goldie was sniffing at the fish behind the youth.

The big lad, Jake, grabbed Bobby by the collar of his scruffy shirt and began to walk away with him. He turned to the lad with the fish. "Come on, leave the snivelling wretch. He ain't gonna say nothing to nobody." He turned round and glared at Jamie, his eyes screwed up and his teeth showing like a snarling dog. "Are you, boy?"

The other one kicked at Goldie, who squealed and slunk off. He then smacked Jamie round the head, growling, "Of course he ain't," before he followed them. Bobby turned and gave Jamie one more look, as if pleading with him to do as they said, then they all disappeared round the back of the hedge.

Jamie lay back in the grass, his arm around Goldie, too afraid to move. He hoped she wasn't hurt. His own neck still felt sore, and he prayed there wouldn't be a mark left for Auntie Ruby's eagle eyes to see. How would he be able to explain that away? There was no way he was going to tell anybody about the last ten minutes. Bobby's cousins might come and torture him some more.

After a while, still shaking, he drew in a deep breath and looked around tentatively. He couldn't stay there all day. They might eat the fish and come back for more. Goldie was licking her paw. He checked it to make sure there was nothing wrong with it. He couldn't see any blood or anything, so, rubbing his neck, he picked up his cap and ran for his life. He thought he heard them again so ran even faster, with Goldie seeming to be just as desperate to reach home as he was.

After putting Goldie in her kennel with a bowl of water, he managed to get to his room without anybody seeing him. Flinging his cap onto a chair, he unbuttoned his shirt to look at his neck in the wall mirror. A large red weal had appeared. He poured some water into the bowl on the dresser and tried dabbing the mark. It just seemed to make it even redder. What was he going to do? How was he going to hide it? Maybe he could put on a different shirt that had a higher collar. Rummaging through his wardrobe, he found his best one. It had a high collar, but everyone would ask why he was wearing it when it wasn't a Sunday or a special occasion, so there wasn't much point in putting that on.

"Pity it isn't winter," he muttered. "I could wear my striped, woolly scarf." It was summer though, so that would look silly.

All his other shirts were the same as the one he was wearing, so he was stumped. Refastening the buttons, he tried different poses, raising his shoulders and putting his head to one side so his neck was hidden. That worked. The sore patch couldn't be seen at all. He tried walking around the room to see if he could keep up the position. It was possible, but could he do it without anybody noticing? It would be easier just to keep out of the way.

Opening a drawer, he took out a wad of paper and a box of crayons. His tree house seemed the safest place, and he could sketch some pictures. He hadn't done any for a while. Better not speak to his papa about the school matter while he still had the dreaded mark.

He realised he wasn't going to be able to visit Bobby any more, so there was no chance of seeing his pretty sister again. Her gorgeous eyes, though—they just needed drawing. He made sure there was a green crayon in the box so he could do a portrait of her.

If he could just keep out of Auntie Ruby's way, as she was most likely to notice, he might get away with it. He hurried down to the kitchen. Luckily, there was only Freda there. Standing sideways, he gabbled, "I'm going to me tree house, Freda. Please can you tell Mama or Auntie Ruby if you see them?"

Maisie came out of the pantry carrying some carrots. "Hello, Jamie," she said rather shyly.

Oh, no, she was on his bad side. Would she notice?

"It's *'Master* Jamie' to you now, Mary." Freda corrected her without looking up from the pastry she was rolling.

Maisie's face crumpled. "Sorry," she muttered, looking down.

"I don't mind," began Jamie, distressed at his little friend's face.

"It doesn't matter what you want, young man. It's how things have to be," the cook continued, the rolling pin moving back and forth. "And anyway, it's almost time for your lunch."

Jamie shuffled round so that Maisie was on his good side. "Please, may I take it with me? It'll be quicker."

Freda put the pastry into the dish and began spooning apples on top of it. "You'll have to wait 'til I've finished this, then."

Jamie didn't dare wait any longer. Auntie Ruby could come in any moment. The door opened, and for a second he thought that it was her but, luckily, it was only Martha.

"I'll just go and check on Goldie then," he mumbled quickly. "I'll call back for my sandwiches in a few minutes." He hurried out, thankful he had got away with it for the time being.

* * * *

Tillie finished writing her letter to Emily and rubbed her belly. She didn't know whether her friend's baby had been born, so prayed she would have a safe delivery. The pain of losing hers still lingered, but not as sharply as before. She could think about it without weeping. There were still moments of desolation, though, when she thought about little Annabella stuck down the well, needing her mama.

Standing up, she decided she was going to be more positive. There was plenty of time for her to have lots more children—that was, if David ever came near her again. She'd heard him in the other bedroom during the night, tossing and turning and groaning in his sleep. She had wanted to go in and comfort him, but had been hesitant, remembering the way he'd spoken to her the previous day.

Recalling that she'd promised Jamie she would help him with some schoolwork, she brushed her long auburn hair, deciding she wouldn't bother with a bonnet as it looked such a nice day, so she tied it back with a black ribbon. The dress she was wearing was her favourite. It fitted her so well she didn't mind wearing it. In fact, she thought she might wear it sometimes after the period of mourning was over. But she might be sick of it by then.

Standing at the window, she saw Jamie hurrying down towards the woods carrying a bag. It looked rather bulky, so probably contained lemonade and books. That meant he was going to his tree house. So much for doing schoolwork, unless David had given him some sums to do but, since the accident, Tillie couldn't remember him doing so.

Sealing the envelope, she closed her writing bureau, took the letter and placed it in the silver salver on the table in the hall, knowing that Purvis would arrange to have it delivered to her friend.

She went up to the nursery to check on Alice, but she was

having her afternoon nap. Ruby sat at the window, looking very pensive. It was unusual for her to be doing nothing, she was always so busy.

Tillie walked over to join her to see what she could be looking at. Sam was in the distant field, exercising the new mare that David had sent him to buy from the horse sales the week before. Normally, he would have gone with him, but was still not well enough.

Her sister looked up sadly.

"What's the matter, Ruby?" Tillie asked anxiously, putting her hand on her shoulder.

"Nothing, I'm fine."

"Come on, tell me. This isn't like you."

"I…no, it's nothing."

"Ruby? You haven't fallen out with Sam, have you?"

Her sister shook her head. "No, it's nothing like that, quite the opposite, actually."

Alice began to stir, so Ruby started to move away, but Tillie pulled her back, whispering, "Leave her. Tell me what's bothering you."

Ruby began to cry. "I've let you all down."

She took her sister in her arms, trying to think what horrendous misdemeanour she could have committed.

After a moment, Ruby pulled away, wiping her face on her sleeve. "You'll all hate me, I know you will."

"What have you done?"

Looking up with tear-filled eyes, she took a deep breath before blurting out, "I've committed the biggest sin in the book."

"Well, I haven't seen any dead bodies lying around, so you can't have murdered anyone," Tillie tried to joke.

"It's worse than that."

"Ruby, just tell me."

"I've lain with Sam."

"Oh." Tillie hadn't thought of that.

"I knew you'd hate me." Ruby began to cry again, running towards the door.

"Don't go, Ruby." Tillie hurried after her, caught her as

she opened it, and pulled her back. "Of course I don't hate you."

"Really?"

"How could I hate you? You're my sister, whatever you've done, I'll always be there for you. And anyway, lying with your fiancé isn't exactly a mortal sin. It's just…" She shrugged her shoulders, unsure whether it was or not. "If it hadn't been for the accident and Annabella…you would've been married by now, so don't cut yourself up about it."

"I wanted so much to wait 'til we were married, but Sam got carried away and…" Ruby looked so forlorn that Tillie hugged her again. Then a horrible memory crept into her head, a memory of a certain blacksmith. Pushing Ruby away, she looked deep into her eyes. "He didn't force you, did he?"

"Oh, no, I wanted it as much as he did. Does that make me a bad person?"

She breathed a sigh of relief. "No, my darling sister, of course it doesn't. It just means you have womanly needs."

"But I might be…you know…"

"Oh." That hadn't occurred to her either. "When did it happen?"

"Yesterday."

"And when did you last have your fairies?"

"I don't remember. They've never been regular." Ruby began to cry once more.

"Well, we'll just have to arrange the wedding as soon as we can."

"But we can't. What about the period of mourning?"

"We'll sort something out."

Alice was wide awake by this time, so Tillie picked her up and gave her a cuddle. Breathing in her sweet babyish fragrance, she heard the door open and, looking up, saw Ruby go out. She was about to call her back, but decided against it. She hoped she had allayed her sister's fears. There was always the possibility that she might not be pregnant, of course, but she didn't want to take that chance. If they didn't plan the wedding and she was, then it would be rather late to get it all organised by the time they found out.

Her main problem was telling David. He was the stickler for protocol. Would he agree to the wedding before the allotted time? Placing Alice on the floor with some toys, she tried to work out what she would say to him.

She sighed. She still hadn't been able to sway her husband from sending Jamie away to school, so how on earth was she going to persuade him to let her sister get married during their mourning period?

Ruby came in carrying Alice's tea on a tray, her eyes downcast.

"Thank you, Ruby," Tillie said hesitantly as she put Alice into her highchair and began to feed her.

Bending down to pick up the child's toys, Ruby gave a heartfelt sigh.

With a spoonful of pink blancmange in mid-air, Tillie said, "Don't look so worried. We will work something out."

Ruby merely nodded, not looking at all convinced, as Alice grabbed the spoon from Tillie's hand. The blancmange flew across the room, landing on the rump of the rocking horse in the corner.

Alice squealed with laughter and, before Tillie could stop her, dipped the spoon into the dish and threw another spoonful after the first one.

"No, that's naughty," Tillie cried, grabbing her hand before she could repeat the action. "You mustn't play with food." She could tell Ruby was having trouble keeping a straight face as she went across and cleaned up the mess. Trying not to smile, she turned back to her daughter who, by this time, had both hands in the sticky pudding and was squeezing it between her fingers. "No...oo," she yelled, the smile immediately disappearing. "Bad girl." She grabbed the dish as Ruby rushed over to wipe the little girl's hands.

She was about to admonish Alice with the words, 'Just wait 'til I tell your papa', but stopped herself. Her ma had always said that, whenever she or Ruby or their brothers stepped out of line. It sometimes put the fear of God into them, dreading the time when their father walked through the door, so she had vowed at quite a young age that she would never use that as a form of punishment. For punishment it was. They, especially her two brothers, Matthew and Harry, would sometimes spend the rest of the day so afraid of their father's return that the whole day was ruined. In a way, the admonishment worked, for they never did whatever they had done wrong again, knowing they would feel the sharp edge of their father's belt if they did.

Cleaning up her daughter, she thought about her brothers. Neither of them had been able to attend Annabella's funeral, so she hadn't seen them for ages. She had received a letter from Matthew a few weeks ago, telling her that Jessie had been delivered of a healthy baby boy whom they had named William after their father. He'd moved on to a larger farm and was very happy. He was now head herdsman, in charge of three other men and two milkmaids, so it was a real step up.

Tillie was so pleased for him. With three young mouths to feed, he must have been struggling, but now he could look forward to a brighter future.

Harry, she hadn't heard from since the twins were christened and didn't even know if he was still in the same place, but she would have to find out somehow, if he was to be invited to Ruby's wedding.

She grimaced, wondering once more how she was going to broach the subject to David. A promise was a promise, so she would just have to find the right moment.

Taking Alice, now blancmange-free, out of her chair, she placed her on the floor with some bricks. Ruby tidied up the nursery, stopping every now and again to look at Tillie with her eyebrows raised.

"Are you sure?" she eventually asked. "Do you really think the master will be in favour of...?" She tailed off, obviously certain the opposite would be true.

Tillie shrugged, not at all sure, but determined not to let her sister down.

"We'll sort something out, dearest sister." She patted her arm. "In fact, I'll go now and..."

"Please don't have an argument over me, Tillie." Ruby grabbed her dress as she was about to leave. "Please don't fall out with him. I'm not worth…I'd never forgive myself if…"

Tillie kissed her. "What have I told you about thinking yourself worthless? It will sort itself out, trust me."

As she went downstairs, she didn't feel at all hopeful, or positive but, as she'd said before, a promise was a promise.

Chapter 13

A few days later, David was sitting in the lounge, reading his newspaper, when Tillie walked in. She went over and kissed him. He looked rather surprised, but also pleased for he put down the paper and took her hands in his.

"That was nice," he drawled, "and unexpected."

Tillie smiled as she sat down next to him, giving him another kiss, this time a more lingering one. It felt so good to be near him, she wondered why she didn't do it more often. Then she remembered his attitude the other day. But there was no point raking up old grievances.

His hand caressed her cheek as she snuggled down into the crook of his arm. Was it the right time to ask him? Not yet, her inner self told her. Just enjoy the moment a while longer. It'd been so long since they'd had any intimacy, she was loathed to break the spell. A few more minutes wouldn't hurt.

She felt David sigh. Was he thinking the same? His hand began to reach lower, down her neck and across her shoulder, down towards her breast. Moaning, she clutched at it, pressing it closer.

The door burst open and Jamie came running in.

Sitting up quickly, she heard David's sigh mirror her own feelings. "Mama, Papa, I've just seen a buzzard, really close. It was circling round, right above my head."

"That's lovely, Jamie." Was that all? Their most tender moment for a long time interrupted by a bird?

He grabbed her arm. "Do come and see, Mama. It might still be there."

David's voice surprised her. "I will come with you, Jamie. I could do with some fresh air. Help me into the wheelchair."

"But Papa, it might fly off and…"

Tillie could see he was eager to go back outside before the bird disappeared, and it would take some time for his father to clambour into the chair.

Raising his eyebrows at her, he opened his mouth to speak again, but closed it and selflessly manoeuvred the chair into position in front of David.

Her heart went out to him. He was prepared to sacrifice his own pleasure at seeing the magnificent bird so closely, in order to help his father. Taking his hands from the handles, she nudged him out of the way. "I'll help your papa into the chair, Jamie. You run out and check that the buzzard's still there, so we know which way to look when we get outside."

His face lit up again. "Thanks, Mama," he called as he ran back out.

"I have not seen a buzzard for ages," David remarked as he pulled himself into position. He was becoming quite adept at it, and it didn't take them long to reach the hall. Purvis appeared and helped them down the step. Tillie pushed him along the drive, wondering in which direction Jamie had gone. Craning her neck, she looked upwards, but couldn't see anything besides crows and starlings.

"Can you see it?" she asked.

David shook his head. "No. Take me down there, away from the trees. We will have a better view then."

Out of the shelter of the avenue of horse chestnut trees that lined the drive, they looked up again as a loud raucous cry of crows made them look behind. Several of the crows were harassing another bird that didn't look much bigger than them. Tillie could hear a high-pitched, sweet-sounding, mewing cry coming from the one that was being attacked.

"There it is," cried David, pointing upwards towards it. "That is the buzzard."

"But I thought they were birds of prey. How come the crows are…?"

"They are warning it off. It was probably threatening their young."

All of a sudden, the buzzard swooped down and, in midair, grabbed one of the crows that had got separated from the others and flew with it to the shelter of some low-hanging trees further down. The other crows bombarded it, squawking and squealing, but it held its own, holding out its wings over the young crow—she assumed that was what it was—until they gave up, realising they couldn't help their fellow bird, and one by one they all flew off.

"Phew, I've never seen anything like that before," gasped Tillie. "I hope Jamie…" She'd been about to say she hoped he hadn't missed it, but wondered if it was rather too grisly for a child to witness.

David looked up at her with an amused grin. "Do you mean you hope he saw it or you hope he did not?" he asked.

She shrugged, not really sure.

"It is nature, my dear. Buzzards have to eat."

"I know, I know," she sighed. "But it was hardly any bigger than the crow. I'm just astounded it could catch such a huge prey, and then fight off all the others when they tried to rescue it."

Jamie came running up from the other side of the field. "Did you see it? Weren't that amazing?"

"Yes, it certainly was," David replied.

Tillie wasn't quite so sure.

"I wish I could've got a closer look, though."

"Yes, that would have been good," David replied.

"Oo, you two are so gruesome." She couldn't understand how they could contemplate such a thing.

David continued as if she hadn't spoken. "I have seen an advertisement in the newspaper for a new type of spyglass called 'binoculars' that make faraway things look even closer. What do you think, Jamie? Shall I send away for some?"

"Aw, yes, that would be wonderful, wouldn't it, Mama? Just think, we'd be able to see all the blood and guts up close."

"Oh, my goodness, why on earth would you want to do that?" Tillie put her hand up to her mouth. "Ugh, I feel quite nauseous just thinking about it." She pulled such a face that Jamie burst out laughing.

"Oh, Mama, I'm glad I ain't a girl. They're so—what's that word? Squee…squimsh?"

"I think you mean 'squeamish'," laughed David.

"Yes, that's it, squeamish."

"Please can we drop this topic of conversation? I've had

quite enough of it, thank you." Tillie pushed the wheelchair forward.

"I'll push, Mama. Where we going?" Jamie reached in front of her and took the handles.

Tillie took hold of her husband's hand and began to walk beside him. "Yes, now that we're out, where shall we go?"

"Oh, I care not, but perhaps we had better not go down there."

Tillie looked to see where David was pointing. She could make out the buzzard, still under the overhang, picking at the carcass of its victim, continuously looking around to check for danger.

Jamie laughed. "I don't think Mama's belly would take it."

She cuffed the back of his head. "You cheeky boy. But you're quite right. I'm glad we haven't got guinea fowl or goose or any other bird for dinner tonight."

They all laughed as they wandered along the lane.

"Talking about dinner, we'd better not go too far," Tillie said after a while. "It must be nearly time."

David took out his pocket watch. "Yes, we had better be on our way back. That is the trouble with these light evenings, one can never judge what time it is. We do not want to incur Nellie or Freda's wrath by being late."

The next morning David seemed in a much lighter mood. As Tillie sat eating her breakfast with him, he suddenly surprised her by asking, "Do you think I would be able enough to go rowing?"

She looked at him in amazement. "What's put that idea into your head?"

"It was something I was reading about in the newspaper yesterday."

That, the bicycle and the new spyglass for seeing gory details up close, she thought. *Whatever next?*

"Where?" she asked. "There aren't any lakes around here large enough."

"Oh, I do not know. It was just a thought, something to do to relieve this boredom. And something that Jamie could partake in as well during the summer, before he goes to school."

"Well, I've been meaning to speak to you about that."

She'd gone over and over in her mind what she was going to say but, now that the right moment was upon her, she couldn't get the words out. He looked at her from under his eyebrows as if to say, 'Don't start an argument', and she was almost deterred from continuing.

"Don't look at me like that," she began, putting down her fork and dabbing at her mouth with her serviette.

"But you know my wishes on the subject."

"Yes, but…" She sighed. How could she persuade him? She watched as he continued to eat his liver and sausages, shovelling them in as if it was his last meal on earth. The sight gave her hope that he wasn't as calm about the idea as he made out.

"He really doesn't want to go and, for that matter, I'm not at all happy about it either, as I've said before. I've tried so hard to get used to the idea, and I know it's tradition, but the thought of losing him again just fills me with despair." Her words caught in her throat as she reached out and put her hand on his.

He stilled, putting down his knife and fork, not looking up.

"Please, David, please reconsider." She looked expectantly at him. His jaw was still moving up and down, the only movement he was making.

He didn't speak for some time, merely carried on chewing.

He swallowed with an exaggerated gesture and wiped his mouth.

Not looking her in the eye, he fumbled with his necktie and ran his finger under his collar before saying, "What will be, will be." Then he wheeled himself out of the room before she could say any more.

Sitting back with her mouth open and a frown creasing her forehead, she shook her head. What had he meant by that? She wondered whether to follow him and ask him to clarify his remark, but knew deep down it would be pointless. He could be so infuriating at times. Just when she thought she was getting to know his character, he sprang something like that on her, something so ambiguous she was none the wiser about his feelings or intentions.

But at least he hadn't said a definite 'he's going', so perhaps he was wavering. She would let him mull it over, and occasionally drop little hints into their conversations, without actually having an out and out battle about it.

Remembering Ruby's predicament, she slapped her forehead with the back of her hand. She hadn't mentioned it, and she'd promised her sister. Better wait until later, though; one problem at a time.

Her cold breakfast looked very unappetising. She half-heartedly picked at it for a few minutes, then gave up.

Martha came in and gave a critical look at the uneaten food. She knew better than to say anything, but Tillie could tell from her actions, as she scraped the remains onto one plate, that she disapproved. She, herself, hated waste. The maxim 'Waste not, want not' sprang to mind.

"The dogs will be happy today with all that meat," she tried to justify herself. She knew she didn't need to, but felt guilty. She was always telling Jamie not to leave his food and there she was, doing just that.

Her son walked in as Martha went out, carrying the tray.

Reaching out her arms to him, he ran and gave her a hug.

"I've just seen Papa, and he said he's going to take me rowing," he said proudly as he pulled away.

"Oh, did he say when or where?"

"No, just that he was going to find out about it."

"Did he say anything else?"

Putting his finger up to his mouth, he frowned. "No, what about?"

"Nothing, darling. How are your lessons going?"

He seemed surprised at the change of subject, but looked down sheepishly.

"I promised to help you, didn't I?" continued Tillie. "What do you need most instruction on if Miss Hetherington doesn't come today?"

He shrugged. "There don't seem no point in doing stupid lessons if I got to go to boarding school."

She hesitated. Should she tell him she was trying to convince David to change his mind?

He looked up at her with such a hangdog expression that she hugged him again.

"Mama?"

"Yes, darling?"

"Do I really have to go? I been trying to talk to Papa 'bout it for ages, but every time I 'fink I will, I get wobbles in me belly and…what was it you said to Auntie Ruby before you telled me 'bout George? Leaves me nerves behind?"

Tillie could tell he was agitated for he had fallen back into his old style of speaking. "It's 'lost your nerve', Jamie."

"Aye, that."

"I know it's hard but, to be truthful…" No, she'd better not get his hopes up. She straightened his neckerchief and, taking off his cap and shaking it, she flattened his already tidy hair, trying to think of a way to allay his fears, but couldn't think of a way to do so without actually telling him what she'd said to David earlier.

She heard the front doorbell ring and wondered who it could be. A few minutes later, her question was answered when Purvis came in with a letter.

Tillie reached to take it but the butler handed it to Jamie. "It's addressed to the young master, ma'am."

"For me?" Jamie jumped forward and took it. "Who's it from?"

Turning it over and over, he peered at the handwriting.

"Open it and see." Tillie laughed.

"I think it's from Sarah." The delight on his face was a joy to behold. He quickly opened it and began to read.

Tillie waited patiently for him to finish, watching the expressions on his face. He was growing up, she suddenly realised with a shock. His face was changing shape. He wasn't her little boy any longer, and she didn't know if she was prepared for it.

"She says she's better, and…guess what?" Jamie interrupted her reverie.

"Tell me." She actually had a good idea of what it contained, as David had received a letter from his sister, Annie, a few days previously, asking if they could come for a week or so. He had replied immediately that they would love to see them, but she wanted Jamie to have the pleasure of telling her.

He jumped in the air, waving the letter above his head. "She says she's coming to visit."

"That's marvellous news." Tillie smiled. His excitement was infectious. Even though she already knew, it felt so good to see him in high spirits. They danced around the room together, singing and laughing.

Ruby came in with Alice clutching her rag doll. She looked like a doll herself, in her matching green dress and bonnet. "I thought I heard gaiety," she said, looking disapprovingly at her sister. "What's made you two so cheerful?"

"Oh, Auntie Ruby, I'm so excited. Sarah's coming." Jamie ran and wrapped his arms around her.

Tillie took Alice, not daring to look her sister in the eye, feeling guilty that she'd failed her, that she still hadn't spoken to David.

"Is that all?" Ruby asked.

Jamie's face lost some of its sparkle. "It's the bestest news I've heard for ages," he declared, looking puzzled that she didn't feel the same. Then it lit up again. "P'raps Sarah can come rowing with us?"

"Rowing?" Ruby's eyebrows shot up.

"Yes, Papa said he'll take me."

"I've never heard anything so ridiculous in my life." She turned to Tillie. "Where on earth has he got that idea from?"

"David mentioned it this morning. I didn't realise he was serious. He said he needed something to relieve his boredom."

"Pah." Ruby's expression changed as she looked up hopefully. "Did you have chance to mention…?"

Tillie knew straight away what she meant. She shook her head. "No—but I will as soon as…when I can…"

"I knew it was a fantasy." Taking Alice back, she began to walk out of the room, her head down, shoulders slouched.

"I will, honestly," Tillie called, wanting to go after her, but knowing it would be useless until she'd delivered her promise.

Jamie looked up from re-reading his letter. "Sarah says she doesn't have to go to school no more 'cos she's been so poorly. She's got a new governess."

Tillie was still thinking about how she could get round David. "That's nice, dear," she said absent-mindedly.

"She's older than me, so it's not fair if she don't have to go to school."

"She's a girl, Jamie. It isn't so important for girls."

"I know, but—"

"Anyway, we need to know if Miss Hetherington is coming today. Come on, let's see if there's a message."

"Can I just finish me letter?"

"Very well. I'll come and find you when I know."

Chapter 14

A week later, Jamie was awake early. Auntie Annie and Sarah were due to arrive that day. Uncle Victor was too busy working to take the time off. He'd been very ill earlier in the year, and the business had suffered from the time he'd been absent, so he needed to build it up again.

Jamie jumped out of bed, eager to get downstairs so he could be at the door to welcome them. He'd had a bath the previous evening, and had scrubbed every bit of his body so that he was extra clean. The mark on his neck had almost faded. Nobody had noticed it, so he'd got all worked up and worried about it for nothing.

His hair was shining as he brushed it. He wished he'd had time to have it cut as it almost reached his collar, but when he put on his cap—a new one that had been bought the previous week—his hair would be hidden.

Opening his wardrobe door, he wondered what to wear that would make him look his best. Taking out his best suit, he looked it up and down, but he would only be told to take it off, so he hung it back up.

Pulling up his black trousers—he was allowed to wear long ones now—he adjusted his braces to make sure they were comfortable, and looked for a shirt. His dark grey checked one felt quite soft but didn't fit properly—the sleeves were too short—but he decided that, covered by his favourite waistcoat, also grey with coloured stripes down the front, and his jacket, he looked good enough to meet his cousin.

Checking himself in the mirror and satisfied that Sarah wouldn't be able to find fault, he went downstairs. For a brief moment, he wished Bobby's sister could see him. He felt sure she would approve as well, but there was no chance he would ever see her again, so what was the point of even thinking about her?

Several hours later, his patience was beginning to wear

thin. He'd been sitting on the front step for ages.

"When are they coming?" He went in and asked Tillie for about the tenth time.

"Jamie, I've told you, I don't know, darling. It's a long journey, as you well know yourself, and they've probably had to make more stops than usual. You know Sarah's still not fully recovered."

He heaved an exaggerated sigh.

"I'm afraid you'll just have to be patient."

"Where's Alice?"

"She's having her afternoon nap, why?"

"I just thought she could come outside and play with me while I wait."

"Well, she can do if they're not here when she wakes up, although it'll probably be her teatime by then. Why don't you practise your spelling or…"

"But Mama, it's Saturday."

"Well, get your book and write a story for Sarah, or draw her a picture." She continued with her sewing.

He was too excited to do anything like that. He turned and went back out before his mother could make any more useless suggestions.

Goldie and her mother, Lady, followed him out. He half-heartedly threw them a ball but Goldie was back with it before he'd had chance to breathe, so he threw it again, this time much harder. Every time he played with that ball he was reminded of Bobby's horrible cousin, Jake. Half expecting him to appear out of the bushes, he glanced up and down the drive. Of course he didn't. He wouldn't come near the house, as he would be too likely to get caught.

Fiddling with some ivy that clung to the side of the wall, his thoughts returned to Bobby's sister and her friends. Maybe the nasty girl who had taunted him was Jake's sister. She was the same sort of bully. He prayed he would never see either of them again, but the girl with those green eyes…

Feeling guilty at thinking about another girl when his lovely cousin, whom he had adored since their first meeting, was due to arrive any minute, he was suddenly aware that something was coming in the distance. He squinted, then jumped up and down. It was a carriage.

Whooping and waving madly, he ran down the drive. Goldie and Lady followed, the younger dog almost tripping him up as she weaved in and out between his legs. Sarah stuck her head out of the window and waved back. Yelling at the dogs to come away from the horses' hooves, he stood to one side as the carriage went by, then turned and ran back alongside it. He was so excited he thought he was going to burst.

They pulled away, but he soon caught up again as it circled in front of the house and drew to a halt with a crunch of gravel. The driver climbed down and went to open the door, but Jamie beat him to it.

"Sarah!" he screamed, reaching in and almost pulling her out.

"Be careful, boy." The voice of her mother stopped him in his tracks. The dreaded Auntie Annie! He'd known she'd be there, but had put it to the back of his mind, not wanting anything to spoil his delight at seeing his cousin. Her attitude towards him hadn't really changed since their first meeting, even though he was now a member of her family.

"Good day, Auntie Annie," he said politely, as Sarah was assisted down by the driver.

The front door of the house opened and Tillie came running out, followed by Nellie. They greeted the visitors warmly, asking about the journey and talking about the weather.

Sarah took Jamie's hand and they walked into the house. Jamie was shocked to see how pale and thin her face was. He knew she'd been poorly, but thought that now she was better she'd be back to normal. She seemed to be breathing oddly as well. He ushered her into the lounge to greet his papa.

"Uncle David," she cried, hurrying over to embrace him. "I hope you are well."

"I am very well, thank you, Sarah. I trust you and your mother are, also."

Her mother followed them in and gave him a peck on the

cheek. "David," she said, looking around the room as if inspecting it. "I was so sorry to hear about little Annabella. We couldn't make the funeral because...well, you know."

"And again, my condolences to you for young George. I trust Victor is fully recovered?"

Jamie didn't want to hear all this adult talk. He'd been taught manners and knew it was important to them, but just wanted to spend some time with his cousin. Waiting politely, he smiled at Sarah and, although tempted to raise his eyebrows, he resisted doing so. As soon as there was a lull in the conversation, he quickly asked, "Shall I take Sarah to the kitchen and get her a drink?"

"Yes, that's a good idea, Jamie," said his mama as Martha came in with a tray of tea.

They made their escape and sat down at the kitchen table. Maisie stood, peeling some potatoes. Sarah looked at her and then at Jamie.

"Yes, it's Maisie. She works here now," he explained, knowing what she was thinking. At his parents' wedding, Sarah had taken Maisie under her wing and looked after her.

"Oh," she replied as Freda put two glasses of her home-made lemonade in front of them.

"Mrs Button couldn't keep her any more, so she come...came here." He turned to the new scullery maid. "But you don't mind, do you?"

Shaking her head, Maisie looked down.

"She's a bit like Katy, isn't she?"

Sarah looked puzzled.

"Don't you remember? The maid that you had when I come—came—to stay at your house that time I got lost..." his voice tailed off. Why did he have to bring that up? He shook his head, annoyed at himself. This was supposed to be a happy time. Why was he thinking about sad things?

"Oh, yes, I remember," Sarah said between sips of her drink. "She didn't stay very long." She shook her head. "None of them do."

Jamie was itching to say it was because of her mama's treatment of them, but he knew Sarah was very loyal, and didn't want to upset her. Instead, he changed the subject. "What do you want to do? I could take you down to my tree house, if you like."

"I'm sorry, Jamie, but I'm too tired to do much. Maybe tomorrow?"

Slightly disappointed, he was determined not to show it. He'd been told she was still weak, but hadn't realised what that meant. He tried to think of something else that might impress her.

Freda, cutting up meat and putting it into the stew pot over on the other side of the kitchen, turned and suggested, "Why don't you show Sarah some of your pictures? You've drawn some really good ones lately."

"That would be nice," Sarah said.

Maisie looked up and opened her mouth as if to say something, but kept silent and looked down again. Jamie remembered when they were children, after they'd left the Gypsy camp and gone to stay with Mrs Curtis, she'd drawn some lovely pictures of flowers and trees. Now she had no time to do anything like that. All she did was slave away in the kitchen.

He looked up at Freda, wondering whether to ask if Maisie could join him and Sarah, but thought better of it. She'd already been told off for calling him 'Jamie'. He didn't want to get her into more trouble.

Sarah finished her drink. "Thank you, Freda," she said. "That was lovely lemonade. I wish our cook could make it like that."

The cook looked pleased. "It's an age-old recipe, handed down from my grandmother."

Jamie didn't remember her mentioning a grandmother before. It seemed odd that she should have one. She looked as old as one herself. "I didn't know you had a grandmother," he said.

"Oh, I don't, not any more. She died years ago, long before you were born, before your mama was born, in fact."

"I thought you must be too old to have one."

Sarah looked shocked. "Jamie, it's rude to say things like

that."

The day wasn't going at all as Jamie had hoped, and he'd been so looking forward to it. "Sorry, Freda," he murmured, looking up at Sarah to see if she forgave him. He didn't want her to be out of sorts with him.

Breathing rather heavily, she took his hand. "Come on, let's see your pictures."

He hoped that meant he was back in favour. Sarah wasn't one to stay cross with anyone for long, even George when he was at his most…Ohhhhhhh…He felt like slapping himself. Why did he keep forgetting that George wasn't there any more? He was D-E-A-D.

Sarah suddenly said, "I still miss George." He swivelled round, flabbergasted. How could she know he'd been thinking about her brother? Was it his fault she was now sad?

"Even though he was a little brat, he'd started to grow up and not be quite so awful."

Jamie put his arm around her. He was as tall as her, as well. At that rate, he would soon be the tallest person in the world.

They spent a while going through Jamie's drawings, Sarah smiling and nodding at them, but not with any great enthusiasm. Disappointed, he showed her the one he'd saved till last, expecting her to be thrilled. In his opinion, it was the best picture he'd ever done. It depicted Sarah bending over a flower as if she was sniffing it.

She merely said, "That's nice," and put it down on the table. Maybe she was just tired from the journey. He would show it to her again later.

"I'm really shattered," she said, looking at him with such weary eyes that Jamie took her hand.

"Let's ask Mama which room you'll be sleeping in. You could have a nap before dinner." He felt so grown up, taking charge of the situation. It had always been Sarah who'd done so before. Now he could repay her.

"Thank you, Jamie. I think I will."

Dinner was ready to be served before Sarah re-emerged.

She and Jamie were allowed to eat with the adults as a special treat. They all sat in the dining room—Jamie on his best behaviour as he'd been warned—talking about nothing in particular. He felt he would never get used to tittle-tattle. He couldn't really see the point in it. He couldn't wait to get away and have a meaningful conversation with his cousin, but sat quietly half listening, thinking about what he could tempt Sarah with the following day. Would she be strong enough to walk down to the lake? He could show her the ducklings he'd seen the previous day. She would love that.

Suddenly, his attention was alerted when he heard Auntie Annie mention Eton. His eyes opened wide as he looked from his mama to his papa, holding his breath.

"Well…" Mama began, also looking towards his father, who slowly wiped his mouth with his napkin, keeping his gaze down, and looking rather uncomfortable.

"You are sending him, aren't you?" Auntie Annie put down her knife and fork and wiped her mouth vigorously. "It's just what the boy needs, some discipline."

There was an awkward silence for a moment. His mother stared at his father, Sarah looked at Jamie, and Auntie Annie glared at everyone with a ferocious glint in her eye.

"I…um…"

"You know all the male Daltons have gone to Eton since time began. You can't change the tradition." Auntie Annie was seemingly just getting into her stride. "Just because he's not actually your own son…"

"Annie, that has nothing to do with anything." His father tried to pull himself up. "Jamie is as much my son as any others we might have. I will not have you…" At that point, he lost his grip on the edge of the table and began to fall. His mother jumped up and stopped him reaching the floor as Jamie grabbed the wheelchair and wheeled it behind him in time for him to land in it.

"Uncle David," cried Sarah, jumping up to go to his side. "Are you all right?"

Nodding, he made himself comfortable. "Yes, thank you, Sarah." He looked across at his sister, who had resumed eating her meal, then back to his niece. "Thank you for your concern."

Auntie Annie looked up from her plate, chewing as if she hadn't eaten for a week. Glancing around at everyone watching her with disdain, she dabbed at her mouth. "What are you all staring at? Aren't I allowed to finish my meal? I could see you had enough attendants, David, to ensure your safety." She purposely put another piece of meat into her mouth. "Sit down, everyone, and eat your dinner. It would be a pity for it to go to waste after—whatever your cook's name is—has gone to so much trouble."

David wheeled his chair under the table. "Yes, please, finish your meals." He picked up his cutlery and half-heartedly resumed eating.

"I have had enough, thank you," said Sarah, although she sat down.

Jamie looked at his mama, who nodded to him to do as he was bid, and they finished the course in silence. Martha brought in the dessert and looked from one to the other, clearly surprised that no-one was speaking. She gave everyone in turn a disapproving glare as she began to clear away the plates, which were by no means empty.

Jamie was still none the wiser as to his father's intentions on sending him away, but he drew hope from the fact that he hadn't said anything positive. He enjoyed his pudding, feeling more hopeful than he had for a while, even though Sarah, sitting beside him, looked exhausted.

"Eat up, darling." Her mother shovelled spoonfuls of the crispy, chewy meringue into her mouth. "You know you need to build up your strength."

"I've had sufficient, Mother." Sarah turned to her uncle and aunt. "That was a lovely meal, thank you."

Jamie still had some of his pudding left. Meringue was one of his favourites. He couldn't bear the thought of leaving any, but would Sarah think it bad manners if he continued eating when she'd finished? He had a quick look round to see what everybody else was doing. As Auntie Annie was only just finishing hers, he quickly spooned the remainder of his into his mouth, even taking a peek at Sarah's half-eaten dish, wondering whether he dared sneak a morsel while nobody was looking. Sarah must have realised his intention and she pushed her plate towards him. "You may as well finish mine, Jamie. I couldn't eat another mouthful."

Jamie looked at his mama to see if he should but, as she nodded, the plate was whisked away from the other side, and Auntie Annie dipped her spoon in and golluped it all up before anyone could say anything. Jamie reluctantly put down his spoon, not daring to glance at Sarah in case she saw the disappointment on his face. When he looked up at his aunt though, he thought he could see an evil smirk on her lips.

* * * *

The next morning, Tillie lay in bed wondering what she could do to entertain their guests. She'd forgotten how awful her sister-in-law could be. Fancy taking the food from under her nephew's nose! Anybody would think she was starving. The look on Jamie's face! It was a picture. It was a pity a camera hadn't been available.

Sounds of movements could be heard from the bedchamber next door. David must be getting up. Hope reared inside her bosom. He hadn't actually admitted he'd changed his mind about sending Jamie away, but he hadn't denied it either. Maybe it was just to spite Annie, but Tillie didn't think he would do that with something so important.

Feeling revitalized, she pushed aside the bed covers and stepped onto the rug, wriggling her toes in the soft rags, remembering how good it had felt when she'd first returned to The Grange. Such a lot had happened since that day, a lot of it sad. But she wasn't going to feel dejected today. She was going to…She hadn't actually decided on a plan of action yet, but maybe David had something in mind. Wrapping her dressing gown around her, she tapped on the dividing door.

"Yes?" he asked as she entered. He was sitting on the side of the bed, stark naked. Somehow, not expecting to see him like that, she was taken aback by the rush of desire, unable to move until, with a moan, he held out his arms. Rushing into them, she knocked him backwards onto the bed. His kisses were like a heady wine, and she didn't want him to stop as he yanked off her gown and ran his hands down her body until she was begging for release. Eagerly, he obliged, and they made passionate love, all the more intense because of their long abstention.

Afterwards, she lay in his arms, stroking him and teasing the short hairs on his chest. One or two were turning white, she noticed, but didn't spoil the moment by telling him. She didn't want to speak at all, just immerse herself in the aftermath of the lovemaking they'd just shared, feeling that words would take away some of the enjoyment.

After a few moments, he said, "Sarah still looks very poorly, does she not?"

"Um." Tillie didn't want to break the spell but felt she should make some sort of comment.

"Did you not notice?" He pushed himself up and looked into her eyes.

"Yes, darling, of course I did."

He dropped back down, wrapping his arms around her. "Annie does not change, does she?"

"No." She traced her finger down his stubbly cheek. The mention of his sister set her off again on the subject of Jamie's schooling. "You didn't contradict her, though, did you?"

"When?"

"When she asked if Jamie was still going to Eton."

He gave a sharp intake of breath, pushing her away. "Is that what all this lovey-doveying was all about? To make me change my mind?"

"No. not at all." She sat up, trying to convince him. "Please, David, you must believe me."

"You had better go now. John will be here any moment to help me dress."

"But…"

He turned his back on her. "Just go, Tillie."

Running her hands down his back, she tried one more time. "David, my darling, you can't think that I would do something like that. You have to…" She felt his muscles contract as if her touch was burning him, and he pushed himself closer to the wall.

Inhaling deeply, she picked up her dressing gown and made her way to her own room. For one precious moment, she'd thought their relationship had recovered, but now they'd taken another step backwards. Dressing herself, she faced up to the fact that maybe that was how her life was going to be. She would just have to accept it. Things couldn't be easy for David, with his bad leg, she knew that, but why couldn't he share some of his frustrations with her? Why couldn't he see she could help him through them?

Bracing herself, she finished dressing and went downstairs to face her sister-in-law. What mayhem would she create today?

Fortunately, the dining room was empty.

Breathing a sigh of relief, she went up to the nursery. Alice was sitting on the stool, and Ruby was taking the papers out of her fair hair. It must have grown as it was the first time Tillie had seen it like that. She waited for her sister to finish, then picked up her daughter and gave her a big hug.

"Who's a big girl now, having ringlets in her hair?"

Alice put her podgy arms around her mama's neck and hugged her. "Mama," she pouted.

Ruby was watching them. Pretending to pick something out of Alice's hair, Tillie managed to prevent a groan escaping her lips. There was no chance of her speaking to David now about bringing the wedding forward.

She could have jumped for joy when her sister murmured, "It's all right, Tillie, you don't have to avoid me any longer. My fairies arrived this morning, so I'm not…you know…"

Putting Alice down on the carpet, Tillie hugged her sister.

"I would have spoken to him, honestly, when I had a chance, but now we can concentrate on arranging your wedding properly, without having to rush."

"S'pose." Ruby finished dressing Alice, but Tillie could tell that something was still bothering her.

"Really, Ruby." Tillie tugged at her sleeve. "You can have the finest wedding imaginable now, so why the glum face?"

Her sister shrugged. "I'm not sure that Sam still wants to marry me."

Tillie's mouth fell open. "But he adores you. Anyone can see that. What makes you think he doesn't?"

Ruby picked up Alice and made towards the door. "I'm going to take this little one out for a walk. Do you want to come?"

"But she hasn't had her breakfast yet. What's the rush?"

"I gave her something earlier."

The door opened and Jamie came tumbling in. "Me and Sarah's had our breakfasts and we want to go out. Can we?"

"Yes, of course." Tillie brushed off a crumb from the side of his mouth and flattened a hair that was sticking up. "But don't go too far. Sarah's not very strong."

"Yes, Mama. It'll be me looking after her now, 'stead of the other way round like it always used to be."

"So it will. Where are you thinking of going?"

"Just down to the lake to see the ducklings."

"All right, be careful."

With a wave, he was gone. Ruby made to follow, but Tillie pulled her back. "Please wait." Her stomach started to tell her she was hungry, but she needed to speak to her sister, to sort out what she had just said. "Have you eaten?"

She received a shrug in reply.

"Come downstairs to the dining room with me, and we'll talk while we have some breakfast."

"I can't eat in the dining room, especially if Madam Annie's there."

"Well, she wasn't there earlier."

They met Martha coming out of the dining room with some dirty dishes.

"Is Mrs Smythe up yet?" asked Tillie.

"Don't know," she replied, then added, "ma'am" as if on an afterthought.

"Well, has she eaten yet?"

"If she'd eaten, I'd know that she was up…ma'am." The

maid's brown eyes battled with her mistress's green ones for a second before she looked down and continued out of the door.

"That woman is getting too disrespectful. I shall have to have words about her with…" She had been about to say, 'David', but the mood he was in, he would probably back the maid, so she said, "Nellie."

The dining room was deserted. The dirty dishes that Martha had been carrying must have been David's, but there was no sign of him.

"Put Alice on the floor, Ruby. She can play with her doll." Tillie went across to the sideboard and lifted up the lids. "What do you fancy, kidneys or sausages?"

"Really, I don't want anything."

"Nonsense, you have to eat something." The sight of the congealed food didn't really appeal to Tillie either, but she spooned some sausages and mushrooms onto two plates and placed them on the table. Alice toddled over to see what they were eating. "Would you like a sausage, Alice?" Picking up the little girl, she sat her on a chair next to her and tucked a napkin into the top of her blue dress before placing a sausage on a plate that Ruby quickly reached for.

"Sossis." Alice's eyes lit up as she grabbed it before Tillie could cut it up, and stuffed it into her mouth.

"Not like that." Tillie and Ruby both tried to stop her. Ruby managed to take it from her, but the look of disappointment on her face made Tillie smile. "You can still have it, but not all at once." She cut it up into small pieces. "It's a good job your father can't see you eating like that. He'd go barmy."

Eating her own food more delicately, she turned to her sister. "Now, tell me what you meant upstairs."

Ruby took her time chewing, looking as if she was engrossed in her food, but Tillie noticed a slight shrug of her shoulders.

Waiting patiently for a reply, she put down her knife and fork.

Ruby looked up, her grey eyes brimming with tears.

"Come on, sis, you know you can tell me. What's happened?"

"Sossis," repeated Alice, so Ruby put one of hers onto her niece's plate and slowly cut it up. Just as she opened her mouth to speak, Annie flounced in, her hair tied up in rags, her silk dressing gown half open, revealing large bosoms spilling out over the top of her pink nightdress. Tillie had never noticed before how big they were.

A low moan from Ruby brought her eyes back to her daughter. Alice was wiping her greasy fingers down her dress, completely missing the white apron, leaving dark fingerprints on the bright blue material.

"I'd better go and change her," mumbled Ruby, wiping the little girl's hands on a napkin.

Annie helped herself to food with her back to them, but Tillie heard her murmur, "I don't know what the child's doing here in the first place."

Tillie chose to ignore her sister-in-law and said to Ruby, "Wait for me in the nursery so we can continue our conversation."

Ruby picked up Alice and went out without replying.

Annie brought her plate of food over to the table. "I can't believe I have to help myself. The standards in this establishment are definitely dropping."

"I'm sorry if you're not satisfied." Closing her eyes, Tillie sighed. "But since David's accident…" She shrugged. Why should she have to justify herself?

"Where is my brother, anyway? I thought he would be here to greet me."

"I'm not sure. He's already eaten, so I expect he's in his study. He has a mountain of work to catch up with."

Annie looked up, her fork halfway to her mouth. "Is everything well between you two? I don't mean to pry, but I sense a…what can I call it? A chill in the air whenever you two are together."

Tillie was taken aback. She hadn't expected her normally selfish, cold-hearted sister-in-law to pick up on the atmosphere she was trying so hard to hide. "Yes, yes, of course, everything's fine." Rushing over to the sideboard, she picked up the now cool platter and took it over to the table. "Would you like some more kidneys?"

"No, thank you, my dear." Annie dabbed at the corner of her mouth. "I have sufficient here."

Taking the platter back, Tillie tried to think of a change of topic of conversation, but was forestalled when Annie said, "Why don't I arrange a party for all your neighbours while I'm here? You're both in sore need of some diversion."

"But we're still in mourning and, come to think of it, so are you." *Although nobody would know it by the way you're dressed at the moment*, she thought, taking another peek at the large bosom and, folding her arms around her midriff, feeling quite inadequate at the size of her own.

She looked up with surprise when Annie continued, "Well, my mourning time is over. They were only children. You can't mourn them forever." She delved into the depths of her chest, producing a handkerchief to dab at the side of her eye. "Although I miss my Georgie so much. He was such a delightful child, wasn't he?"

Choking, Tillie wasn't sure which statement shocked her more. Her sharp intake of breath caught in her throat, and she started coughing. Once she started, she couldn't stop.

Annie jumped up and patted her on the back. "Oh, my dear, I do hope you're not coming down with anything infectious. I don't think my disposition could stand any more upsets."

Shaking her head, Tillie tried desperately to control herself. She reached over to the pitcher of water on the table.

"Here, my dear, let me." Pouring some out, Annie held it at arm's length as if she couldn't bear to approach too closely.

Tillie gratefully accepted it. "Thank you," she croaked after drinking the whole glassful.

"Are you better? You gave me quite a scare."

Tillie nodded.

"Well, where were we? Oh, yes, I was arranging a get-together for you, wasn't I? It doesn't have to be a grand affair, just a few friends." She put her finger up to her mouth. "You do have friends, I presume?"

Tillie had recovered enough by this time to retort, "Yes, of course. We have many friends." What was the woman trying to suggest?

"Yes, yes, certainly. We'll have to draw up a list."

"Don't start anything just yet. I'm not sure if David will approve."

"Oh, don't worry about my brother. I can take care of him."

Tillie wasn't too certain, though.

"And Sarah can play the piano for them," her sister-in-law continued, clearly oblivious to Tillie's concerns. "She's just learnt a new piece, by Beethoven, I think it is."

"Are you sure she's well enough?"

"Oh, yes, she loves playing. It will do her good." Her fingers drummed on the table as she sat lost in thought. Then she asked. "Has James begun pianoforte lessons yet?"

It took a moment for it to dawn on Tillie to whom she was referring. "We call him Jamie, although he was christened 'James' and, to answer your question, no, he hasn't. But it's a splendid idea. I shall have words with David later about starting them."

"He will have to get used to being called by his correct name when he goes to Eton. They don't allow abbreviations there, although he will probably just be called 'Dalton' like his fa…like my brother."

Tillie pursed her lips together before she retorted with anything discourteous. Just bringing up the subject of school was enough to get her riled, but for Annie to stop herself calling David his father was too much to bear. Turning away, she started towards the door, pulling at her sleeves and patting her apron, anything to stop her putting her hands round her sister-in-law's neck.

"Don't go yet, we haven't arranged the soiree." Annie jumped up and pulled her round to face her. "What's the matter, dear? Are you feeling out of sorts? Then, that's all the more reason to cheer yourselves up."

Shaking her head, Tillie drew in a deep breath. "I'll go

and find David and see what he says." She knew full well what it would be. His strict sense of decorum wouldn't allow him to abandon the period of mourning before the end of the six or nine months. She wasn't sure how long it should be, actually. Just because Annie was prepared to cut hers short, didn't mean that everyone should do so.

Walking to the study, she began to work out how long it had actually been. George had died in November, so perhaps Annie was right about him, but her Annabella had died in February, which was barely four months past. Remembering her baby daughter, she hugged herself. These days she tried not to think about her, to avoid the pain and heartache, but sometimes she couldn't help it. She changed direction and went upstairs to the nursery. Cuddling Alice sometimes took the edge off the pain. She hoped she wasn't asleep.

Entering the nursery, she sensed that something wasn't quite right, but wasn't sure what. Rushing over to the crib to check on her daughter, a feeling of panic overtook her as the child lay still and unmoving. Grabbing her, she yelled, "Alice, wake up!" The little girl squirmed, opened her eyes and began to cry.

Ruby came running over. Tillie hadn't realised she was there. "What's the matter? Why are you screaming?"

Trying to breathe in, but not succeeding very well, Tillie half noticed that Ruby's eyes were red, as if she had been crying. Cuddling her daughter close to her, she tried to apologise, to set her sister's mind at rest, but no words would come out.

"Tillie, what's going on? What's wrong with Alice?"

Tillie shook her head. Alice was still bawling and wriggling, obviously not taking kindly to being woken up in such a manner. Holding her at arm's length, she looked at her, and then pulled her towards her again, crooning softly into her hair.

"Tillie, please tell me what's happened." Ruby's worried face peered at her.

"Nothing, dear sister, I'm really sorry for upsetting you like that. I just had this feeling that something was wrong, and after Annabella, I...I get so scared sometimes that the same thing will happen to Alice."

"What...that she'll get stuck down a hole?"

"No, not that, specifically, just that she'll die."

Ruby put her arms around her. "And here's me, worrying about something as trivial as...as..."

Alice had calmed down by this time, so Tillie put her back into her cot and settled her down in the hope that she would go back to sleep. Her thumb in her mouth, she snuggled into the blanket and closed her eyes.

Standing up, Tillie straightened her dress and turned to her sister. "Now, tell me what all this nonsense about you and Sam is about."

Ruby looked at her shamefacedly, opened her mouth, but closed it again without saying anything.

"Come on, sis, out with it."

"Well, you know I told you that I'm not...that I wasn't...you know?"

"Yes, it's wonderful news."

"I know it is, but I was a bit disappointed."

"Surely not?"

"You know how silly I am. I'd just convinced myself that I was, and I'd got quite excited about it."

"What, even if I hadn't been able to convince David to bring forward the wedding?"

Ruby shrugged. In a way, Tillie could understand her sister's feelings about being pregnant. Hadn't she felt so a few times, when her fairies had been late?

"But what were you saying earlier about Sam?"

Ruby shifted her feet, then walked over to a pile of clothes on a chair and began to fold them. "I don't think he wants to marry me any more," she mumbled, not looking around.

Tillie couldn't believe that was true. Inhaling deeply, she took the folded apron from her sister and, looking her in the eye, held her hand. "Why ever not?"

"He...when I told him the good news...he..." Ruby's grey eyes looked bleak.

Tillie arched her eyebrows, nodding slightly, trying to encourage her to continue. "He what?"

"He was glad, said it was a good job we didn't have to bring the wedding forward."

"I expect he was—any sane man would be."

"But it seemed as if he was too glad."

"Why, what else did he say?"

"Well, nothing much, but when I told him we wouldn't be…you know…doing it again until we were married, he walked off in a huff."

Tillie cupped Ruby's face in her hands. "I'm sure it didn't mean that he doesn't want to marry you. He's a man, and men like to sow their oats whenever and as often as they can. He'll come round, you see."

Ruby didn't look too convinced, so Tillie suggested, "Would you like me to have a word with him?"

Ruby pulled at her arm. "No, no, please don't do that."

"All right, but look, I'll stay up here while Alice is resting. You go and find your lover-boy and have it out with him."

Shaking her head, Ruby picked up the pile of clothes and put them in the drawer. "No. Thank you, anyway. I'll wait 'til he speaks to me. He was the one that walked off."

Tillie could see her sister was adamant. Helping her put away the rest of the clothes and tidy up the nursery, she said, "You'll never guess what my charming sister-in-law suggested."

Ruby shook her head again, still clearly upset.

"She only wants to arrange a get-together with some of our friends."

That made Ruby look up in surprise. "When?"

"Within the next few days, I suppose." Then a thought struck her. "Hey, it'll be Jamie's birthday soon, maybe we could…" But she hoped Annie would only be staying for a week at the most. Perhaps they could celebrate his birthday early. It was something to think about. Surely, David couldn't object to Jamie having a birthday party.

"I'll go and find David and see what he says, while it's still fresh in my mind." She turned to go out. "Do you feel happier?"

A Dilemma for Jamie

She received a nod, which was all she expected to receive, if she was truthful. Her sister was not renowned for saying a lot at the best of times.

She found David in his study, chewing the end of a pencil, looking concerned. She bent down to kiss him, testing his reactions, unsure of her reception. He went through the motions of kissing her, but she could tell that his thoughts were elsewhere.

"Am I disturbing you, darling?" she asked, straightening up.

"What? Oh, no."

"You look worried. Is there a problem?"

"Um."

He was clearly not in a mood for conversation. Should she abandon her quest or just go for it? There seemed to be quite a few quests to corner him with, lately. Why couldn't she just take charge of things herself and not trouble him with them?

"David, darling..."

He didn't even look up from his desk.

"It's about Jamie's birthday."

"What about it?" He did look up then. "I am rather busy. Can we discuss it later?"

She sighed. "Yes, I wouldn't want to disrupt your work for something as trivial as your son's birthday," she murmured as she backed towards the door, not even sure whether he'd heard her.

"We will speak later, I promise," he said as she went out.

I suppose that's some concession, she thought, crossing the hall as Jamie came flying down the stairs. "Mama, I've been looking for you. Sarah's fallen over and cut her knee."

"Is it badly cut?"

"Well, it's bleeding a lot."

"Take me to her." Not another crisis! They seemed to be going from one to another. "Have you told Auntie Annie?"

"She's having her morning nap, so Sarah said not to disturb her."

That sounded about right. However did the woman get

anything done? She seemed to sleep half her life away.

Chapter 15

The following day, as they were sitting in the lounge, Miss Augusta Hetherington was shown in, wearing a red and black dress covered by a light grey shawl. Black curls showed beneath her red bonnet, framing her heart-shaped face. Looking at her closely, Jamie decided that perhaps she wasn't so old after all. Was thirty-five old?

They hadn't been expecting her but, having been asked if she was better and all that sort of stuff, his papa told Jamie he should go to his lessons.

"Aw, Papa, do I have to? What about Sarah? I need to look after her, with her sore knee and…and everything." Jamie looked across at his cousin, hoping she would look in pain and say she needed him, but knew she was far too polite to do anything of the kind.

"Well, Sarah can join in. There isn't much she can do otherwise with her leg bandaged like that—if that's all right with you, Miss Hetherington?" his mother suggested.

The governess opened her mouth to speak, but Jamie forestalled her. "That's a good idea." He felt a lot happier at that suggestion. He would have the best of…what was the saying? The best of two places, or something like that. "Do you want to do that, Sarah?"

"Shall I, Mother? What do you think?" Sarah asked.

Annie was lounging on the sofa, flicking through a magazine that David had ordered in especially for her. She began to giggle. They all looked across at her. "It says here…" She looked up, and must have realised she was being spoken to. "What?"

Sarah rolled her eyes, sighing. "Never mind, get back to your magazine."

Her mother did just that, chuckling again.

Jamie's mama gave his father a look as if she thought he ought to tell his sister she was being impolite, but his father merely looked away.

"Off you go then, you two." He shooed Jamie and Sarah out, saying to the governess, "Good day to you, Miss Hetherington," and bowed his head. If he had been able to, he would have stood up and bowed. Jamie felt his frustration at not being able to, and went over and kissed the top of his head. He looked rather surprised, but patted his arm and said, "Good boy." That gave Jamie the incentive to try harder at his lessons, much as he didn't want them that day of all days, while Sarah was there. There were so many other, more exciting, things they could be doing, even though she was injured.

They followed Miss Hetherington along the hall and into the library. Jamie rather naughtily mimicked her gait, hoping that Sarah would be impressed.

"I know what you are doing, you bad boy. Your Mama would be very cross if she could see you," said Miss Hetherington without looking around. How did she know what he was doing? Did she have eyes in the back of her head? He had heard that adults sometimes had them, but he had never seen any.

He thought Sarah was sniggering with him, but as soon as Miss H—as he liked to call her—spoke, his cousin thrust her shoulders back, assuming a ladylike pose, her nose in the air. Oh, dear, another blot on his copybook! Would he ever find anything that would put him in her good books?

"Sorry, Miss Hetherington." Maybe apologising would put him back in her favour.

"I hope you have been keeping up with your lessons while I have been ill." He'd forgotten she spoke in such a very particular way, sounding every consonant and vowel separately. She'd once tried to teach Jamie how to do so, but it was too much bother and he'd given up.

"Um..." He looked across at Sarah, wondering if she would be able to tell if he told a little lie by saying he had. He didn't want anything else to go against him. "Sort of." That wasn't really a lie. He'd done some mental arithmetic now and again, but only because he enjoyed it, not because he was supposed to.

A Dilemma for Jamie

He tried to imagine what Sarah would like to learn about. "Can we study birds today, please, Miss H, um, Miss Hetherington?" Oo, nearly forgot to use her full name.

He turned to his cousin. "You like birds and things like that, don't you?" he asked excitedly, but then another thought dawned on him. "But you probly know everything about them already."

"I couldn't possibly know everything, so that would be good."

Jamie knew she was just being nice. They entered the library, and he found her the most comfortable seat so she could rest her leg.

Miss H took off her bonnet, and her black hair cascaded down her back. Jamie looked at it in wonder. It was so long! How had all that hair been hidden under a bonnet? And how come he'd never noticed it before? He caught Sarah looking at him with an odd expression and closed his mouth, realising he'd been staring at the governess.

Quickly looking away, he went across to the bookshelf to find a book about wildlife. It was fascinating to find out how birds had feathers instead of fur, and how they were formed, and he had to admit at the end of the morning that he'd really enjoyed himself. It hadn't seemed like a lesson at all.

After luncheon, Sarah was tired, so she went for a lie-down. Miss H had some business in town to catch up on so couldn't stay much longer, but promised to return the following day. Jamie wanted to ask her if it was to do with her wedding that he knew was coming up. But he wasn't sure whether it was polite to do so. Not that he was really interested, but he thought Sarah might be. It could be something that would please her.

He decided to go out for a walk. It had really tired Sarah the previous day, just going down as far as the lake, and he felt like going farther than that. After telling Auntie Ruby where he was going, he collected Goldie and set off for his tree house, racing the dog to see if he could beat her. But she just kept to his side, so he couldn't decide whether he had done or not.

Approaching the woods, he heard voices. His stomach

turned over with belly bubbles as he stopped, looking around anxiously in case it was that awful Jake person.

It sounded more like girls' voices, though. Goldie began to bark, and he pulled at her, whispering, "Shh."

Two girls emerged from the woods. One was the horrible one who had made fun of him, and the other…the girl with the green eyes—Bobby's sister. His heart leapt in his chest as they came closer.

"Well, look who it is," scoffed the horrible one. "It's Bobby's friend."

The other girl gave a half smile that lit up her beautiful eyes. Jamie's breath caught in his throat. He wanted to speak but found he couldn't.

"Cat got your tongue?" sneered her friend.

Goldie growled, and he pulled her behind him, forced to look away from the green eyes. Taking a deep breath, he said, "Good day to you, ladies." Even as he said it, it sounded stupid, but he couldn't take it back.

"Oo, ladies are we? Did you hear that, Beth? He thinks we're ladies."

Beth—he knew her name now. He could stand up to them now he knew her name. Sticking out his chest, he asked, "Well, what would you like me to call you?"

The horrible one opened her mouth, but Beth spoke first. "We don't mind being called 'ladies'. Thank you very much."

She had such a soft voice, Jamie could barely hear her.

"Anyway," continued the horrible one, "you, what did Bobby say your name was?"

"It's Jamie, isn't it?" came the soft voice again.

Wow, she remembered his name. "Yes, it is… Beth."

"When you two have quite finished going all gooey-eyed at each other…" The horrible girl screwed up her face and pulled her friend away. "Come on, Beth. We only came out to get away from the camp for a while. My brother Jake's been caught stealing a bicycle and poaching, and the camp's in an uproar."

That was fabulous news. Jamie tried to keep the smile that he felt creeping up his face from bursting out.

"Oh, dear," he managed to say.

He kept his face as straight as possible, until Beth said, "Yes, and Bobby as well."

"Oh, no, that's dreadful. Poor Bobby."

"Oh, it's all right for Jake to get arrested, is it?" The harsh voice was even more grating. "But as soon as little Miss Perfect here mentions *her* brother, you're all sympathetic."

Jamie couldn't deny it, so he kept silent as she pulled her cousin back into the woods. He remained watching until they were almost out of sight, when Beth turned and gave him a little wave. She received a nudge in the back and was dragged along until he could no longer see them.

He continued to his tree house, hugging himself and grinning. Was he in love? He didn't really know what it meant, but could you be in love at eleven?

Climbing up the ladder, he wondered if there were any pencils and paper up there so he could draw her picture while her face was still sharp in his mind—he'd tried many times, but just couldn't get her expression right. He didn't really think there would be, he hadn't been for a while. Anyway, the paper would be soggy because it'd rained a few days previously and the tree house wasn't waterproof.

A baby squirrel came and sat on the railing when he got to the top, reminding him of the story he'd written about a squirrel called Sid when the tree house had first been built. He would have to find the story when he got back and show it to Sarah. They would be able to laugh at his wonky handwriting and the awful spelling.

Should he tell Sarah about Beth, or should he keep it a secret? He didn't know if she'd ever liked a boy, besides him of course, but they were cousins so that didn't count. Maybe he would ask her that first and then decide whether to tell her.

There wasn't any paper there, either soggy or dry and, after the squirrel had puffed out his tail so it covered his back, and scampered away, he climbed down the ladder and called Goldie, who had been ferreting around in the undergrowth. She couldn't climb the ladder, so she always stayed at the bottom, sometimes lying down and going to sleep, or at other times exploring. She never went very far, so he was never worried about her.

He didn't feel like racing on the way back, he just wanted to remember Beth, how her green eyes…actually, they were quite like his mama's. Hers were green, but not quite such a bright colour, and more round. Beth's were a sort of oval shape, framed by long black eyelashes, and her hair was the colour of corn.

What colour dress had she been wearing? He hadn't noticed, but it was pale and rather tatty, so was probably very old. When he got round to painting her, he would dress her like a grand lady, in a beautiful pink dress or, maybe, a green one to match her eyes. He wondered whether she would like to be a lady, or if she was happy living in a hut in the middle of the woods. Maybe, when he grew up, after he'd been to the dreaded school, he could take her away from her poor surroundings and make her into a grand duchess or something like that.

* * * *

Tillie sat in the lounge doing some embroidery, a particularly intricate piece, much harder than she had ever done before, but she was really enjoying it. The tiny stitches made her concentrate, and she felt a real sense of achievement as the colours began to spread across the fabric.

David wheeled himself in. "Where is Annie?" he asked.

Finishing a difficult stitch, Tillie bit off her embroidery cotton. "Probably having her afternoon nap, or is she still on her morning one? I'm not sure."

"There's no need to speak about her like that."

"It doesn't matter to me what she does. She's free to do as she pleases."

He pulled up in front of her. "Anyway, what was it you wanted to ask me about this morning?"

The weary tone in his voice took her by surprise. Threading the needle into the fabric to prevent it getting lost, she pricked her finger. "Ouch," she squealed, sucking her finger so blood wouldn't drip onto her work. The sampler put to one side, she stood up and kissed him. "You seemed very preoccupied. Are there problems with the estate?"

He kissed the back of her hand, keeping hold of it. "Nothing for you to worry about, my dear."

"Oh, David, why won't you share your concerns with me? I am your wife, and they should be mine as well."

"The estate went into a slight decline while I was ill, that is all, and it is taking a great deal of effort to get it back on course. As I said, there is nothing for you to fret about. It is all in hand." He wheeled himself away to the other side of the room. "I thought you had come to bring up the subject of Jamie's school. I have decided that we should take him for a look around it, just to put his and your minds at rest."

He hasn't changed his mind then, Tillie thought but kept silent. It wasn't the actual school that she was bothered about, it was the fact that he would be going away and she wouldn't see him for weeks on end.

"And do you remember me talking about rowing some while ago?" When she nodded, he continued, "Well, I am thinking of asking Charlie Hodges to take Jamie as a special treat for his birthday. I would not be capable of getting into the boat myself, but if you would like to go, to keep your eye on him, that would be acceptable."

"So I can only go if I want to 'keep my eye' on Jamie then, not just to enjoy myself?"

"I did not say that."

Well, that's what it sounded like. Was she reading everything he said wrongly? They used to be so attuned to each other but, since the accident, she couldn't fathom him out at all. "I'm sure he'll be thrilled." She tried to put some enthusiasm into her reply, hoping that David wouldn't notice the lack of it.

He obviously didn't, for he continued, "And I have also been pondering on the idea of organising a ride in a hot air balloon."

"A what?" When were the surprises going to stop?

"It is something else I have been reading about in the newspaper."

That damned newspaper again!

"It is only a thought. I have not done anything about it yet and, of course, it would not be for a while yet. I shall have to show you the article. I am sure it is not as hazardous as it sounds."

Tillie hadn't even considered it might be dangerous, but once he'd put the idea into her head she was convinced it wasn't anything she could condone. She had to change the subject. "Has Annie spoken to you yet about the get-together she wants to organise?"

It was his turn to look surprised. "No. How can we do anything like that? It is much too soon."

"That's what I told her, but you know your sister, she lives by her own rules."

"I shall have to have words with her."

"Thank you."

"Anyway, to get back to the subject I brought up earlier, do you want to ask Jamie about going rowing for his birthday or shall I do it?"

"I think it would please him more if you did so, as it's your idea. He'll love the fact that you've organised something especially for him."

The look he gave her made her wonder whether she'd said something wrong again. Sighing, she stood up. "When do you propose going to the school?"

"Not until Annie and Sarah have gone home."

"Have you any idea how long they're staying?"

"Why, are you tired of their company already?"

"No, David. Why do you insist on putting the wrong interpretation into everything I say? I can't have a simple conversation with you nowadays. I…" Why was she bothering?

"I am sorry. I have a lot on my mind."

"Then do as I suggested and share it with me."

He hesitated, looking up at her as if about to do so, then turned his gaze away again. "Where is Jamie, by the way?"

"I think he went out while Sarah has a lie-down."

"Is Maisie settling in?"

She looked at him in astonishment at the change of subject. "Um, yes, Freda's teaching her everything she needs to know. I'm amazed you even realised she was here."

He gave her an offended glance. "I keep up to date with all the servants. I would have thought you would know that."

"Yes, of course. I apologise." She turned towards the door, thinking she had better retreat before she said anything else to upset him.

"Sam tells me he cannot wait until he and Ruby can be wed."

Tillie knew why. "Yes, Ruby says the same." She wondered whether to share her sister's secret—she would have done at one time—but decided not to. It might have caused another argument. He would have probably taken Sam's side, for he, himself, would definitely have done it before they'd been wed if she'd allowed him to.

He turned to go out. "I shall go and find that newspaper and show you the article about hot air balloons."

Hot air balloons, rowing—what else was her irritating husband going to spring on her? Sighing, she picked up her embroidery and put it out of the way, then went upstairs to the nursery.

Alice was just waking up when she entered. Ruby had been about to pick her up, but Tillie gently nudged her out of the way. "Thank you, Ruby. I'll get her."

Cuddling her daughter, she studied her sister's face. "Have you sorted things out with Sam yet?" she asked.

Ruby shrugged before turning away. She picked up a stocking and began to darn a small hole in it.

"Oh, Ruby, you really ought to go and have it out with him." Putting Alice down on the floor, she went to the toy cupboard and found a wooden train for her to play with. "Choo choo," she said, pushing it along.

"Choo choo," the little girl repeated.

Satisfied that her daughter was happily playing, she walked over to Ruby and took the stocking out of her hand. "Put that down and go and find your fiancé. I can look after Alice."

"But you've got Madame Annie to—"

"Madame Annie, as you call her, is probably still having her nap and, anyway, even if she isn't, she can entertain herself for half an hour."

Ruby still didn't move.

"Don't lose a good man, just because you're too proud."

"But…"

"You do still love him, don't you?"

Ruby nodded in reply.

"Then go, shoo." She practically pushed her sister out of the door and, repeating, "Go on," she watched to make sure she went down the stairs.

Ruby looked back uncertainly, but Tillie motioned with her hand to carry on down.

"Well, little girlie," she said to Alice as she went back into the nursery. "I hope your auntie does the sensible thing and makes it up with Sam. He'll be your uncle then."

The child looked up and said, "Sam."

"Yes, that's it, Uncle Sam. At least, I hope he will be if your auntie overcomes her pride." She knew it wasn't really pride that was holding her sister back. It was her shyness and lack of confidence. She never had any of that at the best of times and it didn't take much to knock it sideways.

Chapter 16

"That would be the most specialest thing of all," exclaimed Jamie, clapping his hands with glee. "A hot air balloon!"

His aunt put her hand up to her brow. "I have never heard anything so ludicrous in all my life."

"Why, Auntie Annie, don't you think you would like to come up as well?"

Jamie had to try really hard to hold back a smile at the look on his aunt's face. He'd only said it to tease her. He hadn't been serious. If these big balloons went really fast, he could imagine her hair streaming out behind her and her face screwed up with the wind blowing her cheeks so they were red and puffy.

His papa gave him a stern look from under his eyebrows but Sarah asked innocently, "Oh, Jamie, can you really imagine Mama doing that?" Then she grinned, clearly realising he hadn't been in earnest.

"Would you like to try it, Sarah?" asked David, putting down his spoon and wiping his mouth.

Sarah hesitated, her napkin in her hand, as if she would like to say 'yes', but she shook her head. "I don't think so, Uncle David. Maybe if Jamie enjoys it and there's another chance, I might consider it, but not at the moment, thank you."

"What about you, then…Mama?" His father turned to his mother.

Jamie was surprised that he'd used that title, but he looked across at his mother, hoping she would agree. That would be great if she came as well.

"I…I'm not sure. Are they safe?"

His papa rolled his eyes. "Would I let your son do anything that I did not consider safe?"

Now Jamie was really confused. 'Your son' sounded as if

he only belonged to his mother. Why had he said it like that?

He saw his mama give his father a weird look. "Of course you wouldn't," she said with a sigh.

Auntie Annie scooped another spoonful of lemon cake into her mouth. "How can…" she began but, because her mouth was so full, some of the cake spat out onto the table. Everybody stared at her, appalled at her lack of manners. She wiped her mouth and swallowed quickly before continuing, "How can anything that goes up in the air be safe?"

"Well, I suppose it does have a risk," replied his papa with a slight shake of his head. "But I have checked that everything is done to minimise anything untoward happening."

"Wasn't there an accident not long back, when someone was killed?" Auntie Annie seemed determined to cast a blight on the idea.

"Maybe there was, but accidents happen all the time. People fall off horses, and carriages overturn—as we all know to our great distress—but we do not stop using them just because of that. So, if Jamie is prepared to run the risk, then so be it." His papa put his napkin next to his plate. "If nobody minds, I shall retire to my study." He tried to get into his wheelchair, so Jamie jumped up to help him, and then pushed him out of the room.

"I don't care if it's not safe, Papa. I think it's a brilliant idea," he said as they went into the hallway.

"Jamie, it is as safe as anything in life, but if you have any qualms at all, then we will forget the whole matter and pretend that I have not mentioned it."

"Oh, no, Papa, I really would like to. Thank you for thinking of it." Jamie looked out of the window as they entered the study. "Just imagine, soaring up in the sky like a bird." He turned and looked at his father's legs. "I'm just sorry you can't come with me, Papa. That would have been super."

His father shrugged. "I regret there are many things I will not be able to do from now on, son, but I just have to accept the fact and get on with my life."

While they were having this one-to-one conversation, Jamie wondered if he dared bring up the subject of school. He still hadn't plucked up the courage to do so. "Papa?" he began, twisting the tassel of the curtain round and round in his fingers.

"Jamie, if you are going to ask about school, then I must tell you that when your aunt and Sarah have gone home, your mother and I are going to take you to have a look around it. So no definite decision will be made until after you have seen it for yourself."

"Oh." How had his father known what he'd been thinking?

"Does that answer your question?"

Jamie nodded. He couldn't really argue with that.

"Come here." He went across and stood in front of him. "Your mother tells me you really do not want to go, so that is why you need to know what you could be missing out on."

He nodded again.

"So, off you go." As Jamie went out, he heard him calling, "I really do have your best interests at heart, you know."

* * * *

The next afternoon Jamie went to find Sarah to see what she felt like doing, and met Maisie coming down the back stairs dressed in a brown frock and shawl, with a rather tatty yellow bonnet over her loose curls. She looked so like her old self that he was taken aback.

"Do you like me new bonnet?" she asked, putting up her hands to frame it. "Ruby gave it me. It's me day off, so I'm going to see Ma and me sisters and little brother." She hesitated. "Do you want to come with me? Charlotte's taken quite a fancy to you, you know."

Of course! He'd heard she had an afternoon off sometimes, but it was the first time he'd seen her without her mop cap and apron since she'd been there. "I'd love to, Maisie, but I can't, not while Sarah's here."

"It's so nice to hear me proper name for a change," she said, her violet eyes looking up at him sadly.

"Don't you like being called Mary? I can ask everyone to make sure they call you 'Maisie', if you want."

Shaking her head, she hurried on. "I don't want to be no trouble. I don't mind really."

"Have a good time then," he called after her, wondering whom he should ask about her being called by her proper name.

* * * *

The sunshine looked so enticing, so Tillie picked up a basket and some scissors and, taking Alice by the hand, escaped into the flower garden. All around her, different coloured blooms bobbed about in the breeze. Alice ran down the path that ran through the middle, trying to catch a white butterfly and, reaching out, almost overbalanced into a bed of yellow chrysanthemums.

Tillie grabbed her before she fell. "Be careful, sweetheart." She stood the little girl back on the gravel. "There are lots of bees in there that could sting you."

"Bee, bee," Alice sang, jumping up and down. "Bee."

At least she wasn't sucking her thumb for a change. Tillie had tried to get her to stop, but without any success.

She cut a few flowers and placed them in the basket. Alice tried to help but just pulled off the heads.

"Perhaps it wasn't such a good idea to bring you with me," she said, pulling the little girl's hand back, but she just wanted to spend some time with her daughter. She still missed her twin so much she sometimes felt she didn't want to let Alice out of her sight, in case anything untoward happened to her as well.

"Ah, here you are." The voice she least wanted to hear got louder as its owner came closer.

"Yes, Annie, I'm just picking some blooms for the table."

"Haven't you got some beautiful ones? I didn't realise this garden was so big."

"Would you like to help?"

"What colour are you using? I think it's so important to

match them, don't you?"

"Well, actually, just an assortment of pink and purple and maybe some yellow ones."

"Oh, no, they have to all be the same to give the right effect."

Sighing, Tillie handed the scissors over to her sister-in-law and picked up Alice to stop her de-heading any more flowers. "Which shade do you think would look best, then?"

"I've always liked blue, but you don't seem to have many in that colour, apart from those delphiniums over there, and they are too tall for a vase. Maybe we'll have red. What do you think?"

I don't know why you're bothering to ask, thought Tillie, but she nodded. "Yes, red will be lovely." She walked over to a clump of big red spiky dahlias.

"Or maybe yellow."

She walked back, biting her tongue.

"Ello," lisped Alice, pointing to a sunflower that was growing in between the stones and was taller than Tillie.

"That's right, darling, that's yellow. I didn't realise you knew your colours."

The thumb went back in and the little girl rested her head on Tillie's shoulder.

"So she should," said Annie, snipping at some pink asters. "Sarah knew all her colours by the time she was eighteen months old."

Of course she did, thought Tillie. *And she could probably name every flower in the garden by the time she was two.*

"It's all in the way you speak to them," her sister-in-law continued, oblivious to the fact that the last thing Tillie needed was to be preached at on how to raise her child. "That's how they learn."

"Yes, Annie," was all Tillie dared reply. If she said anything more, she was fearful that what came out of her mouth would offend.

"Sarah was such a good baby, George too." Annie straightened her back and looked up at the sky. Tillie's gaze followed hers. The azure sky was peppered by fluffy white clouds suspended on the horizon, and a gentle breeze rustled the leaves on the trees. It was a lovely summer day. Tillie hadn't appreciated it until then. It was ironic that it had taken her sometimes unbearable sister-in-law to make her notice the wonders of God's creation.

"I hope he's happy up there," Annie mused, bringing her gaze back down to earth.

Tillie nodded, breathing in the warm, fresh air.

"I miss him so much." Annie wrapped her arms round her midriff.

"Me too…that's Annabella, I mean."

"But at least you still have her twin here to lighten your grief."

"Well…"

"So it can't be nearly as bad for you." A sob caught in Annie's throat and, much as Tillie wanted to argue with her, she put her hand on her shoulder, wondering if she should go even further and hug her, but no, that would be too much.

Realising that Alice was nodding off, she patted Annie's arm, then walked over and sat down on a secluded bench set back in an arbour of roses. The child should really be taken up to bed, but she just wanted to cuddle her. She didn't get the chance very often, as there always seemed so many other calls on her time, so many other duties to perform. She began to croon softly to her, forgetting her sister-in-law for a moment, lost in a little world of her own, imagining she was holding both twins. Life was so unfair at times.

A loud yelp broke her reverie and she looked up to see blood pouring from Annie's finger. Jumping up, with Alice asleep on her shoulder, she hurried across to her. "What's happened?"

"Isn't it obvious? I've cut my finger on these damned scissors. You shouldn't have them so sharp." The basket was upside down on the ground, the flowers strewn across the path. Tillie had to tread carefully so as not to step on them as she examined Annie's finger. "Squeeze it tightly together."

"Oh, Tillie, do something. I think I'm going to fai…"

Suddenly Annie was prostrate on top of the flowers. Tillie

looked around desperately for help. She ran back and laid her daughter on the bench, trying to make her comfortable on the hard surface by folding her shawl into a pillow under her head. Then, checking she was asleep, she ran back to her sister-in-law. Annie was still unconscious.

What should she do? "Annie," she cried, patting her face to see if that would wake her up, but she didn't move.

"Help, somebody," she shouted. She couldn't leave her, and there was Alice to consider. She might fall off the bench. "Help!"

Something must have penetrated Annie's mind, maybe it was the shouting. She stirred slightly.

"Annie," Tillie called again. "Wake up."

Her eyes opened. "Where am I? Tillie?"

"Yes, Annie, it's me. You fainted in the garden."

Blinking, she tried to sit up, but fell back down again.

Martha came round the corner, smoothing down her clothes. For a brief moment, Tillie wondered what she'd been doing, but it didn't matter.

"Oh, Martha, thank goodness," she said. "Mrs Smythe has had a strange turn. Please would you go and fetch help."

The maid looked up with surprise on her face. "Who do you want me to find?"

"Anyone, just get some help," Tillie growled, seething inside at the surly maid as she turned and walked back. Tillie felt like running up and putting a firework under her to speed her up. How could a person be so unco-operative?

"Are you still there, Tillie?" the plaintive voice of her sister-in-law squeaked.

"Yes, Annie. Martha's gone to find somebody." She knelt down on the cinder path and nestled Annie's head in her lap, stroking her hair, hoping she wasn't as bad as she seemed, knowing how she could over-dramatise situations. "Are you hurt anywhere else besides your finger?"

She picked up the hand. Blood was still seeping out a little, but not too badly. As Annie mumbled something incoherently, she tried to remember which herb was used to stop bleeding. Comfrey was for broken bones, and meadowsweet eased pain, but which one stemmed the flow of blood? Something in the back of her mind whispered calendula. Was that it? She could see a profusion of marigolds further down the garden, their bright orange heads waving to her. Should she pick some? But even if she could get to them, which part of the flower would she use?

As she was still debating, Nellie came running up. "What's happened?"

David came hobbling along behind her. Since he'd recovered some of his physical strength, Tom had concocted a pair of crutches so he could walk about without help. He was still very slow and unsteady, but it was a lot easier than the wheelchair.

"Annie?" he croaked, gasping for breath.

His sister half sat up, putting her good hand to her forehead, then slumped down again. "Oh, David, thank goodness you've come to rescue me."

He looked accusingly at Tillie, whose legs were numb from sitting in an awkward position. She began to get up, trying to lift Annie to her feet. *Surely he doesn't think I've hurt her?* she thought.

"I…I can't remember what happened," Annie said in the most pitiful voice Tillie had ever heard her use. David looked up with raised eyebrows, as if to say, 'Well?'

"She cut her hand and then fainted when she saw the blood," Tillie began to explain as she heard Alice start to cry, over on the bench. David looked across at his daughter with surprise. "What is Alice doing over there?" he yelled.

"She was falling asleep when all this happened, so I thought it best to just put her there. What else should I have done? Leave your sister here to bleed to death while I took my daughter upstairs to bed?" Tillie was getting angry by this time. Why was she being made to feel guilty? None of this had been her fault.

"All right, calm down." David bent down towards his sister. "Can you get up, Annie?"

"I…I'll try," she whispered, her face contorted as if in pain. Tillie still wasn't sure whether it was all an act or if she was genuinely hurt, but helped her to her feet. She wobbled and, with the support of Nellie on one side and Tillie on the other, managed to stand upright.

Alice had sat up by this time so, scared that, half asleep, she would topple off the bench, Tillie tried to disentangle herself from Annie's grip.

"You had better see to your daughter," David said, looking across at the little girl, who had turned onto her stomach and was dangling her legs over the side of the bench.

"I'm trying to, but…Annie, do you think you could stand without me now?"

"I…don't…know. I still feel…dizzy."

Tillie looked up and saw Martha standing watching them from the other path. "For goodness sake, Martha," she shouted. "Please grab Alice before she falls and causes another accident."

The maid sauntered over and reached the little girl as she made it to the ground. Alice ignored her half-hearted attempt at holding out her hands to pick her up, and ran to Tillie, flinging her arms round her legs, almost toppling her over.

David leant down to Alice. "Come here, darling, come to Papa."

Alice refused to budge, clinging on even tighter.

They were at a standstill. Annie was clutching onto her arm and Alice was wrapped round her legs, so Tillie couldn't move. Looking up at the sky, she saw black clouds coming over at quite a speed. That was all she needed—rain.

Ruby came round the corner from the direction of the fields, carrying what looked like a hat box. Never had Tillie been more pleased to see her. "Ah, Ruby, please could you…?"

Her sister put the box down and picked up her charge. Alice immediately put her thumb in her mouth saying, "Ooby," and settled into her aunt's arms quite contentedly.

"Right then, let us get you inside," David said to Annie.

Tillie had noticed her looking quite perky while Ruby had been picking up Alice but, as soon as her brother spoke to her, her face screwed up again and her lips thrust out in a pout.

"Ohhh," she moaned. "I don't know if I could make it.

Just sit me over there on that bench."

As they guided her over, Tillie whispered to Ruby, "Where've you been?"

"I told you it was my afternoon off and I was going into the village."

"Did you? When?"

"This morning. Don't you remember?"

How could she have forgotten something like that? Ruby never went anywhere. "Well, what have you bought?"

"I'll show you later."

As they deposited Annie onto the seat, the clouds Tillie had noticed earlier began to shed large raindrops. Ruby ran inside with Alice and her box, followed by Nellie who called, "I'll go and fetch an umbrella."

Once more Tillie was torn. Should she leave her husband and sister-in-law to the mercy of the weather or save herself?

She was surprised when David said to her, "Go on in. There is no point in us both getting wet."

"But…"

Trying to squeeze himself further into the arbour, where there was only enough room for one person to stand, he pushed her gently away. "Go on."

"But you need to be in the dry more than me."

"It would take me so long to get back that I would be soaked by the time I got there. At least it is fairly sheltered here."

She could see Nellie returning by this time so, already half soaked, Tillie made a run for it, bumping into Jamie and Sarah as she reached the kitchen door. They all tumbled in together.

"Them clouds come over quick, didn't they, Mama?" Jamie smiled as he shook his cap over the sink.

"They certainly did." Tillie took off her bonnet and put it on the table as Sarah copied her, then she picked up a towel to dry her face.

Alice was sitting on a chair eating a biscuit. Jamie went across and pretended to take a bite. The little girl pulled it from him and stuffed it in her mouth. "Oh, can't Jamie have a bite, then?" he teased.

She shook her head, chewing frantically as if she thought he would take it out of her mouth.

Freda walked over with a teapot in her hand. "I think you could all do with a nice hot drink. Sit yourselves down."

Sarah sat down, breathing rather heavily.

"Are you well?" Tillie asked.

"Yes, thank you, just a bit puffed."

Tillie went into the pantry to find some milk. When she came back out, Sarah was munching a biscuit and Jamie was teasing Alice again by holding the biscuit tin just out of her reach so she couldn't get one.

"No, you wouldn't let me have a bite of yours, so I'm not letting you have any of mine," he taunted her.

Alice began to get cross, reaching up and almost falling off the chair.

"Don't tease her, Jamie. Just let her have one." Tillie wasn't in the mood for tantrums.

She thought she heard movements in the hall. "Run and see if that's your father," she said, partly to relieve the situation and partly to find out if David and Annie had got back in without getting too wet.

Jamie put down the tin after one more taunt at Alice. She grabbed it and took out another biscuit.

"That's enough now, young lady, you won't want your tea," scolded Tillie. Offering it to Sarah who refused more, she put it back on the shelf.

Ruby had picked up her box from the sideboard, and gone out without saying a word as soon as Tillie had entered the kitchen. Tillie was intrigued. What could she have bought?

Wiping Alice's fingers, she picked her up and turned to Sarah. "Do you want to come and see how your mama is?"

"Why, what do you mean?"

"Oh, of course, you don't know." Tillie explained what had happened.

"Oh, poor Mother. I'd better go and see her." Sarah rushed out of the kitchen with Tillie and Alice close behind.

Her husband and his sister were in the lounge being fussed over by Nellie. Sarah knelt at her mother's feet, in tears.

Tillie wondered if anything else had happened. "What...?" She looked over at David.

"She's just upset," he said. His black hair was plastered to his forehead, giving him rather a comical look. She wanted to smile but thought it would be taken the wrong way, so turned away.

Alice squirmed in her arms, so she let her down and she ran to her father. "Pa," she cried, putting up her arms to be picked up. David reached down and picked her up, bouncing her on his good knee.

Annie moaned, putting her hand up to her forehead in her habitual manner.

Jumping up, Sarah bent over her. "Mother, are you in pain?"

"I just want to go home."

"Well, you cannot do so if you are unwell," David said to her as he tickled Alice under her chin, making her giggle.

"What I need is some peace, then I'll feel better."

Holding his daughter out to Tillie, David gave a sigh. "You had better take Alice up to the nursery, my dear." He turned to Nellie, who had been about to go out of the room. "Help me up, please. I think we had better leave my dear sister to rest."

Jamie ran up to him. "Let me help you, Papa." Between them they managed to get David up and across the room.

"May I stay, Mother?" Sarah half stood up.

"If you wish, as long as you don't make any noise." Laying her head back, Annie closed her eyes. Sarah sat back down and rested her head on her mother's knee. Annie's leg twitched, nudging her off, so she went and sat on the other sofa. Tillie's heart went out to her. She clearly wanted to comfort her mother, and all she got was rejection.

"Are you sure you wouldn't like to come and play in the nursery with Alice and Jamie?" she asked her. "Just while your mama has her rest?"

Sarah shook her head. "I'll finish my Jane Austen novel, if that's all right." She got up and walked over to the cabinet in the corner. "Ah, here it is. I left it there this morning. It's called

A Dilemma for Jamie

'Pride and Prejudice'. It's about…"

Annie moaned again.

"Sorry, Mother." With a dejected air, Sarah sat back down and opened her book.

Tillie gave her a little wave, not daring to say anything further as she adjusted Alice into a more comfortable position in her arms and followed her husband and son out of the room.

What had Ruby been to buy? Eager to find out, she went to find her. How could she have forgotten it was her sister's afternoon off and that she had gone into the village? *The effects of David's infuriating sister, that's what,* she told herself as she tried the nursery first, then Ruby's bedroom. She looked around the room with its single bed and blue washbowl and jug on the washstand, just as it had been when they'd arrived at The Grange all those years before—two shy little girls feeling abandoned by their sick mother, who had died not long afterwards. How circumstances had changed since then.

Ruby was sitting on her bed, holding out a pretty new white bonnet in front of her.

Alice reached out to her aunt saying, "Ooby," so Tillie put her down and took the bonnet from her sister.

"This must be what you went to buy."

Ruby nodded, picked up the little girl and sat her on her knee.

"It's beautiful." Tillie examined the lace round the brim. "It must have cost you a fortune."

"It's for my wedding."

"Oooh, it is still on, then?"

Another nod.

Tillie sat down beside her and enfolded her in her arms. "I'm so pleased for you. For you both. That problem got sorted out, then?"

Ruby nodded again. "It was all a misunderstanding."

"What did I tell you? Listen to your big sister." She gave her another squeeze. "Have you arranged a date?"

"No, but it'll be as soon as is suitable." Ruby bounced Alice on her knee, saying quietly, "Do you think you could ask the master when that would be?"

"Of course. Oh, I'm so happy. Have you decided what sort of dress you would like, because Nellie will make it for you? I'll help as well. You mustn't. That would be bad luck."

Ruby pushed out her lips, shaking her head slightly. "You did say…"

"What? What did I say?"

"It doesn't matter."

"Come on, Ruby. I know I've got a terrible memory, so remind me."

"You said I could borrow yours."

Tillie threw her arms in the air, almost dropping the bonnet. "So I did. I'd forgotten about that. But wouldn't you like one especially made for you?"

"No, yours was perfect, just what I want."

"Come on, then, let's go and try it on you." Tillie pulled her to her feet and dragged her down to her own room. Her dress was folded neatly in a drawer, wrapped in tissue-paper. Sitting Alice on the floor with her doll, they took it out and Ruby ran her fingers over the soft material before holding it against her.

"Do you think it'll fit me?" she asked anxiously.

"We'll make it fit. Luckily, we are of a similar height and you're only slightly more slender than me, or than I used to be. I've become rather flabby since I had the twins. I probably wouldn't get into it now."

Ruby took off her black dress and tried it on. "Is it all right to be putting on a white dress?" she asked nervously, "when we're still in mourning?"

"I won't tell if you don't," whispered Tillie, smiling conspiratorially.

The dress was almost a perfect fit. Ruby was even more flat-chested so the bodice was too big, but a tuck here and there would bring it in.

"Are you sure you wouldn't rather have your own?" Tillie watched her sister staring as if mesmerised at her reflection in the mirror, joy radiating from her grey eyes as she ran her fingers over the soft ivory silk. She didn't really need a reply and didn't receive one, just a rapturous smile.

Alice came across and looked in the mirror as well. "Liss." She pointed to her reflection. Tillie bent down to her. "Yes, that's Alice. Wouldn't you like to have a gorgeous dress like that at Auntie Ruby's wedding?"

"Ooby," she answered, smiling at her auntie who bent down to her and said, "Would you like to be my bridesmaid?"

The little girl nodded vigorously. She couldn't possibly know what her auntie had suggested, but was clearly thrilled to agree to it.

Tillie was itching to try on the bonnet, but it wasn't hers to do so. She put it on her sister, who hadn't taken her eyes off the mirror.

"Ohhhhhh," Ruby wailed. "That's a perfect match." Her eyes filled with tears. "Thank you so much. I shall be the happiest woman in the whole of Yorkshire, in the whole world, in fact."

Not in her entire life had Tillie ever seen her sister so enraptured. Her own eyes filled up at the sight as she gave her a hug. Not too tightly, she didn't want to spoil the dress. If Ruby was this joyful now, what would she be like on the wedding day itself?

"You'd better take it off now. We don't want any mucky fingers making dirty marks on it, do we? Nellie made such a good job of cleaning it after someone spilt ale down it at my wedding." Tillie examined the front section in question. There was only the very slightest hint of a mark. She undid the buttons that ran down the back, and Ruby stepped carefully out. Between them, they folded it and put it back into the drawer, wrapped in the tissue paper.

"Let's go and see Nellie and get this wedding planned."

"Are you sure it's all right to talk about weddings while we're still in mourning for baby Annabella?" Ruby asked as they went downstairs.

"I'm sure it is, as long as we don't hold the actual wedding during the period," replied Tillie, although she wasn't really one hundred percent sure, but didn't want to dampen her sister's happy spirits.

"And you said you'd ask the master's opinion on when it can take place?" Ruby reminded her.

"He is your brother-in-law, so you would be perfectly entitled to call him by his given name."

Ruby's shocked expression made Tillie smile. "Oh, no, I couldn't do that. He's the master first and foremost. No, no." She continued to shake her head all the way downstairs and into the kitchen.

Chapter 17

The following day, with her finger patched up, Annie was feeling a lot better but eager to go home. David and Tillie didn't try to dissuade her, and it was only Jamie who was reluctant to let his cousin go, one of the reasons probably being because he knew that the visit to school was imminent once they'd departed.

The good thing about them leaving earlier than they had originally planned was that the subject of the party had been scrapped. Tillie was not unhappy about that, it was one less thing for David to complain about.

Maisie came out to see them off, surprising everyone by giving Sarah a little present for the journey, a biscuit made in the shape of a heart with a red ribbon attached.

"Oh, that is so lovely," exclaimed Sarah as she hung the ribbon round her neck. "Thank you."

"Come on, Sarah, stop dawdling," called Annie from inside the carriage.

"Coming, Mother." Sarah gave Maisie a kiss on the cheek, then turned to Jamie, hesitating for a moment before kissing him and then hugging Tillie and David. "Thank you so much for a lovely time," she said, climbing in.

They traipsed back inside, but Maisie stayed outside. When Jamie went to call her in, Tillie caught his sleeve. "Leave her, she's probably thinking there's no possibility of her ever riding in a carriage like that."

"Will she always have to work as a scully maid?"

"It's 'scullery', but no, probably not. As she gets older, she should rise in the ranks to be a parlour maid like Martha or a nursery maid like Auntie Ruby or even a cook like Freda."

"But you were a maid, weren't you, and you married Papa? P'raps Maisie'll marry a rich man too."

Tillie straightened his cap. "Who knows?" She turned to David, who was going into his study. "What was that saying you told me once? About things in heaven and earth?"

David turned and smiled. "Do you mean the piece from Shakespeare's Hamlet? 'There are more things in heaven and earth, Horatio, than are dreamt of in your philosophy'."

Jamie looked taken aback. "What does that mean?"

"You will find out when you study Shakespeare at school." David disappeared into his study and closed the door.

Jamie looked bleakly at Tillie. "It looks like I'm still going, then."

"We'll have to see. Your papa's making the arrangements for us all to pay a visit at the end of the week. You might like the look of it when you get there." She tried to put some enthusiasm into what she was saying, but in her heart she was quaking at the thought.

* * * *

"How far is it, Papa?" Jamie watched the fields and trees rushing by. They seemed to have been on the train for ages. As much as he was excited at travelling, his insides were bubbling up at the thought of seeing the school.

"Not too long now." His papa seemed deep in thought.

"I'm so pleased you decided against Eton, David," said his mama. "That would have been just too far away."

"Is that where you went, Papa, to Eton?" Jamie jumped up again as the train began to slow down. Without waiting for a reply, he continued. "Is this where we get off?"

"Yes and no."

"What?"

"You mean, 'I beg your pardon', Jamie, not 'what'," his mama scolded. "You really must remember to speak properly."

"Sorry, Mama." He still didn't know if they were getting off but, as the train pulled to a halt, neither of his parents stood up. "We're not getting off here, then?"

"No, we have another three stops before ours." His papa pointed to Jamie's seat.

"As many as that?"

"Yes, so sit quietly, if you please."

Jamie sat back down twiddling his new brown cap in his hands. He could hear the steam gushing out of the chimney on top of the train, and longed to stick his head out of the window and watch it billow up into the clouds. His mama reached over and took his hand, a weak smile on her face.

"Where's John? Why isn't he in here with us?" he asked.

"He's in the third class carriage. It wouldn't do for him to be in here with us, in the first class."

"So, where's Papa's wheelchair?"

"It's in the baggage compartment."

"Oh." He thought of his little sister left at home without her big brother to play with. "I wonder what Alice is doing without us, Mama."

"Auntie Ruby said she was going to take her a walk if the weather keeps fine." They both looked out of the window. Grey clouds were scudding across the sky.

"It looks like it is going to rain," said his papa. Jamie hadn't realised he'd been listening to them. His mama let go of his hand and pulled her shawl closer around her.

"Are you cold, my dear?" His papa sat facing them. He leaned forward.

Jamie looked up at her. Her hand had felt warm enough. She hadn't seemed cold.

Shaking her head, she replied, "No, no, I'm quite warm, thank you."

Jamie replaced his cap and traced his finger along the brown check in his new trousers. All the clothes he was wearing were new for the occasion. The shirt was rather itchy, and he put his hand round the back of his neck to scratch the place it irritated most.

"Do stop fidgeting," his papa said, sitting back.

Pulling at his collar one last time, Jamie wriggled and pulled his jacket tighter.

His papa leaned forward again and reached towards him. "Now your cravat has come undone. Come here, let me redo it."

Raising his head so his papa could tie his cravat, Jamie studied his father's face. He had quite a few more wrinkles than he'd noticed before and his skin looked rather yellowish. There were creases at the side of his eyes, and he had a little black spot on the end of his nose.

"There we are, that looks better." His papa looked directly at him and Jamie could see yellow flecks round the outside of the black bit in the middle of his blue eyes. He'd noticed the same colouring in Alice's and Annabella's eyes. That was odd. His mama's eyes weren't that colour, nor were his own.

"Why are my eyes a different colour to yours?" he asked.

"Because I am not your biological father, as you know."

He looked up at his mother. Her eyes were green, nothing at all like his own. "So, why aren't they the same as mama's then? She's my real mother, isn't she?"

"Of course I'm your real mother," his mama exclaimed, grabbing his hands. "What on earth made you say that?"

"Nothing, sorry." He felt really ashamed, seeing the pain on her face, and wished he hadn't mentioned it. "I am really a Dalton now, though, aren't I?"

"Yes, a real Dalton." His mama looked across at his papa as if she wanted him to agree as well. He just nodded.

"So…"

"Come on, what's worrying you?"

"I was just thinking about something Auntie Annie said to me the other day. She said I would be called 'Dalton', not 'Jamie', when I get to school, so I just wanted to make sure."

"Yes, she said something similar to me." She turned to his father. "Is it true, David?"

"Why does it matter what they call him?" his papa said.

"Because it matters to Jamie. Didn't it worry you before you went?"

His papa pursed his lips. "No, I cannot recall that it did."

His mama looked as if she was going to say something else, but she turned back to Jamie. "Well, if it is true, at least you've been forewarned."

He wasn't sure what that meant, but the train was pulling into a station for the third time and he tried to calculate if theirs would be the next one or the one after that. 'Three more stops', his papa had said when they'd stopped the first time, so that meant there was one more. He sat looking out of the window, trying to see if there were any birds he didn't usually see at home, but they were travelling too fast to tell what they were. He thought he saw a buzzard, but it could have been a kite or a kestrel. There were green fields and trees—green everywhere—green, green, green—apart from a few sheep or cows now and then. They weren't green, of course.

"Would you like a sweetie?" his mama asked, handing him a small paper bag.

"Oo, yes, please." Without looking into the bag, he delved in and felt around, licking his lips and savouring it even before he pulled it out. Just about to put it into his mouth, he looked to see what sort it was. He had to smile to himself when he saw it was a *green* one. Oh, well, he was sure it would taste good. Rolling it around in his mouth, he worked out that it tasted pepperminty.

His mama smiled at him. "Is it nice?"

"Um, lovely," he answered, rolling it around again with his tongue.

She offered the bag to his papa but he shook his head. She took one herself and he could hear her crunching it. His wasn't going to be crunched. It was going to last as long as possible.

Looking out of the window again, he saw some people on horseback looking as if they were racing the train. He waved to them as they drew abreast and one of them waved back.

"Look, Mama." He prodded his mother's arm. "Look at those people. They are riding as fast as us."

"So they are," she replied.

"They will not be able to keep it up for long," his father joined in. "Horses do not have the stamina to run fast for long periods."

True enough, they were already falling back. Oh, well, at least they hadn't been green, although one of the riders had been wearing a green coat.

The train was finally pulling into their station. His stomach churning, he wished he hadn't finished his sweet and wondered whether to ask for another one. His father was looking at him rather sternly, for some reason he couldn't fathom, so he thought better of it. Mama straightened his jacket and cravat as they stood up.

The door opened and John appeared on the platform with his father's wheelchair. They helped him into it and Jamie grabbed his mother's hand tightly as they walked along the platform and out of the station.

* * * *

Lying in bed the next morning, Tillie thought back to the previous day. She'd been rather surprised at the enormity of the school. It was nothing like she'd envisaged. The small schoolhouse she had passed many times on her walks to the village, but had never entered, was tiny in comparison.

One of the older boys had shown them around. She felt sure she would have got lost otherwise. There were hundreds of boys there. How would her Jamie be able to develop his character with so many pupils all vying for the attention of the teacher? They had even been told that if any boy put a toe out of line he would be thrashed with a cane! She had not really ever smacked Jamie hard, nor had David for that matter, no matter how naughty he was. Maybe a sharp slap, but never, ever, using an instrument. The thought of him being flogged and beaten was too much to bear. There was no way she was going to allow her son to go to such a barbaric place. David had said it formed a boy's character, being kept in hand in such a manner, and it hadn't done him any harm, but that was then, in the old days. Times had changed. Slavery had been abolished many years earlier, even before she was born, but she had heard of it. Not that it had anything to do with caning, but to her it was similar. She would do everything in her power to stop her son going to such an institution.

She jumped out of bed, not caring that her hair was dishevelled, and hurried into the adjoining room, marching in without knocking. David was sitting on the edge of his bed, rubbing ointment into the damaged skin on his leg. She was taken aback at the sight. The skin had been eased over the stump, which was just below his knee and it was smooth in the middle, but wrinkled round the edges. The last time she'd seen him naked, she hadn't noticed his leg, she'd been so aroused that she'd run straight into his arms. The memory of that morning made her tingle. That was the last time they'd been intimate.

As he looked up, it suddenly dawned on her that episode had been over a month ago and had her fairies been since?

"Good morning, Tillie," he said.

Standing open mouthed at her realisation, she stood immobile. Come to think of it, she'd felt a little sick lately, but had put it down to worry. She'd better consult her diary just to make sure. Turning to go back out, she muttered, "Good morning," and left, barely registering that David was speaking to her.

Where had she put her diary? Nothing much had been entered in it for some while. It wasn't one of her priorities. But she did usually mark the dates when her fairies started.

Rummaging through her drawer, she was reminded of the lady with the cats whose diary had helped her find Jamie during that agonising time when she'd tramped through the countryside, desperately looking for him. A shudder ran through her body at the remembrance. The lady's diary had impressed her so much she'd started writing one herself. That reminded her of Emily who hadn't replied to the letter she'd sent some while ago, and she hoped the new baby was thriving. She really ought to make an effort to visit her soon.

The diary located, she flicked through it. True enough, the last entry had been over two months before. Hugging her arms around herself, she grinned. Was she going to have another baby? She'd been devastated at losing the baby boy, right at the time that little Annabella had died, but now...Better not say anything to David yet, though. He seemed so preoccupied lately. Going across to the window, she looked out at the blue sky. A feeling of peace descended on her and, taking a deep breath, she offered up a prayer.

What had she been about to confront David with? Oh,

yes, the dreaded subject of Jamie's schooling. Should she go back in or wait for another time? *Get it over with,* a voice in her head told her, so, grabbing her dressing gown from the back of the door for protection, she wrapped it around her and went back in, a little more hesitantly than last time.

"David, I must…" There was nobody there. How had he dressed so quickly? Damnation, she would have to wait after all.

Going back into her room, she splashed water on her face, dressed as quickly as possible in the dress she'd worn all week and had decided needing washing, but would now have to do another day, ran a brush through her auburn curls and hurried downstairs.

On the way down, it suddenly occurred to her that David might have thought she'd run out of his room because she'd been horrified at the sight of his stump. She stopped. Oh, no, he would probably never speak to her again.

The smell of cooked food filled her nostrils, making her feel slightly nauseated as she slowly opened the door to the breakfast room.

David sat eating kidney and sausages and reading the morning newspaper. Looking up, he folded the newspaper and put it down on the table. "Are you joining me?" he asked amiably, patting the chair beside him.

"Um, yes, all right then." Blowing out her breath as relief flooded through her, she helped herself to a small amount of bacon and some toast.

"What was all that about earlier?" he asked, pouring her a cup of tea as she sat down. Thank goodness her fears were unfounded. If he'd had the slightest inkling she'd been appalled or even upset—which, of course, she hadn't been—he would have said something.

Loathed to spoil his good mood by bringing up the touchy subject of school, she hesitated. "Uh…what do you mean?"

"Why did you rush in and back out like that?"

"I remembered something." She knew she sounded vague, but wasn't yet ready to tell him of her suspicions.

A Dilemma for Jamie

He continued, "Shall we see if we can organise Jamie's hot air balloon ride? His birthday is next week, is it not?"

"But I thought his birthday treat was a ride in a boat and the balloon thing would be later?"

"Well, I spoke to him last night, and he said he would rather go up in the balloon. We can do the boat trip any time."

"But your leg…"

"Oh, I would not be going, just you and Jamie."

"Me?"

"Yes, did you not express an interest in it?"

"Um, not really."

"Well, he cannot go on his own." He put down his fork. "But if you are not in accordance with the idea—as you seem not to be for anything I suggest—then we will drop it."

Putting her hand on his arm to prevent him from getting up, she said with a sigh, "I didn't say I was against it, I was just a little taken aback, that's all." It wouldn't be safe if she was expecting. "Maybe Ruby or someone else could go with him?"

"So you are not in favour of it, then?"

There was no option but to tell him. "The truth is…" She looked into his eyes to gauge his reaction. They were almost sparking. Would she make them even angrier with her news? And this meal had started so well. Taking a deep breath, she cast her eyes down again, fearful of what she might see. "The truth is, I might be…I'm late."

An exasperated gurgle made her glance up again. "What are you talking about, woman? Late for what?" he almost screamed.

"I might be with child."

Realisation dawned in his blue eyes, and they softened. "Oh," was all he said.

She waited for him to say something else to convey delight or, at the very least, look a little pleased. It seemed an age before he took her hand in his and replied, "In that case there is no possibility of you escorting Jamie. I shall find some way of going with him myself."

"No, David. I can't let you do that." She had to think of an alternative. There was only one other option—her earlier suggestion. "I'm sure Ruby would be willing," knowing full well that her sister would probably have a fit of the vapours at the thought of it.

Eyebrows raised, he challenged her to retract her statement. "You really think so?"

Shaking her head, she was forced to admit that she didn't.

A huge grin spread across his face. "Anyway, I am thrilled at your news."

"I haven't had it confirmed yet, so it's not definite."

He suddenly sat back. "But when could you have…?"

"Don't you remember?" Disappointment filled her. Had he forgotten? Had it meant so little to him? But they'd parted on rather bad terms that day. "About a month ago. I disturbed you naked one morning."

"Yes, of course." Emotions seemed to be racing around inside him as his eyes scanned her face. "I felt rather guilty afterwards at my harsh words to you."

"You did? I assumed I'd said something wrong."

He reached over and kissed her, a long lingering kiss that made her insides turn somersaults.

Hearing the door open, she pulled back. It was Martha, coming in to clear away. The look on David's face held a promise of maybe happier times as he pushed himself away from the table, stood up with his crutches and left the room without a word. But she still hadn't sorted out the problem of Jamie going away, or—she suddenly remembered—asked him when Ruby and Sam's wedding could be arranged. What on earth was happening to her memory? She was becoming a real dumb wit.

* * * *

Jamie finished his breakfast and went outside. Kicking pebbles in the gravel, he thought about the previous day. The train ride had been exciting, and the school? Well, he'd never seen such a big building, and so many boys in one place. It had been amazing. They'd been shown around the…what were they called? Not bedrooms, dorm-trees or something like that, where lots of boys all slept in one big room. The boy who'd taken them had been very nice, very polite, but quite a lot older. He hoped he would be his friend when he got there.

He hadn't seen Sebastian, but all the boys were very friendly. The dining room had been enormous. One boy had told him the food was awful, that they were only fed gruel, whatever that was, but his papa had reassured him he'd been joking.

He'd lain awake all night thinking about it, or so it had seemed. "Mama's going to be so upset when I tell her I've changed my mind," he said to Goldie, throwing her a stick. "Because I do want to go now I've seen it. And you, you're going to miss me, aren't you?" He stroked her golden coat when she brought back the stick and then lay on her back to have her tummy tickled. Bending down, he happily obliged. Lady came bounding over to them.

"You want tickling too?" he laughed, rubbing her tummy with his other hand. "Do you think you'll miss me as well?"

He hadn't considered the dogs when he'd been weighing up the good things with the bad. Sitting back on his haunches, the dogs nuzzling his hands to play again, he gave a big sigh. And what about Maisie? He'd promised to look after her. But since she'd been there he hadn't been able to help her, he hadn't been allowed to. They hardly ever spoke, so would she really be bothered if he was there or not?

His mama was the biggest problem. She'd often told him she was trying to get his papa to change his mind, and it would seem so ungrateful if he said that, after all her hard work, he'd changed his mind.

It'd looked so exciting, though, so full of different things to do. They'd seen the classrooms. One had pictures of birds all around the walls. That was what had swayed his decision. Miss Hetherington knew a bit about birds, but not that much, so to give up the opportunity to study them in more detail would be a...what was the expression Auntie Ruby used? A crying shame.

A loud squawking made him look up. There was his buzzard being attacked by a group of crows. At least it looked like 'his' buzzard, as he called it, a young one with a white underbelly. It'd probably been about to grab one of their babies. It squeaked its distinctive high-pitched cry as it flew away.

"Better luck next time," he called as it disappeared out of sight behind some trees.

That was another thing he hadn't thought about. He wouldn't be able to wander around, watching real birds flying above him. He would be stuck in a classroom all day. Would he like that? All his life he'd been free to go where he wanted—well almost. How would he like being cooped up inside?

He wandered around the lake, the dogs following, running back and forth. Nearing the woods, he thought about Beth. He wouldn't see her either, but then, he might not have seen her again anyway. Taking off his cap to scratch his head, he stood and peered through the trees, willing her to appear. When she didn't, he considered going in, but decided not to. What if he did meet her? What would he say? And anyway, she'd probably have her horrible cousin, Jake's sister, with her, and he was definitely not in a mood to listen to her taunts.

Turning back, he threw another stick to the dogs and made his way home, his mind still in a mess as to what he should do.

Chapter 18

Tillie sat reading a letter that had just been delivered from her friend, Emily, the vicar's wife. It started with an apology for not writing earlier, but she explained that she'd been so busy since having the baby—a boy whom they'd named Edward Peter after his father—that it was difficult to find time for writing. Emily had been such a good friend. Tillie couldn't wait to visit her. She would know the proper etiquette for arranging weddings during mourning periods, so that would be one less thing to bother David about. Wondering whether her testy husband would mind if she went that afternoon, she quickly finished the letter and went in search of him.

Knocking on his study door, her insides still tingled at the remembrance of the kiss he'd given her earlier, but the worried look on the face that greeted her when she entered caught her by surprise. He shuffled some papers and seemed to hide one of them under a book as she bent down to kiss him, hoping for a repeat of the morning one. She was disappointed when she only received a peck.

"Is everything well, darling?" she asked, straightening up.

"Yes, yes." He shuffled the papers again, stacking them into a neat pile. "To what do I owe this pleasure?"

"I was wondering if you would mind if I went to visit Emily later on. I know it's short notice, and I don't have time to let her know, but she's had her baby, and I would so love to see them both and congratulate her, and Edward, of course."

He didn't seem to be listening to her, his attention was on one of the papers. "That's good," he said, not looking up.

"And the baby's got four legs and three heads." That would prove whether he was taking in what she was saying.

"Really?"

"David!" He obviously was not.

"What, my dear?"

"Did you hear what I just said?"

"Yes, he has four..." He looked up then, his mind noticeably clearing. "I am sorry, my dear, I am a little distracted, but, yes, I will arrange to have the carriage brought round for you. Will you be taking Alice or Jamie?"

"Yes, they can both come."

"Well, make sure neither of them goes near that swing."

Shaking her head, she grimaced as she visualised the previous occasion when Jamie had gone flying through the air when the rope had broken on Emily's swing. It had been a miracle that he hadn't been badly hurt. "Of course not, darling, there's no need to remind me. Anyway, you know they took it all down after that awful incident."

"I know, I know, I was only teasing."

"I sometimes think you take delight in doing that."

"Well, my dear—" He kissed her hand "—it is such an easy task."

Leaning over, she tried to read the paper he was trying to hide. "Are you sure everything's is well, that I can't help you? I would gladly put off my trip if there was anything I could do."

"No, no, off you go. It is about time you had some distraction and a change of air."

Nothing had given her so much excitement recently as the anticipated visit. Remembering how quickly she'd dressed that morning, she went to find Nellie to ask for a bath to be filled. Visiting her friend, smelling of stale perspiration would never do.

Opening her wardrobe, she wondered whether to wear her best dress. It had only been worn for church but, seeing as the period of mourning would soon be over, she wouldn't need it many more times. She took it out and laid it on the bed. There was a small stain on the bodice. "You can come out," she moaned, rubbing it with her handkerchief. When it didn't budge, she went across to her washstand and dipped the handkerchief into the jug and went back to rub it again.

"I think that's done it," she said as Nellie came in, followed by Martha, both carrying large jugs of hot water which they poured into the bath that the housekeeper had already brought up and half filled.

Nellie looked around the room as if expecting to see someone else there. "Who were you talking to?" she asked.

"Me? Nobody." She couldn't admit to speaking to a stain. They would think she'd gone mad.

"Thank you," she said, taking off her clothes. "I can manage now."

"I'll bring up one more jugful. There doesn't seem to be very much in there," said Nellie. "Seeing as Martha didn't seem inclined to suggest it." The maid had already gone out without speaking.

"Don't bother yourself, it'll be lovely." Tillie said, dipping her toe in. "Oo, could you pass me that jug of cold water. It's just a tiny bit too hot."

The housekeeper obliged, and Tillie sank down into it.

"I'll fetch another one to wash your hair with," called Nellie as she went out.

When she returned, Tillie was luxuriating in the balmy silkiness of the warm water. Sitting up, she obeyed the command to 'lean forward' as Nellie rubbed soap into her hair before pouring over the lukewarm liquid to rinse off the suds.

"I can't see David ever doing this again," she rued as Nellie wrapped her hair in a soft towel. "It was one of the tasks he used to love doing before the accident."

"A lot of things have had to change since then. Just thank God he wasn't killed."

"Oh, I do so every day." Tillie finished soaping and splashed herself all over before stepping out and wrapping herself in a white towel.

"I've been meaning to talk to you about Martha," Nellie said as Tillie sat in her chair for Nellie to brush the tangles out of her hair.

"What about her?"

"She just doesn't pull her weight, and there's something shifty about her."

"Yes, I've noticed that. Have you had words with her? Ouch." Tillie yelped as the comb caught on a particularly stubborn knot, bringing tears to her eyes.

"Sorry." Nellie lifted the tangle and tried to separate the hairs by hand. "That's better." She continued combing out the rest of them more gently.

"Yes, I told her yesterday she needed to pull up her stockings and get more work done."

"And what did she say?"

"She couldn't understand why I should insinuate there was anything wrong with her work, which, I suppose, there isn't. She just doesn't seem to get a lot done. Look how hard Ruby worked before you had the twins. She never stopped, did she? Morning to night she slaved away, bless her."

"She still does. Not only does she look after Jamie and the tw...Alice—" How long would it take to stop doing that? "—in the nursery, but I've seen her doing other chores when she hasn't noticed me watching her."

"She's a goodun, is your sister."

"She certainly is, not that she ever realises it herself." Tillie stood up and rummaged in her drawer for some clean underwear. "Did you know she went to the village the other day and bought a bonnet for her wedding?"

"No. When is it?"

"Well, I'm supposed to be asking the master when it would be suitable." She looked hopefully up at the housekeeper. "I don't suppose you'd know?"

"Um, I'm not sure. I've never had to arrange one at such a sad time."

"Never mind, I'll ask Emily. She'll be bound to know."

Once dressed, Tillie went up to the nursery to tell Ruby she would be taking Alice out that afternoon. Ruby sat in the corner crocheting while the little girl lay in her crib, cooing quietly, almost asleep. Not wishing to disturb her, she went over to her sister and whispered the message to her.

After a light lunch, Purvis came in to tell her the carriage was ready. Gathering up her children, she hurried out, and was about to step into it when she remembered Freda had baked a seed cake for Emily.

"Run inside please, Jamie." She turned to him. "Fetch the

cake that's on the kitchen table." As he went back in, she settled Alice in the corner and sat next to her. Being a sunny day, the hood was down. She didn't want Alice to have the full sun on her face, so got up and changed to the other side, tightly tying the ribbons on the little girl's blue bonnet to make sure it didn't blow off, before doing the same to her own black one. Jamie was soon back with the cake and, as soon as he was seated, she called to the driver to proceed.

She hadn't taken any notice of who was sitting in the driver's seat but suddenly realised it was Sam. Rather surprised—she would have expected the new groom to be taking them—she felt rather guilty that she hadn't greeted him, seeing as he would soon be her brother-in-law.

Alice fell asleep before they had travelled much more than a mile, so she put her on her knee as Jamie became quite excited when he thought he saw an eagle flying above them.

Tillie looked up but couldn't see a bird at all. "We don't have eagles in Yorkshire, do we?"

"Oh, no, we don't." He sighed but immediately perked up again. "Maybe it was a red kite. They have beaks like eagles."

"Are they around in these parts?"

"I'm not sure. I've seed 'em in books but don't think I've seed one in real life."

Should she correct his speech? As they were visiting, perhaps she ought to. She didn't like to do it too often, for it seemed as if she was always nagging.

"The word is 'seen', Jamie, not 'seed'. A seed is something you plant in the ground to grow into a plant."

"Sorry. It's hard to remember."

"I know it is, but when we get to Mrs Thompson's house, you must be on your best behaviour."

"I'll try." He squinted up into the sky, eager to spot another bird. "There's a kestrel over there. You can tell them 'cos they hover before they dive down to catch their dinner. That's called 'prey'. Did you know that, Mama?"

"Yes, darling."

He suddenly looked her straight in the eye. "Mama,

would you be very, very sad if I went to school?"

"Of course I would, my darling, and Alice too. We would miss you so much."

He looked away again, nodding slightly.

"I'm still trying to persuade your father to let you stay at home. Please don't give up hope." She hated to see him so downhearted.

He looked back at her and opened his mouth as if about to say something else, but closed it again without speaking. Reaching across, she patted his knee. "It will all work out for the best, you'll see."

He nodded once more and continued to survey the hills around them.

They soon arrived at the vicarage. "Did I tell you Mrs Thompson's had a baby boy?" Tillie asked as they pulled up.

"Yes, Mama, many times. His name's Edward." Jamie sounded rather patronising, as if he was out of sorts with her. But it wasn't her fault he was being sent away. "And their little girl is called Victoria."

"Oh."

She straightened her bonnet as Sam opened the carriage door. Jamie jumped down first and, as Alice was still asleep, she handed her to the groom while she alighted.

"Thank you, Sam," she said, taking her daughter as the front door opened and her friend ran out, her arms wide and welcoming.

"Good day to you all. What a wonderful surprise! Come on in."

The vicar appeared at the door, pulling on his hat. "Good day, Mrs Dalton. How lovely to see you. I must apologise for not staying, though. One of my parishioners awaits me."

"Good day, Vicar. Lovely to see you, too." He still looked as much like a big teddy bear as usual. "I trust fatherhood suits you."

"Oh, it certainly does." He kissed his wife and made off down the street. Tillie always marvelled at the easy relationship the vicar and his wife had, no embarrassment at showing each other affection, even in public.

"Come on in." Emily ushered them all into the living room. Tillie could hear a baby crying upstairs.

"I'm so sorry to land on you like this without any warning. Maybe it wasn't such a good idea. Would you prefer it if we left? I feel really guilty at inconveniencing you."

"No, no. Now that you're here, please make yourselves comfortable. I'll be as quick as I can." She hurried out, and the baby's cries soon stopped. Tillie assumed Victoria was also upstairs, probably having a nap.

Jamie still had the cake in his hands. "What shall I do with this?" he whispered.

"Take it to the kitchen."

When he returned, he went across to a cabinet set in the corner of the large living room and peered inside. "What's all them funny mug things, Mama?" he called.

"They're Toby jugs, Jamie."

"But look at that one. He's got his feet on a dog's back and, ugh, just look, he's got a great big wart on the end of his nose."

Alice had awoken by this time. She trotted over to stand next to her brother. "Dog," she said, pointing to a different jug.

"Oh, yes, they've all got dogs, and mugs of frothy stuff."

"That's probably beer."

Jamie came back to sit next to Tillie. "Why are they there?"

"I suppose Mrs Thompson likes to collect them. Some people do."

"Why don't you?"

Tillie didn't like to tell him she thought they were ugly things, in case he inadvertently said something to Emily, so she merely shrugged.

She wondered whether it would be impolite to make some tea. Deciding it would surely be a help to her friend rather than an indiscretion, she stood up and went into the kitchen. The children followed her, and she sat them down at the table and went across to the kettle. It felt quite full, so she pushed it further onto the range and looked for a teapot. A bright knitted tea cosy caught her eye and, under it, she found a pot, took it over to the kettle and poured some hot water into it.

Remembering from previous visits where the teacups were kept, she asked Jamie to get some. "Very carefully. We don't want any mishaps."

The tea made, she covered the teapot with the cosy and went in search of milk.

They were drinking their tea when Emily came in carrying her chubby baby, who looked replete and sleepy. "This is Edward. Victoria is at her grandmamma's today. She'll be so sorry to have missed you."

"It would have been lovely to see her. I hope you don't mind, but I took the liberty of making a drink," Tillie said quickly, before her friend could feel offended. She was sure she wouldn't do, and was proved right.

"Oh, that's good."

"We brought you a cake," said Jamie, pointing to it on the table. "Freda made it."

"Why, that's lovely. You must thank her for me."

Accepting the cup that Tillie handed her, she sat down next to Alice. "You've grown, haven't you?" she said to the little girl. "I bet I know what you would like." She pointed to an orange biscuit tin on the dresser and asked Jamie to fetch it. He did so, opened it and looked inside, his eyes lighting up at the sight of its contents.

"My favourites, macaroons," he cried. "Freda hasn't made these for ages, has she, Mama?"

He offered the tin to Alice, then to Emily before picking one out for himself.

"What about your mama?" asked Emily. "Doesn't she want one?"

He tried to say, "Sorry," but spluttered half his biscuit across the table. Taking the tin, Tillie glared at him. Why did he always show himself up in her friend's presence? Exasperated beyond belief, she slammed the tin down on the table, feeling even worse as the loud bang disturbed the baby in Emily's arms. Fortunately, he didn't cry, merely opened his eyes.

"I'm so sorry, Emily," she apologised, telling herself to calm down. She would have loved to hold the baby, to get into practice again, but Alice reached over and wanted to be picked up. Had she guessed that was what she intended and felt threatened or jealous? Tillie hoped not, not with another baby on the way. Rather roughly, she put her daughter on her knee, holding her close to try to dissipate some of her irritation.

"How is Mr Dalton?" Emily asked, joggling Edward up and down.

"He's coming along nicely, thank you."

"He can walk with crutches," said Jamie, his mouth now empty. "Tom made them for him."

"Why, that's marvellous news." The baby began to murmur, so Emily put her knuckle in his mouth to soothe him before turning back to Tillie. "How are you coping? It must be so hard when you have lost a little one."

"Well…" Tillie didn't want to start on that subject. She would probably break down, and didn't want to do so in front of the children. Biting her lip, she took a deep breath and fixed a smile on her face. "We are coping quite well, thank you. We do have one dilemma, though." At her friend's raised eyebrows, she continued, "Do you remember my sister, Ruby?"

"Yes, of course."

"She's getting wed," piped up Jamie.

"Please don't interrupt, Jamie," Tillie began but Emily stopped her.

"Let's find some toys." She disappeared and came back, carrying what looked like a wooden boat under her free arm. "Shall we take it into the living room?"

Tillie put Alice down and took the boat from her. Alice tried to reach up to take it but she said, "Wait until we get there. You can see it then."

Putting it down on the carpet, she saw it was a Noah's Ark, full of wooden animals. "Isn't this wonderful?" she exclaimed.

"Do you know the story of Noah and his ark, Jamie?" Emily asked, setting down the baby, now fast asleep, in the corner of the settee, before kneeling down to take out some of the pieces.

"Yes, he had two animals of every sort, didn't he?"

"That's right. Now, you two play nicely while your mama and I have a chat." She stood up and beckoned Tillie over to the sofa on the other side of the room.

"What's this dilemma?" she asked once they were comfortable.

"I don't think I told you last time I saw you—that was at the funeral, wasn't it? It seems so long ago. Anyway, to get back to my problem, the thing is, Ruby and Sam became betrothed just before David's accident, and we didn't have a chance to organise their wedding. Now they're getting desperate, if you know what I mean?" Emily nodded. "And I'm not sure how long we have to wait before we can socialise again. I've been meaning to ask David, but he seems in such a peculiar mood lately that I haven't had the heart."

Emily looked thoughtful for a moment. "Some people say the period of mourning for a child should be a year, but others say six months and, as it wasn't Ruby's child, I think it would be perfectly all right to leave it just the six months."

"But David and I will be attending. Does that go for us also?"

"Well, since Prince Albert's death, things have changed. The queen's gone into such a decline that it seems she wants everybody else who's lost a loved one to mourn with her."

Tillie tried to take in this information as Alice came across with one of the wooden pieces.

"Dog," Alice said, showing it to her.

"No, darling, that's a lion."

"Line."

"That's right. What else have you found?"

"I've found a fox, Mama," Jamie called. "Do you remember Rufus, my pet who got…who ran off?"

"Yes, dear. See if you can find an elephant."

"Here's one, but I can't find the other."

"Well, keep looking." Tillie turned back to Emily. "So you think it will be all right to arrange the wedding for next month, then?"

"Yes, I think so, but just confirm it with your husband first."

"Of course, of course."

"By the way, I seem to remember—" Emily nodded towards Jamie "—it's someone's birthday soon."

Tillie nodded.

"I haven't had much time to make anything, but I have a little gift for him." She stood up and rummaged behind the sofa, bringing out a parcel wrapped in brown paper with a little blue bow on top.

Tillie saw Jamie look up and hoped he wouldn't disgrace himself by asking what it was. He looked at her and she raised her eyebrows, giving him a look that he must have interpreted correctly, for he said nothing, just continued playing with his sister.

"Look at this one, Alice," she heard him say. "What do you think it is?"

Tillie turned back to Emily who smiled, clearly understanding the interaction. "Thank you, that's so kind of you, especially when you must be busy."

"Well, my mother often takes Victoria for the day. Baby Edward is so good, and I now have a girl from the village who comes in three times a week to assist with the cleaning."

"That must be a great help."

At that moment, Baby Edward stirred. Tillie was itching to hold him. "May I?" she asked, going across to him.

"Certainly."

"I know some mothers won't let anybody else pick up their babies for fear of catching colds and things," she said, picking him up gently, then leaning forward and whispering, "I might be having another one."

Emily's look of glee showed how pleased she was. She evidently understood that Tillie couldn't say it out loud for fear of little ears picking it up.

"I'm so thrilled for you," she mouthed.

"It's not confirmed yet," she added, tickling the baby under his chin. He responded by smiling, so she repeated it.

"That's his first smile," cried Emily. "Oh, Edward will be so annoyed that he's missed it. He's been trying to get him to smile for a few days."

"Maybe it was just wind. Sometimes they seem as if they're smiling, don't they, with wind?" Tillie felt guilty. If it *was* the baby's first smile, why had he chosen the time to do it when she was the one holding him?

"No, there's another one. It's definitely a real smile." Emily reached over and took him as Jamie and Alice came across to see what was causing all the excitement.

Alice reached out to hold him but Tillie couldn't trust her to do so. "No, darling, he's not a dolly. You might drop him."

Jamie also tickled him. "Hello, Edward."

Alice tried to copy him but scratched his cheek, making him screw up his face.

Please don't cry, Tillie prayed. Luckily, he only murmured as Emily joggled him on her knee.

"Wood," Alice said. Tillie quickly caught her hand before she could hurt him again, and sat her on her lap, thinking she'd better curtail the visit before anything else happened.

She sent Jamie to find Sam, and they made their farewells.

"Do come again soon," cried Emily as they got into the carriage. "And I hope everything goes well for…you know what."

I bet she's hoping it's not too soon, thought Tillie, straightening Jamie's cap that had almost fallen off when he climbed into the carriage. "Give Victoria a big kiss from us all."

The vicar came round the corner, and he stood with his arm around his wife and baby, waving, as they pulled away. They seemed such a happy couple. Tillie couldn't imagine them ever having any arguments or tiffs.

Chapter 19

The bright sun shining through his window woke Jamie on his birthday. He lay still for a moment, thinking about all the things that were troubling him, especially the problem—which hadn't been resolved—of whether he was going to school. He'd sort of told his father he'd enjoyed the day at the school and would rather like to go there after all, but hadn't told his mother.

What would they be doing for his special day? The hot air balloon had been postponed, but his papa had mentioned a rowing trip a few weeks before, yet hadn't done so since, so he'd probably forgotten all about it.

Jumping out of bed, he dressed in his best clothes in case they were going anywhere special, and ran downstairs.

Freda and Maisie were in the kitchen preparing for breakfast.

"Many happy returns, young man," said the cook, wiping her floury fingers down her apron before shaking his hand.

"Thank you."

Maisie hurried over to the dresser and picked up a parcel, handing it to him. "Happy birthday," she said shyly.

"Thank you, Maisie. What is it?"

"Open it and see," said Freda, turning bacon in the pan on the range. The delicious smell of the food made Jamie's stomach rumble as he opened the little parcel.

"Oh, it's…lovely." It was obviously an animal, made of gingerbread, but what sort?

"Do you really like it?" asked the maid, who was now called Maisie by everyone in the household. Mrs Button and her children still called her Mary, though, but she didn't mind that, so she had told him.

"Can you tell what it is?" she asked uncertainly.

Jamie didn't want to offend her by saying the wrong thing, but he just couldn't work it out. He racked his brain to try to imagine what she would have linked him with.

"May I taste it first, to see if that gives me any clues?"

She laughed. "It'll just taste of gingerbread."

He nibbled a corner of what he assumed was its ear. "Um…elephant?"

"No, it hasn't got a trunk, silly."

Freda cleared her throat and glared at the little maid. The smile faded from her violet eyes as she reached up and tucked a black curl into her mobcap. Jamie was desperate to bring back her smile. It must be so hard for her to treat him as her master's son rather than the friend she'd grown up with. He tried hard to think of an animal she could have thought he would remember.

"It's a rabbit," she said at last, looking faintly disappointed that he hadn't guessed.

"That's just what I was going to say." He knew he shouldn't tell lies, but had to take the sadness away from her face. Something jolted his memory. "Like the baby rabbit we caught in the wire when we were at the gypsy camp. I remember."

Her joyful nod made him want to hug her but he wasn't allowed to do that any more, so he just gave her the biggest grin he could and thanked her again as he ate the remains of the gingerbread.

Martha came in, her face—he'd heard Freda say once—as sour as an unripe lemon. She picked up a tray Freda had prepared and walked out without saying a word. He saw Freda shake her head and continue rolling pastry as Maisie began to spoon mushrooms into a dish.

"Are they for Papa? May I take them in to him?" Jamie reached for the dish.

"Yes, they are," said Freda. "And I suppose you may do so, just this once."

Picking up the dish, he hurried to the breakfast room. His father was reading the newspaper, a cup halfway to his mouth. His look of surprise was just what Jamie had hoped for.

"Well, the maid seems to have changed today." His papa smiled as Jamie placed the dish in front of him. Putting down the paper and the cup, he reached out and took Jamie's hands.

"Many happy returns of the day, son." He looked as if he was going to say something else but stopped as his mama came in.

"Darling," she said, hurrying over to enfold him in a big hug. Jamie looked over her shoulder and saw a strange look on his papa's face, as if he was...not cross, but disappointed.

"Happy birthday," his mama squealed. "I can't believe you're twelve years old already."

"Yes, I know. I feel so much more grown up today than I did yesterday." Jamie really did feel older. He couldn't recall any other birthday feeling like that. It was strange.

His papa laughed. "Ah, the innocence of youth. Have you eaten yet?" When he shook his head—he didn't think gingerbread would count as eating—his father patted the chair next to him. "Sit yourself down, then. You can have your breakfast with your mother and me." The bell was rung and Martha appeared.

"Please would you bring extra food for my grown-up son," his papa said, making his mama grin at him. The maid scowled and walked back out with a slight nod.

His father raised an eyebrow as his mama said, "Freda's had a word with her. I think you should do so as well, unless you would prefer me to."

"No, no, I shall do it later. But let us not spoil this special day." He raised his hands above his head and grinned at Jamie again. "Guess what I have in store for you?"

About to say, "A rowing trip?" he stopped. What if it wasn't that? He didn't want them to be disappointed that they hadn't given him the right present.

His mama frowned as she gave his papa a nudge, whispering, "You mean 'we'."

"Yes, of course, dear," his papa replied to her, then turned back to Jamie. "Give up?"

He nodded. "Yes, Papa, I give up. What is it?"

"A rowing trip."

He was just about to leap with joy when his mother squealed. "But I thought we'd decided against that."

"No." He turned to Jamie. "Well, son, what do you think?"

Jamie looked at his mama. She looked as if she was going to cry. He was so confused. "Um…"

"Take no notice of your mother."

"David!" his mother yelled.

His father reached over and took her hand. "I'm sorry, my dear, I did not mean it to come out like that." He turned back to Jamie. "I mean that your mama wanted to take you to the zoo."

"The zoo! That would be brilliant." Jamie clapped his hands. It was his father's turn to look disappointed. "I'm sorry, Papa…or should I call you 'Father' now I'm nearly grown up?"

"Yes, I suppose so. But you would rather go to the zoo, would you?"

"Yes, please, if I may. Alice could come as well. P'raps I could ride on an elephant. I've seen pictures in one of me books, of folks doing that."

"So be it. The zoo it is."

Martha came in with some more food and served them. Jamie tucked in to the sausages and bacon, then looked up hesitantly. "I don't s'pose Maisie could come, too?"

His mama looked hopefully at his father. "Well, David," she said, her fork poised between her mouth and her plate. "I suppose it wouldn't hurt if we took her just this once, would it? The poor child works hard and deserves a diversion."

"But she's only a maid, and maids don't go out with their masters or mistresses."

"I know, but she is rather special to Jamie. He grew up with her, and who knows? If she hadn't wandered off while we were in that barn, she might have…no, forget I said anything."

Jamie checked his father's reaction. He couldn't imagine what his mama was going to say but wondered if his father could. His face didn't give anything away. He stroked his chin, his mouth moving in time with his hand.

"I shall think about it, so do not go saying anything to her, young man, in case I decide in the negative."

Jamie put some more bacon into his mouth, keeping his

head down, trying to work out what that meant. Negative meant the opposite to positive, he knew that, so he probably meant 'no'. Why did adults have to say things in such a roundabout way? Why couldn't they use simple words that everybody could understand?

Finishing his meal, his father tried to stand. As Jamie jumped up to help him, he said, "I can manage, thank you. Enjoy the remainder of your breakfast, and I shall see you later."

Buttering some toast after his father had gone, Jamie asked his mother, "Do you think he'll let Maisie come?"

"I really don't know, Jamie. We'll have to wait and see." She put down her fork. "Anyway, while he makes his decision, we'd better plan the rest of your day." She looked rather uncertain. "Are you sure you'd rather go to the zoo than go rowing?"

"Yes, Mama, really sure. I can't wait to see all them animals I've only seed in books before." At her raised eyebrows, he realised he'd said something wrong. "Oh, yes, it's 'seen', isn't it, not 'seed'? Sorry."

"And it's 'those', not 'them', but we won't pursue that today. Come on, let's go and find Alice."

Jamie had never seen Alice's eyes so big as she gazed around at all the animals. "Look at that little monkey." A small ape he thought was probably a gibbon was swinging backwards and forwards, eating a banana. "He's just like you." He bent down to tickle her as she sat on her papa's knee. He checked the notice on the wall. "Yes, I was right, it is a gibbon."

"Well done, Jamie." His father put the little girl down to walk. "See if you can tell me what that one is over there."

"Mucky," exclaimed Alice, running over to the cage.

"Don't put your fingers through the bars," called his mama, hurrying after her, dragging Maisie by the hand. "It says they can bite."

Jamie was thrilled that his father had allowed Maisie to come with them. She seemed rather nervous, not letting go of his mama's hand. He followed with the wheelchair. "Phwah, that's a big 'un. That must be an orang-utan. It's got ginger hair just like you, Mama."

His mother looked offended. "Are you saying that I look like a big ape?"

"No," he laughed as Maisie sniggered, covering her mouth with her hand. "It's just got the same colour hair as you."

"Well, that's a relief. Ah, look at that one over there. It's got a baby on its back."

Jamie wondered why she gave his father a peculiar smile but, shrugging, he pushed the wheelchair even harder. "Come on, Maisie, let's see what other strange animals there is."

They spent an hour with Jamie trying to guess the names of everything before he looked at the signs, until Alice became drowsy and fell asleep on her father's lap.

"Shall we find somewhere to have lunch?" his father suggested a little while later as they passed the elephant enclosure and the male let out an almighty roar, making them all jump. It didn't wake Alice. She didn't even open her eyes as she snuggled down closer into her papa's arms.

"That sounds a very good idea," his mama agreed, grinning. "I'm ready for a sit down."

His father took her hand. "You must not tire yourself out, my dear." Jamie was a little surprised at the concern. First he had been asked to push the wheelchair—his papa had thought he would be unable to manage with the crutches—and now this.

"Yes, I'm fine. I don't really feel comfortable, though, staring at all these wild animals caged up when they should be out in their natural habitat in the jungle, or wherever they come from."

"Yes, I know what you mean," his father said. "But at least they are safe here."

"And, Mama, we wouldn't be able to see them if they was in Africa, would we?" Jamie chipped in.

"And that is important to you, is it?"

He thought about that. The animals looked happy enough to him. "Yes."

A Dilemma for Jamie

"Well, come on, then, let's go and find some sustenance."

Sitting in the carriage on the way home, his mama whispered something to his father and then gave Jamie an odd smirk.

"Shall I tell him now or wait 'til we get home?" he heard her ask.

"Tell me what?" Jamie couldn't wait to know what the secret was.

His father appeared to be concentrating on something outside. "No, I think we had better not spoil the surprise."

Jamie strained his neck to see if he could see anything through the window, but there were only fields and trees and a few cows. "Please tell me."

His mama smiled. "We have a treat for you this evening."

He tried to imagine what it could be. "A party?"

"No, not quite. It's too soon for that."

"Is it something I'd like?"

"Well, do you think we would give you something you wouldn't like?"

"No, s'pose not." It didn't seem as if they were going to tell him. He tried to think of things it might be, but every suggestion was met with a 'no' or a shake of the head.

"Do you know what it is, Maisie?"

"No." His little friend shook her head.

He still hadn't wheedled the surprise out of his parents by the time they arrived home, and began to think that his parents were just having him on and pretending there was something.

"Don't go into the drawing room," his mother called. John came out to help his father, so Jamie went indoors first.

Ah, the surprise must be in the drawing room. Dare he go and have a peek? Looking around to see if anybody was in sight, he tiptoed over to the door and began to open it quietly.

"Hey!" a voice called from the stairs. "Where do you think you are going?"

Jamie jumped back in alarm as what looked like a large crow came swooping down the stairs. It was Nellie.

"Um…nowhere. We just got back from the zoo."

"Well, you'd better go and have a wash, then, if you've been cavorting with dirty animals."

Cavorting? "Oh, we didn't go on any, only looked at them through the bars." Was that what she meant?

"That makes no difference. You still need a wash. Ah, here's your mother and father, and little Alice." She came to the bottom step and bent down to his sister. "Did you have a lovely time at the zoo?"

"Mucky." Alice took her thumb out of her mouth just enough to say the one word.

"Yes, Nellie, we saw lots of cheeky monkeys like Alice." Jamie actually felt a bit peevish that the housekeeper hadn't asked him if he'd enjoyed his day out. It was his birthday, after all.

"Well, Jamie, do as Nellie says, and please take Alice up to the nursery," his mama said.

"Yes, Mama."

"And you'd better go and change into your maid's clothes, Maisie."

"Aw, Mama, can't she share the surprise as well?"

"I'm afraid not, Jamie. She's had most of the day off. I expect Freda needs her to help with the dinner."

"Sorry, Maisie." He turned to the little maid, who'd turned away with a sad face, on her way to the back stairs up to her attic room.

His mama opened the drawing room door. "Your father is very tired and needs a rest before dinner." Jamie tried to peer round to see what was inside but she glared at him, so he had no option but to do as he'd been told. His mind was working extra hard to try and work out what the surprise could be.

He and Alice met Auntie Ruby on the landing. "Hello, you two, have you had a good time?" she asked. Well, at least someone was interested in his birthday.

"Yes, thank you, Auntie Ruby. It was…" He tried to think of the best word to use. "It was stupendilious."

"That's a big word. I haven't heard that one before."

"I think I just made it up." Jamie laughed, pleased that his auntie was impressed.

"Mucky," repeated Alice, reaching out her arms to be picked up.

"Who's mucky?" asked Auntie Ruby.

"That's her new word. She means 'monkey'."

"Oh, did you see lots of monkeys?"

Alice nodded.

"And elephants and lions and all sorts of animals," Jamie added. "Auntie Ruby?" he asked as they entered the nursery.

"Yes?"

Would she tell him? There was only one way to find out. "You know…" Washing his hands in the basin on the washstand, he tried to think of a way of asking, without actually letting on that he didn't know what it was. "My present in the drawing room?"

"What about it?" She began to undress Alice.

"Do you know what it is?"

"Yes." She wasn't giving anything away.

"Can you just remind me how it works?"

"I thought you weren't supposed to know 'til later."

"Well, Mama sort of let it slip."

"I'm not sure myself, but you'll soon see."

Drat, that trick hadn't worked. He would just have to wait.

After changing out of his outdoor clothes, he went back downstairs and knocked on the drawing room door. There was no reply. Should he creep in, anyway? But his father might be asleep and would be cross if he woke him up. He saw Martha going into the dining room, her hands full of cutlery and napkins. He followed her in.

"Do you know if Papa is still asleep?" he asked.

"How should I know?" She put away the items she'd been carrying without looking at him.

"Well, do you know what my present in the drawing room is?"

"It's only a blinkin' magic lantern, for heaven's sake. I don't know what all the hush-hush is about."

"A magic lantern, what's one of them?"

She looked up then, her eyes wide and guilty.

"Oh, it's…you'll find out." She hurried out.

A magic lantern! How could a lantern be magic? He was even more puzzled. Maybe he could find a picture in one of his father's books. He hurried to the library. Where to start? He didn't even know what it did, so how would he know what sort of book to look in? If it was magic, would there be a picture anyway?

As he stood looking, Nellie came in. "Oh, it's you, Master Jamie. I wondered who'd left the door open. What are you looking for?"

Still searching the shelves, he murmured, "I'm trying to find a book that'll show me what a magic lantern looks like."

He heard her take a big breath. "How do you know?"

Oh, he wasn't supposed to know, was he? He turned round to face her, feeling his cheeks go red.

"Have you been in the drawing room?"

He shook his head.

"Then who's told you? Not your Auntie Ruby, surely?"

"No, no." He didn't want to get his auntie into trouble for something she hadn't done. "It was Martha."

Nellie looked as if it was going to explode. She stormed out, her arms flapping like one of the penguins he'd seen at the zoo.

Oh, dear, what was going to happen now? Should he stay there or follow her? He decided he might as well stay out of the way. Searching through the books, his attention was seized by one about monkeys. A moment later his mother ran in.

"What's this I hear about your surprise being spoiled?" she yelled.

"It isn't, Mama. I got no idea what a magic lantern is." He looked up at her. She seemed really upset. "Really, Mama." She came across and hugged him, seeming to calm down. "I was trying to find a book that'd show me one, but I found this. Look, it's got monkeys just like what we seed today… I mean, seen."

"You mean 'saw'," she said quietly, looking at the pictures. Now he was even more confused. She kept telling him not to say 'seed' and, when he remembered, she changed it again.

"But, anyway, come and have some tea," she continued. He was about to argue that he'd rather see the lantern thing first, but the sad look on her face stopped him.

"Yes, Mama." All the time he sat in the kitchen his mind tried to conjure up what it could be. If it was magic, then there was no end of possibilities. Getting more and more excited, he jumped down from his stool and ran to knock on the drawing room door once more. This time his father called "Come in."

The room was in darkness but an eerie light was shining on the wall. He could see a baby elephant holding its mother's tail with its trunk. He almost screamed. How could an elephant have got into his house? Suddenly the picture changed and a lion was looking at him. Backing out, shielding the pictures from his eyes, he tried to see if there was anybody else in the room. If his father had called out, then he must be there, but where was he? Surely he hadn't been eaten by the lion?

"Papa," he squealed. "Where are you?"

"Over here, Jamie."

With one eye on the lion, he peered into the back of the room and could just make out figures. Running over to them, almost in tears, he cried, "I thought you'd been eaten."

"What do you mean?" His mother took him in her arms. He was shaking so much he could hardly stand. "Jamie, what on earth is the matter?"

"I thought…"

"David, turn off the lantern," she said. The room was plunged into complete darkness. "Light the lamp, quickly." A faint glow showed his mother and father, quite whole and not at all chewed. He let out his breath.

"What…where…?" He looked at the wall where the animals had been, and there was just a white patch. He looked right around the room. The other walls only held the pictures and portraits that had always been there. "Where've they gone?" he asked, really puzzled.

"They weren't real, Jamie, just pictures."

That really was magic! He took another deep breath. "But how did they get on the wall?"

His father showed him a sort of lamp. "It has a special lens that projects the pictures, see." He tried to show Jamie how it worked, but he was still feeling the effects of his scare and didn't really understand what he was saying.

"Did you think they were real animals?" asked his mother.

He felt rather stupid now he knew what it was, so didn't reply.

"You did, didn't you? Oh, you poor thing. I'm so sorry. It was supposed to be a treat and now it's ruined." She burst into tears.

"Oh, Mama, please don't cry. It is a treat, honest." He turned to his father. "Please may I see some more, Papa." His stomach was churning from the fright, but he couldn't bear to see his mama upset like that. He had to stop her crying.

His father shuffled along the settee. "Tillie?"

She nodded. "Sit down here, Jamie, between us."

His mama stopped crying, just sniffed a bit, so once they were seated comfortably, the lamp was put out and the pictures were back on the wall. All sorts of animals appeared in front of him. Every now and again he reached over to check that his parents were still beside him, the image of them being eaten alive still fresh in his mind.

When the show had finished and the room was lit up again, he kissed his mother. "Thank you for such a…" He tried to remember the word he had made up earlier. "A stupendilious day."

She gave him a hug. "Have you really enjoyed it?"

"Yes, Mama, and thank you, too, Papa, I mean, Father." He reached over to kiss him, but wasn't sure if he was too old to do that now. He did it anyway. "I think I'll go to bed now, if that's all right?"

"Of course, darling, it's been a very exciting day. You must be tired."

He nodded, thinking it hadn't been exciting in the way she meant, but he wasn't going to let her know.

"Oh, Jamie," his father called as he was almost out of the door. He turned back. "Your mother and I have had a long talk and she has finally come round to my way of thinking."

Jamie looked at his mama. She didn't seem very happy as she stood up and walked across to him.

"Your father tells me you've changed your mind, and would now like to go to school. Is that right?"

He nodded. Excitement began to replace the earlier fear. "Yes, Mama, but only if you're not too upset."

"Well, I can't say I'm happy about it, but if it's what you want…"

He reached up and hugged her. "Thank you." Trying hard not to grin too much, he gave a little jump and began to walk out again.

"And one more thing."

"Yes, Papa, I mean, Father."

"Would you like to help out with the harvest in a few weeks?"

"Oh, yes, please."

Maybe his birthday hadn't turned out quite so bad after all.

* * * *

Nellie hurried in as Tillie and David sat on the sofa watching the magic lantern pictures again. Her face was like thunder. Tillie had never seen her so ruffled.

"I've dismissed that thieving Martha. Told her to pack her bags and never come back," she spluttered.

"Why, what's she done?" asked Tillie, jumping up.

"I've had my eye on her for days after I noticed several items of silver seemed to be missing."

"Why on earth didn't you say something?"

"I didn't want to alarm you until I had proof, but earlier, I saw her creeping down to the vegetable garden. She kept looking at something in her hand, so I followed her and hid behind a hedge when I heard her talking to someone. I was too far away to see who it was at first, but then I recognised one of the lads from the village. I showed myself and Martha was so startled she dropped what she was holding. As she was scrabbling around to find it amongst the cabbages, I spied it shining and grabbed it. You'll never guess what it was."

Tillie looked at David to see if could guess. "No, tell me."

The housekeeper held out her hand. Lying in it was the diamond and pearl necklace David had given Tillie for her wedding.

She gasped. "Oh, my goodness. Thank God you found out in time."

"You'd better check if anything else is missing, ma'am."

"Well, if you've already sent her packing, then it's too late." She ran across and gave the housekeeper a hug.

Flustered by the unusual show of emotion, Nellie looked embarrassed as she handed Tillie the necklace, and turned to go out.

"Thank you so much, Nellie." David put out his hand for Tillie to give him the trinket. He turned it over. "It belonged to my mother, you know." He gestured for Tillie to sit down beside him again so he could put it round her neck. "A family heirloom. Thank goodness you caught the thief in time."

Nodding, Nellie left the room.

Tillie stood up to check her reflection in the mirror, stroking the sparkling jewels.

"You should wear it more often," David said.

"There never seems to be an appropriate time."

"Well, once we are out of mourning, we shall have to find 'an appropriate time', my darling. It seems a waste for it to lie in a drawer, untouched and unloved."

Tillie smiled. It wasn't like her usually reticent husband to be so lyrical.

She sat back down next to him. "Are you sure we're doing the right thing for Jamie?"

"What do you mean?"

"Going to…you know where?"

He reached out and enfolded her in his arms. "I know you have your qualms about him going away, but it will be the making of him, believe me. He needs the company of other boys. The only male conversations he has are with Sam or John."

She snuggled into his embrace. "I know, but I'm going to miss him so much."

He lifted her chin and kissed her. "But you will soon have the new baby to look after." He patted her stomach. It was beginning to get rounder. "Now, do not look at me like that, I appreciate it will not be the same."

Tillie sighed. Would she ever get used to her darling boy not being with her every day? He was growing up and she had to let him go, but it was going to be so hard.

David cupped her face in his hands and kissed her again. "I am only acting in Jamie's best interests."

"Um." The feel of his hands stroking her cheek was awakening her senses. Having been seemingly shut out from his affections, she was desperate to bring back their loving relationship. She began to caress his leg, her hand moving higher. His sharp intake of breath as he grabbed her hand and pulled it to its goal gave her the encouragement she needed. "I've missed your loving so much," she murmured against his mouth as his tongue lapped at the inside of her lips.

"Me, too," he moaned, pulling her closer, his hand finding her breast, but he stopped as footsteps were heard in the hall. "Get me upstairs and we can continue this in bed."

Fully aroused, Tillie was loathed to stop but necessity told her she couldn't let a servant catch them making love on the settee. She sat up and straightened her clothes. "I'll go and find John to help you. Wait there, I won't be long." She reached over and kissed him one more time as the door opened and Nellie came in to tell them she had seen Martha off, after checking her bags to make sure she hadn't pilfered anything else.

Lying, replete with love, an hour or so later, Tillie reached across and stroked her husband's back. It was so good to have him back in her bed. He gave a satisfied grunt as she curled up and wrapped her arms around him. She wasn't going to let him ever leave her to sleep in the other bed again. She still hadn't found out what he'd been hiding from her in his study, but she trusted him enough to know that if he said she had nothing to worry about, then she wasn't going to waste her energy doing so.

* * * *

Getting up as red streaks stretched across the clear blue sky, Jamie put on his old worn-out clothes, picked up the packet of sandwiches Freda had left out for his breakfast and joined the rest of the men making their way to the fields. He was so excited at being allowed to help with the harvest for the first time. The shock of the magic lantern was still at the back of his mind, but he kept quiet about it, not wanting anybody to know how afraid he'd been. He felt rather silly that pictures could have scared him so much, so tried hard to forget about it.

Every farm needed harvesting at the same time, and they all helped each other. Men came from farms far and wide, so there were many faces Jamie didn't recognise. He stuck close to Sam and made sure he did what he was told. By lunchtime, when everyone stopped for refreshments, he was exhausted. His face and back were dripping with sweat from his tasks: lifting hay, throwing it onto the wagons, and then running little errands when required. He considered asking if he could stop work and go home, but didn't want to look like a milksop, so spurred his weary body on.

Halfway through the afternoon, he was riding down the lane, lounging, on a brief break from the hard work, on the back of a wagon full of hay, when he saw Bobby emerge from a field in the distance behind them. Sitting up straight, he saw Beth come out of the thicket. His breath caught in his throat. She wasn't wearing a bonnet, and her long fair hair hung loosely around her shoulders. He couldn't quite see her beautiful green eyes but he could picture them.

They began to walk in his direction, so he waved, noticing, thankfully, that the horrible girl and Jake weren't with them. *I hope that awful Jake's in prison*, he thought. Bobby waved back and Jamie thought he could hear him calling his name. Then Beth waved as well. His heart stopped for a moment and his stomach turned somersaults. Even at that distance, he could see her smiling.

The wagon went round a bend and they were immediately out of sight. He let out a deep sigh. As much as he'd enjoyed helping to load the wagons and, even though he'd been disappointed when he hadn't been allowed to cut the corn or the hay, he'd really loved doing all the rest of the chores, and just seeing Beth for that single minute had rounded off a perfect day.

He felt something wriggling in his jacket and, opening his pocket, remembered the harvest mouse he'd rescued from the scythes. Taking it out, he cupped it in his hand. It was tiny.

"What shall I do with you?" he asked, knowing he couldn't keep it. Its little whiskers twitched as it looked up at him. He opened his hand a little way and it shot off to hide in the hay beneath him. He wondered what a tiny mouse would have looked like as a picture on the wall. Not nearly as terrifying as a lion, that was for sure. He still shuddered each time he remembered, and hoped the images would all be gone from his mind by the time he went to school. It took the edge off the thrill that kept entering his body at the thought of going there.

Chapter 20

Ruby tried on her wedding dress once more. In church the previous week, she had felt almost excited when she'd heard the banns being read out, but now butterflies fluttered in her stomach. All manner of fears and doubts invaded her mind. What if Sam changed his mind? What if he didn't turn up? What if he'd realised he didn't really want to get married, but hadn't the heart to tell her to her face? Maybe he would go through with the ceremony just so he wouldn't lose face, but leave her as soon as it was over.

She'd tried to tell Tillie about her worries, but her sister had told her not to be so silly. "It's as clear as the nose on my face that he worships the ground you walk on," her sister said each time Ruby even hinted at anything going wrong, "so why on earth do you think he would do anything like that?"

Ruby felt herself shrugging, just thinking about it. She tried hard to be positive, but it was so difficult.

Taking off the dress, she hung it carefully in her wardrobe, and then climbed into bed. In the morning she would be Mistress Samuel Wright, a married lady. She tried to sleep, knowing if she was tired in the morning she would be testy, but so many things were going around in her head that it proved elusive.

A new nanny would soon be engaged to look after Alice and the new baby when it arrived. She would miss her little niece so much. Sometimes she felt like her own daughter. Turning over to find a more comfortable position, she rubbed her stomach. Maybe she would have a daughter of her own in a year's time. Had she been right in being true to her word and not allowing Sam to be intimate again since that first time? It had been very difficult, but she'd found ways to satisfy him, so he hadn't been too put out, but she'd once heard someone say you needed to practise many times before you conceived. Then she remembered that Tillie had done so on her first experience of lying with a man. *Perhaps it was different when you were forced*, she thought as she drifted off to sleep.

Dozens of white horses surrounded her. Sam was trying to pull her away from them but then the horses changed to sheep that were trying to grab the baby in her arms, charging at her and hooking it with their horns and she couldn't keep hold of it. She screamed as it disappeared down the mouth of the nearest one, a large ram with huge curved horns.

Sweating, her breath caught in her throat, she sat up and tried to get out of bed, but the sheet was wrapped around her leg.

"Get off," she cried, as much to the sheep as to the sheet. Panicking and arms flailing, she fell, landing in a heap on the floor, still entangled in the linen. "Somebody, help me." She knew there was nobody who could do so as, apart from her, there was only Maisie at the other end of the landing and she wouldn't hear her. Tears began to fall down her cheeks.

Was the dream a warning? Did it mean any child she had would die? She curled up in a ball and remained there the rest of the night, too afraid to get back into bed in case the nightmare came back.

* * * *

Tillie found her curled up on the floor the next morning when she went to help her dress for the wedding.

"Ruby, what on earth are you doing down there? You're still in your nightgown," she exclaimed.

"Oh, Tillie, I don't think I should go through with this wedding." Ruby remained huddled in the sheet.

"My darling sister, I've told you, there's no need to be nervous. Sam loves you and can't wait to marry you."

"But I've had a sign."

"What sort of sign? What are you talking about?"

"A nightmare."

Tillie bent down and took her sister in her arms, stroking her head. "Nightmares aren't portents of doom. They're just dreams, that's all."

Ruby laid her head on Tillie's shoulder. "But you hear of

people predicting the future through dreams."

"Oh, you can't believe all that nonsense. Honestly, believe me, you and Sam are going to have a long, happy life together, with dozens of children clinging to your apron strings, and you will be the best wife and mother in the country. There, that's my prediction, and I can tell you that without dreaming at all."

Ruby sat up. "Are you sure?"

"Yes, my darling girl. I'm positive."

"But I don't really want *dozens* of children."

Tillie laughed. "Well, perhaps that was a bit of an exaggeration." Extricating Ruby from the tangled sheet, she pulled her up. "Now, come on, sis. It's time to put on that beautiful dress, and show the world what a gorgeous bride you are."

"Thank you, Tillie, for always being there for me. I don't know what I'd do without you." Standing up, Ruby gave her a hug. "It's just that I was so happy, I thought it was too good to be true."

"Well, it isn't, this wedding is about to happen. Your adoring husband-to-be is awaiting you, to give you the love you so richly deserve."

"But…" Ruby blew out her cheeks as Tillie brushed her sister's hair, pinning it up, leaving a few curls hanging down at the front, and the rest secured in a bun on top of her head.

"No more 'buts'." Helping her into the dress, Tillie fastened the buttons down the back. "And no more uncertainties. Now, look in the mirror."

"Ooh, is that really me?"

"Yes, my darling sister, that is you in all your glory."

Ruby looked lost for words, her grey eyes shining with happiness.

Clearing a lump from her throat, Tillie placed a necklace of pearls interlaced with diamonds round Ruby's neck. "This is my present to you."

"Oh, thank you so much." Ruby twirled around and around in front of the mirror. "I really don't deserve it."

"Yes, you do. You must believe me."

"I'm such a lucky girl."

"And Sam is the luckiest man alive to have such a wonderful, caring wife."

Ruby held out her hands. "No-one could have a better sister than you, Tillie. You will still be a part of my life, won't you?"

"Of course, you try and stop me. I couldn't be more pleased for you than at this moment, and I'll always be here whenever you need me." She smiled, genuinely happy as she placed a sprig of flowers in Ruby's hair and attached her veil, leaving it off her face until they got to the church. "There we are."

Pulling a garter up her leg, Ruby took one more look in the mirror, her face beaming.

"That's the something blue," said Tillie. "What do you have for the 'something borrowed'?"

"Well, I have your dress for 'something old', the necklace for 'something new', although I was going to have my new earrings for that, and…borrowed? Oh, I've forgotten."

Tillie took off her pearl earrings. "Will these do?"

"But, Tillie, what will you wear?"

"It doesn't matter about me. You're the one everyone will be looking at, and they match the necklace perfectly."

Ruby replaced her earrings with Tillie's, saying, "You wear mine, then."

"No, my darling, thank you, but you saved up for those. Keep them for a special occasion—your first anniversary or something like that."

Ruby pulled on her long white kid gloves. "Ooooo, I can't wait now. Shall we go?"

Nellie was on her way upstairs as they emerged from the bedroom. "Thank goodness…" She stopped halfway. "Oh, Ruby, you look beautiful."

"Thank you, Nellie. I actually feel it, for the first time in my life."

Her brother, Matthew, was waiting at the bottom of the stairs. "I was beginning to wonder if I wasn't needed to give you away, after all, sis," he said, reaching out to Ruby. "But I see my fears were groundless. Sam's a lucky man."

"That's what I keep telling her," said Tillie.

"Oooo," Ruby repeated, clearly too excited to say much else.

Nellie shooed them out of the door. "Off you go, then. The master's already taken Jamie and Alice. The wedding breakfast will be ready for you on your return. Freda's been up since the crack of dawn, little Maisie too, preparing it."

Tillie grabbed her new bonnet from the chair in the hall where she'd put it earlier before she'd gone up to check on Ruby. "Better not forget this." She grinned. "I would look very undressed without it."

"It matches your dress exactly," said Ruby as they climbed into the waiting carriage. "It's a beautiful shade of royal blue."

"Yes, isn't it?" Matthew agreed.

Ruby turned to him, seated beside her. "Have Jessie and the children come?"

"Oh, yes, she wouldn't have missed it for the world. They've already gone to the church."

"We haven't seen Baby William yet, have we, Tillie?" Ruby asked.

"No, he must be quite big now."

"You can say that again, he's proper chubby." Matthew's proud face reminded Tillie so much of their pa. How pleased he would have been to have seen both his daughters happily married.

"And what about Harry?" Ruby turned to Tillie. "Is he still coming?"

"Yes, he's bringing his sweetheart. Apparently, they've been walking out for quite a while."

"I wonder what she's like." Ruby looked up, her face aglow. "Ah, listen to the church bells peeling."

"Yes, they're just for you, sis." Tillie couldn't keep the smile from stretching across her face at the delight in her sister's. The sun came out from behind a cloud, lighting up the stained-glass windows of the church in a blaze of colour. "Aw, aren't those windows dazzling?"

"I'll bet they look even more so from inside," said Matthew, stepping down and helping his sisters alight.

Sarah came running out of the church porch, followed by Jamie, dragging Alice by the hand.

"Auntie Ruby, Uncle Sam's been here ages. He thought..." Jamie stopped.

Tillie shook her head at him and he looked at her questioningly.

"We're here now. That's what matters," she said. "Have you got the ring cushion?"

"Oh, I left it on the pew in church."

"And Alice's posy?"

"That's in there as well."

Tillie brushed off a pink petal from her daughter's white dress. "I hope you haven't been fiddling with it and spoiling it." Her daughter merely shook her head, her thumb in her mouth as she held out her other hand for Tillie to take.

"Run and fetch them, Jamie," she told him. She was about to ask about David, but he'd already gone inside. He soon came back out clutching the cushion and Alice's flowers. "Father's sitting near the front, waiting for you." He must have read her mind.

"Good." Fortunately, Alice's posy hadn't suffered too much damage. Tillie turned and gave Ruby a kiss before adjusting her veil. "Right then, Ruby Raven, I'd better go in and tell the organist to start." She smiled. "That's the last time I'll call you by that name. In a short while, you'll be Mistress Samuel Wright."

"Ooooo."

Making sure that Sarah had charge of Alice, she went inside and sat next to David. Sam looked across at her and the look of relief on his face as she nodded removed any qualms she may have had. Not that she'd had any, of course.

The organist started the wedding music and everyone turned around to look at the beaming bride.

Remembering the elation she'd felt at her own wedding, Tillie held David's hand, smiling into his eyes as her sister pronounced her vows clearly and loudly.

Emerging from the church, showered with rice, the happiness of the newly married couple was apparent. Ruby looked radiant. Tillie marvelled at how the love of a good man had transformed her sister into the confident woman she now appeared.

As she felt the baby inside her kick for the first time, she sensed new hope for the future.

About The Author

Married to Don, Angela has 5 children: Darran, Jane, Catherine, Louise, and Richard and 7 grandchildren: Amy, Brandon, Ryan, Danny, Jessica, Charlotte and Ethan.

Educated at The Convent of Our Lady of Providence, Alton, Hampshire, Angela was part owner of a health shop for 3 years and worked for the Department of Work and Pensions for 16 years until her retirement when she joined the Eastwood Writers' Group and began writing in earnest.

Her hobbies include gardening, singing in her church choir, flower arranging, bingo, scrabble, and eating out.

Her first novel 'Looking for Jamie' was released as an eBook in November 2010 and in print in February 2011. It has been hailed as 'one of those books you can't put down'. Without the help and encouragement from the writer's group, she says her book would never have been finished.